42 Months Dry

A TALE OF GODS
AND GUNPLAY

Zachary Bartels

www.gutcheckpress.com

Published by Gut Check Press—Lansing, Michigan

Requests for information may be directed through http://www.gutcheckpress.com

The following is a work of fiction. All characters appearing therein are fictitious. Any resemblance to real persons, living, dead, or assumed into heaven via whirlwind and fiery chariot, is purely coincidental.

Scripture passages are from the King James Version or are the original translation work of the author.

ISBN 978-0-9830783-2-6

Published in association with K-D Enterprises.

Cover copy and editorial services by Syntax Writing Services.
http://www.syntaxwriting.com

The following story is true.
Sort of.

It's true like a big-screen adaptation of a sporting event.
True like the official version of the Alamo or the Arthur
legend or Watergate, with heroes and villains unmistakably
pinned down on a simple spectrum of good and evil. The
details may be specious, diligent reader, but they are such
for your enjoyment.

These events took place in Shomron during the final month
of the great drought. Leaders rose and fell with little
fanfare in those days, and often for no good reason.

But Ahab . . . Ahab had it coming.

הקדמה
prologue

Abner died showing off.

It began with a protest, naturally—a pointless little demonstration, which had blossomed into a halfway respectable mob. It was harmless enough at first: a few dozen malcontents flaunting homemade signs and chanting trite slogans on the hem of the Ephraim Executive Office building. Nothing new. Such crowds had become commonplace in Shomron and they usually lost interest within a few hours, dispersing on their own.

People blow off steam. That's what they do.

And the past three years had produced a record crop of steam, most hissing out in a surge of violent crime. The murder rate had tripled. Sale of all things illegal—goods and services alike—became the driving force behind what was left of the economy. Scrambling to the defensive, an overwhelmed police force assumed a siege mentality, leaving pickets and protests to quell themselves.

But it was a slow news day, prompting a local TV station to dispatch a plucky young correspondent to cover the non-event, adding a few embellishments for broadcast. Channel 8 broke into programming throughout the morning, offering sensational if repetitive updates of the unrest downtown.

The media spin proved self-fulfilling, as the un-employed, uninspired, and unhinged descended on the site. Before long, the crowd boasted several hundred bodies, filling the street outside the steel and glass tower.

Too late, police fumbled to the site in a vain attempt to contain the unrest. They diverted traffic to isolate the affair. Textbook procedure—tie a tourniquet and stop the hemorrhage.

But the tourniquet didn't take. What had early on adopted a rave atmosphere quickly devolved as midday approached and the sun found its mark at the top of the sky. The towering buildings propping up the capital's skyline no longer offered shade to the sweating horde.

Organized mantras disintegrated into a chaotic chorus of shouts and demands. The armed guards inside locked down and stood their ground, weapons at the ready, safe behind three-inch-thick bulletproof glass.

The sun seemed to hang at twelve o'clock for hours, baking the protesters, magnified by a lens of smog, refracting off the vertical glass. Yet not a single picketer gave up the vigil; it was as if they had reached an understanding in advance— some plan of action to which they'd all committed.

Drunk on thirst and sweat and determined not to walk, the disgruntled throng began to swell and pulse, looking for an outlet. The police sensed the shift in the air and all at once ceded the street.

Now unhindered, the crowd went to work. Dehydration and mob-think proved a liberating combination. A few parked cars found themselves tires-up. Roadblocks were re-imagined as battering rams. A wall of protesters thundered on the windows of the government headquarters, demanding what was rightfully theirs.

That's about when Abner arrived.

A self-styled revolutionary, Abner had a gift for turning up at the climax. Rumor was that the Ministry of Justice and Conduct had recently doubled the price on his head to eighty thousand shekels—a real accomplishment for Abner, considering he had none others to speak of.

Perhaps it was the sunstroke and lack of water, but to the crowd, his entrance was purely messianic. They went silent, parting for him as he strode into their midst, and at his request lifted him onto the roof of a double-parked delivery truck.

Standing there on his makeshift stage, Abner held up his hands for silence. The crowd obliged. He had all the command and presence of a veteran candidate, though he looked more like a rock star than a politician, dressed as he was in ragged T-shirt and ripped jeans. He pushed his ratty black locks back from his chestnut eyes and began an impassioned, if rehearsed, speech.

"People of Ephraim, I have a message from Jah!"

A mixed reaction rose up from the crowd and then spun back down to the street. A few cheered. More booed. Most just wheezed their disappointment.

Abner had never been a religious man, but ever since King Ahab had married a Tsidonian woman, he'd been waxing spiritual with sickening predictability. The New Abner couldn't seem to go five minutes without invoking the name of Jah or calling down heavenly judgment on the regime. Abner saw in Jah an untapped mascot for his cause: God and country. A powerful symbol of the good old days before all this. Before the goyim took over.

"I'm not a prophet," he continued, "but I've been poring over their sacred writings these past few months and they would have wanted you to hear this."

He paused for applause. None came.

In reality, the prophets of Jah had never liked Abner. He used Jah just like he used people. But with most of the prophets either dead or banished, it seemed a safe claim to make.

"Ahab and his lackeys are bathing in wine and oil while our families die of dehydration! Our faucets don't run, our toilets don't flush, fires are eating this city alive. And now, we're not even allowed to worship the god of our fathers! Ahab must be humbled!"

His words began to reanimate the crowd. *Humbled.* They liked that. Abner's base began to cheer and whoop and egg him on. The effect was contagious.

"I don't know about you, but I've had all I can take!" More cheering. Pointing to the top of the forty-story building, he dropped his voice into to a gravelly palette. "He's up there right now. Ignoring us. I think it's time we give Ahab a little update on his approval rating."

As the crowd screamed its own approval, Abner fought down a smile. He had them right where he wanted them. Now, to close the deal. He took a deep breath and leaned into the crowd.

"We will never be truly free until we—"

A wall of sirens squashed his call to action. Six hulking, squared armored vehicles roared up to the assembled crowd from all directions, boxing them in. Men in riot gear emerged with silent efficiency, automatic weapons in hand, eyes scanning the crowd.

Abner steeled himself. "Are you thirsty? Are you *thirsty*?"

The people eyed each other, unwilling to take in the sight of the armed troops surrounding them.

Abner shouted, "Courage! Now is the time to fughh—" The word *fight* retreated back down his throat.

Across the sea of bodies, a man had climbed onto the roof of an armored truck and now stood directly facing Abner. He wore all black. His white-blonde hair and light skin—the color of raw pork—stood in stark contrast to the black hair and deep olive skin of the crowd. He spoke into a microphone, sending his voice booming out a massive mounted speaker, filling the street.

"I am El-Baal. This gathering has been condemned. You have fifteen seconds to disperse." He dropped the mic, which bounced twice and squealed a wave of angry feedback. His hand disappeared into the black void of his jacket for two breathless seconds and emerged with a gleaming black handgun.

Clicking off the safety, he leveled it at Abner, then cocked up his left arm, making a show of counting off the seconds on his silver designer wristwatch. For a beat, everything was still. No one blinked. Abner stared back at the gun and swallowed hard. His ratty hair fell back across his eyes.

El-Baal pulled the trigger.

A mist of red filled the air behind Abner's head. His body bounced off the truck's hot steel roof with a hollow *clung* and rolled limply down into the crowd.

Panic set in. The initial wail of protest was quickly swallowed up by gasping and grunting and crunching as the one-time protestors trampled one another, single-mindedly bent on escape.

The armored troops sprayed the crowd indiscriminately with machinegun fire. Desperate men and women clawed and kicked their way to the perimeter and disappeared into the city. Within a minute, the street was empty save a dozen corpses. El-Baal slid his gun evenly up under his arm, back into its holster, and plucked a small two-way radio from his belt.

"The situation is resolved," he spat into the radio.

From forty floors up, King Ahab gave a long, throaty sigh through the tinny speaker before saying, "Next time, maybe a warning shot?"

"That *was* my warning shot."

אליהו

e l i - j a h

The Kerith Ravine Inn was a dump—the quintessential dive motel. One story, ten rooms, separated by paper-thin walls. Even the dim, pre-dawn light couldn't gloss over the chipping paint, mismatched doors, and hand-painted room numbers.

A neon sign loudly thrummed the pleasant name in a sickly red glow, clearly announcing the motel's presence to the few motorists who happened down the gravel road each night.

Inside room 7, an alarm clock came to life with a grating buzz. Eli Tishbi snapped upright out of sheer conditioned response. For a moment he sat half-tangled in the yellowed sheets, staring dazedly at the screaming contraption, as if trying to determine exactly what it was. Then, snapping awake, he silenced it with the heel of his hand and rose. He had slept in his clothes again—black dress pants and a half-buttoned white shirt. He shuffled over to the bathroom sink, clicking on the old television as he passed.

Also by force of habit, he'd slept with gun in hand—a Maqil .60 etsba semi-automatic pistol with a seven-inch barrel, which he unceremoniously plopped down on the vanity. He blinked away a layer of crust and purposefully avoided meeting his own gaze in the mirror. Years ago, he'd perfected a dark, smoldering glower that unnerved even the most hardened men. Somewhere along the way, he'd forgotten how to turn it off.

His eyes skipped instead to the reflection of the television behind him. A peppy meteorologist was announcing that the drought had begun exactly three and a half years ago today. Three and a half years and Eli still caught himself reaching for the knob on the faucet. As if anything was going to come out. He gave it a spin anyway, just because. Maps materialized behind the weatherman, adorned with numbers that would have seemed absurdly high just a few years ago.

Eli grabbed up a bottle of amber mouthwash. He popped the cap, emptied the contents into his mouth, and after a few swishes, spit it back into the bottle. He winced. Eight days was pushing it, he decided, and dropped the bottle in the trash.

From a finger-sized glass vial, he applied a few drops of oil to his fingertips, which he rubbed into his freshly shaven scalp in tight circles.

The sound of his name snapped his attention back to the television. Eli always felt a little childlike thrill when the news was about him, followed closely by a sense of embarrassment. Eyes glued to the screen, he nimbly buttoned his shirt and began looping a simple black necktie.

A pretty young anchor was building an awkward segue from the drought to the recent search effort—the "most intense international man-hunt in recent history," she called it, and added, "Eli Tishbi remains at large today, as the this leg of the search comes to a close."

"At her weekly briefing, Queen Isabel Ahab had this to say. . . "

A pre-recorded clip replaced the anchor on screen: a beautiful fair-skinned woman in her late thirties standing at a podium, flanked by two pairs of broad shoulders in black suits. She wore her long blonde hair down against a slightly provocative silk blouse.

Expertly playing the teleprompter she spoke articulately, with a hint of anger. "We hold fast in our position that Eli-Jah Tishbi is an extremely dangerous individual. His disgusting brand of religious exclusivism is no longer welcome in our society, nor does it have any place in modern civilization. I can assure all of you that, despite the failure of our recent efforts, we will continue our search for Mr. Tishbi and when we find him, we will bring him to justice as we have the rest of these religious zealots. Please bear with us as we continue our search here in Ephraim and contact local authorities with any helpful information. Thank you and Baal be with you."

Cameras flashed and reporters bellowed questions after the queen as she brisked away.

The anchorwoman reappeared on screen. Above her shoulder materialized a black and white still of a bearded, long-haired man shouting and waving a gun.

Eli pulled on a well-oiled calfskin shoulder holster and buckled it in place.

"This photo of Tishbi was taken two years ago," the anchor was saying.

Eli glanced at his reflection with a smirk. *It's amazing the difference a cubic foot of hair makes.*

"Tishbi is wanted for multiple religious and political violations," she continued. "And more recently, several leaked documents have suggested that some within King Ahab's regime believe that Tishbi may actually be in some way responsible for the ongoing drought. If you have any information, you are ordered to contact your local

11

authorities or to call the King's Security Taskforce at 8812-003."

Eli holstered his gun, and concealed it with a thin trench coat.

Three and a half years. Today was the day. Forcing himself to take in his reflection, Eli administered a mental self-pep talk. He couldn't help think that his eyes read twice his thirty-three years. Then again, prophets were in a high-stress line of work.

Snagging a small suitcase, he happily left the dank room behind, a prisoner finally making bail. It was, for the moment, a nice morning, the sun just beginning to spin some color onto the rundown stretch of highway.

A boxy rust bucket of a car sat waiting for him, a twenty-year-old Rekev IV—top of the line when it was new. Now it stalled if idle for more than a few seconds, the engine ejected coolant at an impressive rate, and the interior had developed a smell that could only be described as rotting mildew.

Eli loved the car anyway. It had become his only friend and companion during the past couple of years. He called the old Rekev "the Wreck" in his mind, an endearing pun of which he was simultaneously proud and ashamed.

The engine woke with a huge, deep growl. Eli looked at his watch. 5:30 AM. It was a two-hour drive to Shomron.

By seven, the oppressive early morning heat seemed to be singling out the Trembling Cup Café, a closet of a coffee shop just south of downtown Shomron. Cool mornings were a distant memory for the city and even now, with the sun barely above ground, the day was more thirsty than pleasant. A neon sign in the window read "Espresso," while a larger, hand-lettered sign beneath it advertised "Drinking Water."

Inside, Mishael stood behind the counter, carefully filling little plastic bottles with clouded water. He expertly topped off each, not spilling a drop, and screwed their little caps in place with a surgeon's precision.

The door swung open with a jingle and three men entered. The one in the middle was tall and thin, wearing wire-rimmed glasses and short-cropped hair. His confident strut and designer suit projected an air of authority as he strode up to the counter. The other two—thick-necked non-descripts in generic black suits and sunglasses—waited at the door, hands clasped in a fig leaf stance, stiffly taking in their surroundings.

Mishael smiled at his patron. "Let me guess: grandé mocha with three shots of espresso?"

"If you've got it."

"Are you kidding me?" The older man laughed, enjoying the same old banter and the distraction from his busywork. "You're the only guy, and I mean the *only* guy, buying coffee anymore. They say the caffeine sucks the water out of your system. And bein' that we've got a severe shortage of the stuff, people have resorted to actually sleeping at night."

"Desperate measures, my friend." He passed Mishael a colorful bill. Same as every morning, and the bill was always crisp.

The bell jingled again and Eli filled the room with his presence. The two gorillas by the door tensed, gave him the once over. Mishael rested a hand on the sawed-off he kept under the counter in case someone tried to get grabby with his precious water. Then he remembered the government thugs at the door. Pros and cons to their daily visits. He hadn't been held up once this year. Hadn't missed a quarterly tax payment either.

Nose buried in his cash drawer making change, he recited, "The *Pretty Clean* is fifty shekels. *Really Clean* is seventy-five. I'm out of steam distilled, but I should have some day after tomorrow." As he spoke, he poked his thumb at a price list taped to the wall behind him.

Eli studied the larger menu above it for a moment. "Hmm. Tempting, but I think I'll go with a red eye, three shots, and just a touch of that caramel syrup."

Mishael looked up. "That so?"

"If it's not too much trouble."

He shrugged and pulled out a second coffee cup.

Eli was studying the thin, bespectacled man to his left.

"Don't I know you from somewhere?"

The man cleared his throat uncomfortably. "You might. I'm in the papers once in a while."

"Yeah, that's it! You're Obadijah Whats-his-name. The government bigshot. I've read about you. Tight with the king and everything." He flashed a big smile. Maybe too big.

"Yes, that's me. I'm not a bigshot, though. Just a working man like yourself." Obadijah took his coffee from Mishael, muttered *thanks,* and turned to leave. Eli hooked his arm with a firm squeeze.

"No, don't be coy. You're right in the middle of things. You're a mover. Possibly a shaker, but definitely a bigshot."

אליהו

The two brutes were between Eli and Obadijah in an instant. One of them reached into his coat and growled, "That's enough. I suggest you move along, sir."

Eli snickered. "Look, you've even got two of the famous Shomrey-Melek watching your back. I mean, everybody knows they're a dime a dozen, but come on—only a major player would have some of the king's own bodyguards at his beck and call."

They escorted Obadijah to the door, one eye on Eli, the bigger of the two grunting, "You better hope I don't see you again."

"Wait—one more thing," Eli called when they were halfway out the door. "You must be a well-read guy. You ever heard this before?" He produced a pocket sized spiral notebook, flipped it open, and read,

> *"For as you have drunk from my holy mountain,*
> *So shall all the heathen drink continually.*
> *They shall drink and they shall swallow down*
> *And they shall be as though they had not been."*

Sudden recognition spilled across Obadijah's face. His mouth fell open, but he missed a breath.

Eli turned to Mishael. "How about you, Whiskers? Ever heard that before?"

"Uh, can't help you out there, buddy."

Obadijah recovered at once and shot an order to the two guards. "Bring the car around and wait for me." They didn't question the command, but stared a warning into Eli as they left.

Mishael plopped the second coffee down on the counter. "Ninety-five shekels," he announced.

Eli retrieved a roll of bills from his pocket and peeled two of them off, hesitating a moment as he peered dubiously down into the cup. "Did you brew it with the 'pretty clean' or the 'really clean'?"

"You tell me."

Eli snorted, flipped the bills onto the counter, and found a seat at the farthest corner table. He pulled out an ash black cigarette, lit it, and snapped his chrome lighter shut with a satisfying *schick*. After some wavering, Obadijah pulled up a chair and joined him.

For a moment they both stared at the table.

Obadijah broke the silence. "Nice haircut. I'd have never recognized you." He toyed with a packet of sugar, balancing it on its side, and quietly adding, "What are you doing here, man?"

Eli's eyes rumbled. "Oh, I don't know. I thought I'd do some sightseeing. I heard rumors about a bunch of new tourist attractions in town. You know, shrines to Baal. Ishtar poles. Other idols. I thought I might come and have a look. Maybe get a souvenir T-shirt." He laughed darkly. *"I sold my soul to Baal and all I got was judgment and condemnation. And this T-shirt."*

Obadijah half sighed, half wheezed. "This is *not* a good idea."

"Well, it didn't really look like anyone else was addressing the problem. Besides, Jah told me to come back."

Obadijah raised a finger. "Don't preach to me. Especially not on things you know nothing about."

"So now I don't even know what Jah is saying to me?"

"No, the other thing. You have no idea what I've been up to on this end. While you've been hiding out in the boondocks, I've been getting things done."

"Oh, I'm so sorry." Eli tipped back in his seat. "I must be confused. I thought I was talking to—now let me make sure I get this right—'Obadijah Uzzi, the Chief Officer of Domestic Issues Subject to the King' or some such nonsense. I mean, don't get me wrong; I'm sure you've been *getting things done.* Picking out the king's curtains. Setting up monuments to devils. Maybe offering up a nice—"

"*That* brought you back? You think it all falls apart when you leave town? Man, you really are out of touch. Always got a sickle when you need a scalpel. Do I need to remind you what our queen has been up to these past couple of years?"

"Oh, you mean your *boss's wife*? I believe she's been killing people like us by the hundreds. No one has heard jack from the prophets of Jah in months. In fact, she's done such a thorough job that I'm the only one left."

Obadijah put down his coffee and chuckled. "Yeah, man. That's right. You're the only one."

Eli drew down his brow. "What?"

"Nothing. I'm just saying you're right. You are the man." He laughed again. "Jah's last hope."

Eli stared at his friend for an awkward moment, trying in vain to read him. "Just tell me!"

Obadijah exploded into laughter. "Okay, check this out. Just after you took off, I get promoted to the Office of the Interior. I'm working real hard, trying to keep a steady paycheck and put water on the table. The work sucks, but it's work and I'm thankful. Then one day, my supervisor gets appointed as an advisor to the king. He's a nice guy and he likes me so he offers me a deal: if I agree to do this soul-suckingly dull housing commission job for six months, get their books under control, he can guarantee I'll get promoted too. Of course I take him up on it. Now this is right about the time that Isabel goes all Rameses on us and starts killing the prophets of Jah like she's trying to beat a high score. Says it's *his* will. You know who she means."

"Baal." Eli let the two syllables roll off his tongue soaked with disgust.

"Idol du jour in Shomron." Obadijah took a drink of his coffee.

"So then what?"

"So then I'm getting there! You wanna blow that poison the other way?" He slid the heavy glass ashtray across the table toward Eli. "So I find myself in the unique position of feeling an obligation to my God and my fellow prophets, while at the same time employed by the very people trying to kill them. Then it hits me—the perfect solution." He paused. It always felt good to have the information Eli didn't.

"Which was . . . ?"

"Massive reorganization of the housing projects. This drought, compliments of Ahab, has pistol-whipped the economy. We've got legions of new homeless on our hands. So, we build a few more low-income units, juggle everybody around, and before you can say 'shibboleth' we have a building in the projects solely dedicated to housing the prophets of Jah."

"How many?"

"A hundred. Up in Kishon Heights."

"And Ahab's footing the bill." A smile stretched slowly across Eli's face.

"Now you're catching on. So, it looks like maybe someone else is working to improve the situation after all."

Eli gazed into his cup. "I apologize. I've been out of the game too long. Forgive me."

"No big deal. If you weren't so intense, you wouldn't be any fun. So, are we cool? You going back to the boondocks?"

"I'm afraid not. I need a favor from you. Give your boss a message for me. Let him know I'm back in town."

Obadijah inhaled some coffee and hacked it back into his cup.

"You want me to *what*? Are you trying to get me killed?" He slid his chair back and took off his glasses. "There's not a mercenary or bounty hunter in Ephraim who isn't after you. Ahab wants you, man. Bad. And Isabel wants you worse! She even had LOCUST running the search for the last couple months."

Eli's head tilted cynically. "*What—*" Laughter swallowed his first attempt at finishing the question. "—is 'Locust?'"

"Liberation Of Countries Under Sovereign Tsidon. Or something like that. They're sort of a special forces team from Baal country."

"Wait a minute—the countries are liberated *to* Tsidon?"

"Or *for* Tsidon, take your pick. Isabel uses them for her dirty work, all the ultra-classified stuff. Not many people know about it."

Eli was busy spelling in his head. "I don't think words like 'of' are supposed to factor in to acronyms, are they?"

"Either way, they're nasty guys. I don't care how tough you are, you *don't* want LOCUST on you. They're the ones who killed Ben Hadad's son last year. Put a bag over his head and cut his throat while he was taking a leak at Damesq airport. Effective if not subtle."

"Yeah, I think I had the action figures when I was a kid. Look, Jah's kept me safe this long. Why don't we just trust him to be a little more sovereign than Tsidon. Give Ahab the message for me, okay?"

"You act like it's no big deal. But it is for me."

Eli leaned back, unamused.

"I don't know where Jah's spirit is going to send you next. If I tell Ahab that you're back in town and then you disappear, I'm a dead man."

"As Jah is my witness, I will present myself to Ahab today." He drained the rest of his coffee. "It's a good thing I'm *not* the only one left. This could get messy." He mashed the cigarette butt into the ashtray and stood.

Obadijah nodded slowly. "I'm sure it will. Watch your back." He poured the last few drops of coffee onto the smoldering cigarette butt, killing the flame with a *tsst.* "You really ought to quit that. It's horrible for you."

Eli shrugged. "Everybody dies, right?" And made his way to the door.

As he pulled it open, Obadijah offered, "You know, you wouldn't be the only one left anyway. I'm still here."

He nodded at his old friend and walked out.

Chaos on Shlomo Avenue.

Obadijah had waited an hour before calling King Ahab and reporting Eli's reappearance, giving the prophet plenty of time to hide himself away in advance of the inevitable building-by-building search, which began in the Trembling Cup and moved out in concentric circles.

Troops in desert fatigues poured in and out of apartments and businesses, searching closets, ransacking storerooms, and emptying walk-in freezers. Several fights were in progress as business owners defended their property from the soldiers' careless rifling. Backup arrived from the Ministry of Justice and Conduct with batons, stun guns, and little restraint.

Only one person stood still amidst the confusion; a lone tranquil figure planted like a cedar, his hands behind his back, watching a stack of televisions through an electronics store's display window.

An elated news anchor broke the story. "Once again, we have confirmed reports that a high-ranking government official has spotted Eli Tishbi here in downtown Shomron. A door-to-door search is currently being conducted. This is the most recent photo we have of Tishbi." The same picture of a bearded, long-haired Eli appeared on the screen. Apparently, Obadijah had left out some details of their encounter.

"Citizens are advised not to approach the fugitive, as he is considered armed and extremely dangerous. Anyone with information about his whereabouts is ordered to contact their local authorities."

Eli turned on a heel and walked away from the store, unnoticed.

The king's limousine zipped past the last checkpoint, through the gate, and down into the secure underground parking lot. It passed ten identical limos, several sports cars, and a few heavily armored vehicles—all parked in neat rows—before gliding to a stop. Two Shomrey-Melek agents, their business suits clinging to their lumberjack frames, spilled out of the front seats. One produced a bulky pistol from his jacket and scanned the dimly lit garage as the other opened the limo's back door.

King Ahab emerged. A smarmy man, he was ridiculously dressed in a billiard red suit. His hair was impeccably groomed, his beard neatly trimmed, and his shoes un-scuffed. He kept his skin baby soft and his thick eyebrows plucked down to the shape of two fat caterpillars.

The click of metal on an oiled spring echoed across the garage as Eli stepped quickly from the shadows, gun trained on the king.

"This is some security you've got here, Ahab. I was barely able to waltz right in undetected and catch you completely off guard." He motioned to the two agents. "Hands on your heads."

Ahab nodded at the agent with the pistol. He dropped it and both men raised their hands and interlocked their fingers, mortified and frightened. Ahab narrowed his eyes for a moment before recognizing the prophet.

"Eli. Smart. Hitting me at home while all my men are out looking for you."

"Yeah. I'd have to be a real genius to outwit you, right?" Eli said absentmindedly. His attention was on the taller of the two agents. "Joab? Seriously? You're still working for this loser. I remember when you used to be a stand-up guy. And now you're just another of Ahab's yes-men. Congrats."

Joab straightened to his full six-foot-four and dropped his hands to his sides. "I'm captain of the Shomrey-Melek, Tishbi. I guard the king's life with my own. I wouldn't expect someone like you to understand that."

"And I guess it doesn't bother you that he serves Baal. Doesn't seem to bother many people anymore. Hence the homecoming."

Ahab smiled a slimy smile. "What is this, Eli? Hmm? Are you going to shoot me now?"

"Probably not. Not while you're Jah's anointed, anyway. I would like a favor from you, though."

Ahab rolled his eyes. "Anything you want. Anything at all. Just make it *rain* and I'll give you a third of my kingdom! Otherwise, I don't grant favors to dead men."

"Soon," Eli replied. "I promise. But this search-and-destroy crap has got to stop. Killing me is not going to get you anywhere. You *need* me. Remember that."

Ahab's lower lip slid forward as he considered the comment. "Point taken. So I need you. So what? I don't think you came all the way here to tell me that. Am I right?"

"Very astute."

"Well then, what do you want? You've cleaned yourself up a little bit. I'd be glad to help you land a decent job."

"Call off your little manhunt. Just for a couple of days. Cancel the price on my head. Convince me, and tomorrow I'll come and see you at the office. We can sit down like a couple of gentleman. You offer me a drink and a cigar and we sort this thing out."

"If I agree?"

"Then maybe it'll rain. No more angry mobs. No more riots. No more large-scale sanitation issues. Get it?"

Ahab was mumbling. "Isabelle would never go for…"

"Well then don't tell her! You're the king, remember? She's a foreigner. Man up."

Ahab swallowed the thought.

"Be in your office tomorrow morning," Eli continued. "Leave your pride at home. Maybe you still have a chance to restore the glory to your kingdom."

The king glanced at Joab and then back to Eli. "Okay, I'll play along for now. But make this easy on me. Stay out of sight. Don't make one of your *scenes* for the cameras."

"Gladly. I'll be back when the mood has cooled down a little around here." Eli made for the exit, gun still covering the three of them.

Ahab called out after him, "I'm doing you a favor here! You don't show and bad things are going to happen!"

"Bad things are gonna happen anyway." The prophet backed into the door and spun out.

Eli knelt on the dirty carpet of Room 49 in the Tirat Motel. Larger than the Kerith Ravine but just as run-down, the Tirat was well-known as a place to lie low or conduct illicit business of all varieties. Everything about it, from the cigarette smoke soaked into every surface to the lethargic man at the front desk to the blinking, buzzing fluorescent lights screamed, *We don't care.*

The prophet, however, was not truly in the Tirat Motel. His shirtless body was next to the bed, prostrate, palms down to the floor, shaking violently. But Eli was elsewhere. He couldn't smell the rotting walls or feel the smashed carpet. He was standing in a field, in the midst of a cloudy night, staring up at the sky, which bore a deep orange tint. Something about the place set off warning flares in his mind.

Why am I here, Jah? Show me.

Lightning jumped from cloud to cloud and the air crackled with thick, electric tension. With a spike of thunder, the orange clouds began to grow and expand, becoming deeper, thicker, shifting into huge masses of burning gas, bleeding into one another, squeezing out the black night.

Until the entire sky was on fire. Slowly, the flames began to churn around and around, forming a gigantic inverted vortex, picking up speed, swirling around the dome of heaven, giving Eli the feeling that it was the ground that was moving.

Fire was piling up at the center of the vortex, growing into a bulbous mushroom of flame that seemed to stretch thin its skin as it expanded. Eli held his breath. Adrenaline coursed through his body. *Calm down. It's a vision, it's not real.* But he could feel the heat breathing down on him.

Then the bulb burst. A huge column of fire shot down from the sky, thundering into the ground and exploding on impact. The force of the explosion slammed Eli off his feet and into the sky. He hung there in mid-air for a moment, then twisted over backwards as gravity did its job and yanked him back to the earth, where he landed violently, face down.

Eli opened his eyes.

He was drenched with sweat. So was the carpet beneath him. His heart was pounding and he gasped for breath. Cautiously, he pulled himself from the motel room floor, sat back against the bed, and mopped the sweat from his face, willing his pulse to slow.

What was *that*?

אחאב
a h a b

All was peaceful and protest-free outside of the Ephraim Executive Offices as Eli made his way in the front door the next morning. Still, the Abner incident had clearly prompted some heightened security measures. In addition to the normal metal detectors and bomb-sniffing dogs, several Shomrey-Melek were randomly selecting visitors for a more personal touch.

Eli placed his car keys, cell phone, and money clip on the little conveyer belt and passed under the metal detector. Nothing beeped and the agents apparently did not deem him worthy of a pat-down. This relieved Eli who was chastising himself, thinking that even an empty gun holster would probably arouse suspicion.

Less than a minute later, he was standing in the middle of the sprawling atrium. He flipped open his cell phone and punched a button.

"O. I'm here. Two minutes. Right. Lift number four."

He snapped the phone closed and dropped it back into his coat pocket. Walking up to a large elevator bay, Eli pushed the "up" button. He glanced around at the few employees milling about and wondered how anyone could work in this place. Were memos routinely distributed, updating the workers on the newest demonic policies? *Next week is bring your daughter to work (and sacrifice her to Baal) day.* How could they all be so mundane about the national slide into idolatry? Eli popped his knuckles impatiently. He couldn't get to Ahab soon enough.

One of the dozen elevators arrived with a *ding*, slid open, and spit out a white-haired senior Shomrey-Melek agent and a jowly administrator. A couple of chatty women boarded, but Eli let it depart and hit the button again.

While he waited, he popped a lithium pill and clenched his eyes shut for a few seconds, trying to balance things out. The choice elevator arrived, and Eli boarded.

The car stopped at the second floor and Obadijah stepped in, clearing his throat nervously. When the doors had closed, he turned to face Eli and whipped his coat open wide. Twin pearl-handled silver pistols hung snugged into shoulder holders at Obadijah's sides. Eli grabbed them both, quickly snapping one into his own shoulder holster and slipping the other into his waistband at the small of his back. Without a word, Obadijah then retrieved a small key from an inside pocket and handed it to Eli. At the tenth floor, he casually exited, leaving Eli alone in the elevator.

Eli slid the key into a slot on the elevator panel and gave it a turn. Number forty lit up.

The waiting room for Ahab's penthouse office was just what Eli expected. The atmospheric ceiling was accented by tasteful lighting that illuminated an assortment of plush furniture. No one was actually waiting to speak to the king, but a dozen extra-imposing Shomrey-Melek agents stood at attention around the perimeter of the room, like guardian statues in a Persian temple. Large bulges betrayed the hand cannons in each agent's suit coat. Ahab's version of a red carpet for his old nemesis.

Visitors to the king's office normally exited the elevator on the 39th floor, where they were painstakingly searched and then escorted up to the reception area by two Shomrey-Melek. Eli savored the look on the agents' faces as he stepped out of the elevator all by his lonesome and strode right up to the receptionist. Even she had a bulge in the jacket of her joyless, gray pantsuit.

"Ahab is expecting me," he said flatly. "My name is Eli-Jah Tishbi."

"We all know who you are," she droned as she mechanically opened the oversized appointment book on her desk and ran her finger down to the only entry of the day. "The king said to have a seat and he'll send for you when he's ready."

Eli strolled over to the longest of the leather couches and flopped down. He could feel every eye in the room boring into him as he propped his feet up on the armrest and yawned boisterously.

During those years in hiding, the showman in Eli had been building and building under the surface. At the height of his career, he'd been known for public spectacles. The kind that are banned from the evening news, but get repeated over every backyard fence and tear their way around the Internet. Why just announce Jah's message to the people, Eli reasoned, when you can burn it into their minds with style?

He glanced around at the Shomrey-Melek agents adorning the walls. Some he recognized from years past and offered an acknowledging nod. Others were clearly new recruits. His review was stopped short as his eyes fell on two men who did not fit in.

Eli had never met El-Baal or Luli—Ephraim's high priests of Baal—and it immediately occurred to him that they couldn't stick out more if they tried. All the color from their pale skin and hair seemed to have drained into their black turtlenecks. Both priests wore gold amulets of Baal around their necks, black sport coats, and meticulously shined shoes. Eli pegged them at about forty.

He studied them curiously. They glared back. For half a minute, the tension grew between them, Eli unwilling to break off his gaze and El-Baal hatefully fingering his gold amulet. The moment ended with a sudden buzz at the receptionist's desk and a flinch from the high priests.

"The king will see you now," she announced. Eli winked at the two light-skinned men and pulled himself to his feet.

The king's office was even more extravagant than the waiting room. Ahab sat, carefully posed behind a huge mahogany desk, which boasted artifacts from all over the world, including a foot-tall golden statue of Baal. Floor-to-ceiling windows offered a breathtaking view of the entire city. Two high-backed leather chairs sat facing the desk and Joab stood between them, arms folded.

Eli pointed at the captain of the Shomrey-Melek. "I thought we were going to speak in private, Your Highness."

"I know you're not stupid," was the king's dispassionate reply.

"If I was going to kill you, I'd have done it yesterday when I had a chance to escape, not today with no way out and a dozen of your goons waiting for an excuse to perforate me."

Ahab mulled it over for a moment and gestured for Joab to leave.

"I'll be right outside," Joab said—to Eli more than to Ahab—and walked out, closing the heavy door behind him.

Eli made himself at home, sinking into the oiled black leather of a designer chair. He picked up the statue of Baal, looking it over with contempt.

For a minute, Ahab sat quietly watching him, unwilling to speak first.

Eli broke the silence by announcing, to no one in particular, "Look at this cursed thing. This is what I'm talking about. How could you possibly let Ephraim get tangled up with this devil?"

"You say devil, I say to-*mah*-to."

"Your Kingdom is on the verge of imploding because of your apostasy, and you're making yucks."

Ahab sighed dramatically. "When are you going to realize that you're an anachronism, Eli? Progress's worst enemy: a man who can't let go of the way it used to be."

"The way it *is*, Ahab. The way it is. You and your blonde harlot can't change that."

Ahab assumed what he hoped was a diplomatic smile. "What have I done to make you so angry? I think you're making things out to be far worse than they really are.

"Baal's not a jealous god. I'm not sure he's even capable of that kind of emotion. You can serve him *and* your god. He doesn't care. In fact, your god is part of Baal. Just like you and I are part of Baal," he recited, Isabel's words marching out of his mouth.

He stood up and added with a flourish, "All gods are part of him. Everything is part of the great and mighty Baal. He's what holds it all together!"

Eli let him stand there for a moment, frozen awkwardly with upraised hands, before slowly responding, "Wow. That was a really boring speech."

Ahab's face fell.

"You're a spoiled rich kid, Ahab. Don't wax theological. Jah has always protected us. He has always kept his covenant with us. Now you've broken that covenant. I can't let that stand."

"I refuse to have this conversation with you again. So pointless. So hopelessly small-minded." Ahab held out his hands sympathetically. "It's okay;" he reassured, "I used to be the same way. Luckily, Isabel opened my mind to greater things."

Getting no response, Ahab stood up straight and tried another tack. "Let's get real," he said with all the sincerity of a door-to-door used car salesman. "Let's talk terms. Exactly what are your demands? What must I do in order for it to rain?"

Eli stroked his chin. Nonverbal sarcasm, the showman coming out again. "Hmmm. What *are* my demands? How about this? You destroy every idol, every little statue, every Ishtar pole, every high place dedicated to worshiping evil.

"Send the prophets of Baal into exile and make your wife understand how things work around here. Turn from Baal, cry out to Jah and return Ephraim to her former glory. Here," he lifted the solid statue off the desk and shoved it into Ahab's chest. "You can start with this one. Smash it."

Ahab teetered, and fell backwards into his chair, struggling to lift his god back onto the desk.

"Out of the question!" he exploded. "I will not allow everything we've achieved to be undone at the whim of a criminal! Eventually, it will rain. It has to. Baal's prophets have assured us of this. If you aren't willing to make a reasonable deal, then maybe I'll just have you publicly executed. Isabel would really like that. She's been itching to complete the set!"

The king's airway suddenly closed, and he was yanked to his feet by Eli's meaty hand. He tried to yell for his guards, but only managed to produce a sick gargle as he found himself looking down the barrel of one of Eli's guns. His eyes doubled in size and all traces of the cool, in-control demeanor vanished.

Rage oozed off of Eli's words. "Do not speak lightly of your slaughter of Jah's prophets. If you do not repent, you and that harlot will both pay dearly for your crimes. I have seen your deaths and this is what Jah says: *In the place where you have spilled the blood of the prophets, dogs will lick up your blood. Yes, yours!*" He released Ahab's throat and shoved him back into the chair by his face.

The king gasped for breath and rubbed his throat gingerly. He started to speak, but Eli shut him down with a single look. "This is my show. That should be clear. Now tell me—who are the two ghouls out in the lobby?"

"What are you talking about?"

"The chalk-white goyim sporting amulets of Baal around their pasty necks! They were eyeballing me. I don't like it when people eyeball me."

The color drained from Ahab's own face as he realized who was waiting just outside his office. "Those . . . would be high priests of Baal. Isab—" he caught himself—"we granted them authority to enforce Baalic law last year. If they know you're here, then Isabel knows you're here. And if that's the case, you'll probably be dead before you step out on the sidewalk."

"Let me worry about that."

Ahab buried his face in his hands. Eli fidgeted.

"Look, I told you before—I won't kill you while you're Jah's anointed. You still have a chance to make this right. I wouldn't be here if you didn't. Are you really comfortable turning your back on the God who rescued our people from Mitzrayim and brought us into this land? Can you really do that?"

"Eli, that's a myth," Ahab condescended. "Do you understand the difference between reality and myth?"

"If it's a myth, then where did your fathers get these relics?" Eli motioned to the small Egyptian statues on Ahab's desk. "If Moshe didn't deliver our people from Mitzrayim—if he's a myth—then how can his descendants be your advisors? Think!"

"Look, Eli. I don't disagree that these stories are important. They inspire our people, foster national unity. They're part of who we are. But they're just that. Just stories! Yes, our ancestors came from Mitzrayim. Yes, they were probably led by a man named Moshe. But the rest is just nonsense. It's legend. An exclusive god like Jah isn't big enough for our people or our times. We've made a lot of progress in the last few years and people like you need to step into line or you'll be *forced* into line."

"And who's going to do that? You?" Eli laughed.

"Someday they're going to write a book about you, Eli-Jah Tishbi. And you know what they're going to say?"

"Enlighten me."

"You'll be remembered as an antique—someone who fought to maintain the status quo while the progressives of the world moved on to better things. Men like you invariably fail, and history is never kind to them."

Eli rolled this around in his head. It snowballed into an idea. He wasn't sure if it was his or if . . . No, it was definitely Jah.

"Okay," he said, "this is how it's going to be. Tomorrow morning, we all get together. Everyone. We'll decide once and for all whose god is greater. The 450 prophets of Baal will show you their lord and I will show you my Lord. Whoever proves himself to be greater is truly God. Should Baal prove to be greater, then I—and all the prophets of Jah with me—will turn ourselves in and you can do to us as you please. Banish us, kill us, whatever. Either way, if you follow through on this, you have my word that it will rain tomorrow. Now, is that a 'reasonable deal'?"

"Yes. And it's about time."

Eli stood. "Isn't it just wonderful when everyone gets what they want?" He snapped the handgun back into its holster and smiled broadly.

"But what if, uh," Ahab cleared his throat. "What if your god proves himself to be greater?"

"You're not starting to have doubts, are you, Ahab? I think you know the answer to that one." Eli picked up the statue of Baal with one hand and dropped it the six feet to the marble floor. It shattered into a thousand little gray pieces with a deafening crash.

The heavy office flew open and in rushed the Shomrey-Melek, guns drawn and ready for the worst, only to find

Ahab sitting sheepishly behind his desk. They surveyed the scene with some confusion, not sure whether to detain Eli or let him go. Eli laughed as he kicked a chunk of the statue, sending it skidding along the marble. "14-Karat concrete, eh Ahab? Kind of a metaphor for your whole regime."

Joab stepped back to let the prophet pass and the other agents followed suit. Only the two high priests remained in the doorway, blocking the way. Eli burst between them, giving both a taste of his broad shoulders and nearly knocking them off their feet.

He took the elevator back down to the lobby, replaying the meeting in his head the whole way. What had he agreed to? He needed a place to think it through and receive his instructions from Jah. The Tirat would do for another night, he thought.

As the doors parted on the first floor, two priests of Baal stood in his path, dressed very much like their superiors upstairs.

"The queen would like to see you," said the taller of the two. "Come with us please."

איזבל

isabel

Eli glanced from one man to the other.

"Sure, no problem," he replied cheerfully, and shot three knuckles into the short priest's throat, sending him convulsing to the ground, clutching at his neck, kicking frantically, struggling for air. Eli exploded from the elevator, slamming the other priest to the floor in the process. As he instinctively located the exits, his peripheral picked up five more priests converging on him. One was speaking into a radio, while two others reached into their jackets for guns. A handful of Shomrey-Melek had also noticed the commotion and were moving in.

Instantly, Eli produced his pistols and, swooping down, hooked the gasping priest under both armpits. He extended the two handguns, lifting his half-conscious human shield, and began dragging him toward the door. Taking aim at the two closest priests, he issued the warning, "Count the cost, my friends."

They brought their hands back into sight, empty, and put them in the air. Agents in the distance drew their side arms and waited for the clean shot. Confused glances. How could anyone smuggle guns into the most protected building in Ephraim during a time of heightened security? As he neared the door, Eli's shield began to struggle, and the prophet shifted one pistol to the man's head, calming him instantly.

A shrill alarm filled the building as Eli's back hit the emergency exit's crash bar. He launched his hostage back into the atrium with a well-placed kick. Half a dozen bullets bound for Eli were stopped short by the building's bulletproof windows. Keeping his frame near the ground, he sprinted to his waiting car. He had parked on the curb, next to a big red NO PARKING sign, collecting an assortment of tickets throughout the morning.

The priests were pouring out of the building as Eli fumbled with his keys, dove into the car, started the ignition, shifted into drive, and stomped the accelerator. The Wreck squealed away from the curb, joining the mass of speeding commuters, all seemingly running late, all honking and yelling. Gunshots rang out behind him as he disappeared around a corner.

At the first entrance ramp he encountered, Eli pulled the big silver car up onto an elevated freeway and poured on the gas. Weaving in and out of traffic at ninety miles an hour, he was singularly focused on his goal: put miles between himself and the Executive Office building. Regroup, re-center, re-connect with Jah.

He was so focused that he barely noticed the two black Susah LE sedans—windows tinted—pulling in behind him from opposite sides of the freeway. The twin government plates and flawlessly polished armor performed a perfect duet in the rearview mirror—standing out against the muddled lunch hour traffic. Eli leaned harder on the accelerator, but gained no ground. A third pursuer fell in behind at the next ramp.

One of the sedans overtook him on the passenger side and the mirrored window came down. Eli expected to see an agent of the Shomrey-Melek behind the wheel—

probably someone he knew from the old days. A little banter. A little fancy maneuvering. Call it a day.

No such luck.

A pale face greeted him, crowned with slicked-back blonde hair and dead eyes. The driver leveled a shotgun at Eli and issued a monosyllabic command, lost in the wind but apparently meant to convey the message, *Pull over.*

An overhead sign warned of a sharp corner: REDUCE SPEED. Eli floored it. The buckshot left a pock-mark pattern on the passenger door and window, but didn't touch the prophet as he fought the steering wheel around the banked bend. The three sedans behind him fell back, navigating the curve with skill, one of them bouncing easily off the guardrail and back into the right lane.

The superior horsepower to Eli's right matched him inch for inch. Eli braced himself, ready for more shots to find him.

As they rounded the corner, however, the sedan came upon a backlog of cars obeying the speed limit. The priest slammed on the brakes, fishtailed and recovered, scraped along the guardrail. The other two sedans blew by the first, skillfully playing all five lanes of traffic, slowly but certainly gaining on the prophet's older car.

From the sky above, Eli heard the unmistakable *whup-whup-whup* of a helicopter joining the chase. He could almost feel it descending on him. Soon, they'd have him boxed in on all sides.

Jah is an ever-present help in times of trouble. Whom shall I fear? Suddenly, he found himself looking down a quarter mile of completely open expressway. Grabbing the opportunity, he shoved the gas pedal to the floor until his foot hurt.

His eyes fell on a crude toggle switch mounted on his dashboard. An inch of label tape identified it: NOS. The car's previous owner had installed the nitrous oxide tank years earlier. When he sold it to Eli, he was adamant that it still worked. "Try it," the punk had urged, "It'll blow you away." But the prophet had never considered it worth the police attention he would likely receive—yet another disadvantage of living as a fugitive from the law. Doubting there was anything left in the tank after two idle years, he flipped the switch. There was a brief *hsshhh* swallowed up by the thick growl of the engine burning with increased oxygen.

The needle on the speedometer pulled down and the freeway did the same, turning to a decline and passing under a web of crisscrossing bridges. Eli heard the helicopter pull up, narrowly avoiding a collision with an elevated highway. He checked the rearview mirror and found the sedans were disappearing fast.

Just ahead, the freeway forked, the left arm curving up and around to merge with a six-lane throughway above. Eli flipped off the nitrous and guided the car to the right, down into a tunnel. The solid blur of light on either side slowly gave way to individual mounted lamps as Eli eased on the brake. A minute later, the road split again. This time, Eli pulled left and emerged from the tunnel.

He took the first exit he encountered. Pulling back into city traffic, he negotiated a hard right onto a narrow industrial access street, blew through a red light, and cut back through an abandoned factory toward Jeroboam Drive. Glancing to the mirror, he let out a sigh of relief— no one behind him. No sound of a helicopter either. He'd lost them for now. His heart was pounding. He needed to double back, slip past Isabel's men, and get to the south side of town where he could stash the car.

Faintly, the *whup-whup-whup* of the chopper returned overhead. Had they found him already? *Not so fast, Eli. Probably just combing the area. Might not even be the same chopper; could be a news helicopter for all you know.*

He spotted a cluster of apartment buildings ahead. A carport could hide him from the searching eyes above. He picked a particularly dense complex and sped toward it. This would work. This would buy him some time.

He mashed the brakes. The smell of rubber and brake fluid steamed up off the asphalt. Blocking the road in front of him were three black government cars, parked bumper-to-bumper. Four priests took cover behind them, guns trained on Eli as he sat dumbfounded in his car, engine idling.

How could they have gotten ahead of him? Known which road he'd choose? *Impossible*, he thought.

Eli never knew how much power to attribute to Baal. He usually told himself that Baal was just a ghost story. An excuse to do evil in someone else's name, more or less worshiping one's own basest instincts. But then something like this would happen, leaving him to wonder in a secret part of his soul whether Jah and Baal were more evenly matched than he dared imagine.

All other things being equal, Eli would not have been out of the game. He could have done a 180-degree turn and fled the way he'd come. Experience told him that the chase was far from decided, that odds were good no bullet would find its way to the driver's seat or the gas tank. Or he could have gained some speed and smashed his way through the crude roadblock—if it hadn't been for El-Baal and Luli standing in front of the barricade, guns poked to the back of a kneeling woman's head.

The cowards.

They couldn't outmaneuver him, so they had tracked his course from above, brought a civilian into the mix, and showed themselves to be utterly unworthy adversaries for a prophet of Jah. Whatever power was at their disposal, they were nowhere near Eli's league; he was sure of that. *Goyim. Foreigners. They have no covenant with the Living God.*

Slowly, he kicked open the door and exited the car. He made a show of dropping his guns to the gravel. Luli tossed the older woman to the side of the road like a trash bag and the two high priests advanced warily toward Eli, hugging their triggers. The other men circled around behind. Eli swallowed hard. Surrounded, six guns pointed in his direction, he weighed his options and didn't come up with much.

Jah, I'm going to need a way out of this. The next thing he felt was a sharp pain in his back. Electricity ripped through his muscles, setting off a series of spasms. The pain faded and his vision swam.

Then everything went black.

Eli found that dreams from Jah were markedly different from visions. Visions usually came while he was awake. They might envelop his mind while he prayed or they might slam themselves into his senses while he drove down the street. Either way, visions *seemed real*. He could feel his fingers moving, could look around at his surroundings, even interact with them.

In dreams, however, he was just an observer. Events unfolded before him, but he was not present in any corporeal sense. He couldn't speak, couldn't look down and see his body—he could only watch as images unfolded before him, as if projected directly onto his mind. And dreams had an ethereal quality—a concentrated reality with a higher resolution and more extensive palette than the physical world.

This hyper-reality was present now as Eli absorbed the scene before him. It was a temple room of some kind. He couldn't be sure where—probably not Ephraim, as he didn't recognize the art or the architecture. Not Tsidon either. There was something paradoxical about it, as if the ancient past had collided with the future in this place. The room was small and perfectly round, its walls meticulously engraved and overlaid with gold. At its center, on a raised altar, sat an idol of Baal, arms twisted obscenely, his pointed crown forming a tall spike at the top of his head, face expressionless.

In front of the altar, two men argued. Both were dressed lavishly in royal robes and jewelry. One was thin, short, and clean-shaven. The other was muscular, with a thick black beard that reached to his stomach.

Eli's attention was drawn to the smaller man. A faint orange flame flickered and danced above his head. Eli had seen this phenomenon before, floating above the heads of Jah-El, Obadijah, and other prophets, when Jah's spirit was especially strong with them. He had no idea whether anyone had ever seen such a flame above his own head; it was not the sort of thing Eli would ask.

A small silver crown was perched on the tall, bearded man's head. But without the crown, Eli could have identified the kingly authority that he projected. He was clearly not of The People, but for some reason, Eli liked him immediately. There was an openness about him that made him seem worthy of leadership. The two men spoke a language that was at the same time familiar and foreign. By listening carefully, Eli found that he could make out enough to follow the conversation.

The king spoke passionately, running a hand softly up and down the idol. When he would pause, the Prophet gesticulated wildly to accent his responses, matching the king passion for passion. The flame above his head burned brighter, flaring into a gaseous blue with each punctuated word. Eli made out the name of Jah and the name of Baal. The king seemed offended. Then indignant. Then concerned.

Their tones softened as they neared an agreement. It was clear that the men were laying out guidelines for a challenge of sorts. A contest for the god on the altar. It was all too familiar. As they worked out the details, a pair of men in priestly garments entered the room. They went rigid at the sight of Jah's Prophet.

These priests were the opposite of El-Baal and Luli in almost every way—their skin was olive, their eyes dark and round, their beaded beards hung to their belts—yet they shared some indefinable quality with their ghostly white counterparts, like a different instrument playing the same ugly tune. The king greeted them warmly and began to explain the test. Eli strained to hear the rules of the challenge, but the scene was fading quickly.

"Wake up, dead man." The voice was soothing and sing-song. Eli's head pounded. He experimentally opened one eye.

"Wake uuuup."

His vision slowly came into focus and he found himself face-to-face with Queen Isabel. She pushed a strand of her long blonde hair behind an ear and straightened her low-cut top.

"He's awake," El-Baal growled. He and Luli stood at her left and two other priests at her right. She softly stroked Eli's cheek a couple of times before slapping it with surprising strength.

Eli jerked alert. He found himself sitting in a rusty metal folding chair, hands cuffed behind his back. He sneered at Isabel. "Hi, honey. How was your day?"

"Oh, my day is going just fine. But yours is about to get a whole lot worse."

"You can't hold me here," Eli chided. "Get with the program. Ahab and I reached an agreement this morning. We're going to sort everything out tomorrow."

Isabel laughed.

"Call him up," he demanded. "Ask him yourself."

"No, I don't think I will," Isabel said. "My little puppet can make all the 'deals' he wants if it makes him feel important. It makes no difference to me. I rule as I see fit. Besides, if you'll have a look around, you'll realize that this isn't exactly *official business*."

Eli surveyed his surroundings. They were on the second floor of an abandoned factory. Several windows were broken and refuse lay strewn across the floor. The place reeked of human stench. Clearly, some homeless people had been living here recently and for a moment Eli could only think of what Isabel might have done to them. Then he noticed that, even in a knee-length skirt and designer blouse, Isabel somehow didn't look out of place here. He met her eye line with contempt.

"You've been a very naughty girl."

She leaned in to his ear and whispered, "You won't tell anyone, will you?" The sensation caused every tiny hair on his neck to stand at attention.

Eli grinded through his teeth, "Jah already knows your deeds, harlot. And he's going to make you *pay!*" He shouted the last word right down the queen's ear, sending her reeling, stumbling in her high heels.

"This displeases me," she said. "El-Baal, would you please help Mr. Tishbi with his attitude?"

El-Baal stepped forward with a mean little smile and smashed his fist into Eli's jaw. Without missing a beat, Eli snapped back to face him. El-Baal punched him a second time, harder. Blood flowed from an L-shaped cut in his cheek.

Isabel stepped between them. "That's enough. We haven't brought you here to hurt you, Eli. Well, not *just* to hurt you. We're all here together in this lovely, quiet place because you know something that I don't."

Eli addressed El-Baal, "You hear that, Blondie? That's what they call an *understatement.*"

Isabel ignored the comment. "So you're going to tell me what I want to know or we're going to spend the whole day taking you apart piece by piece until you talk. And no one—not even your little god—can save you." She drew close, centering herself in his field of vision. "Can you guess what it is you're going to tell me?"

"I can't imagine."

She playfully yanked on Eli's tie with every other word. "Where are the rest of Jah's prophets?"

"Easy—you killed them. Next question."

"No," she said flatly. "There are at least one hundred still unaccounted for. I have reason to believe they're still here in Shomron. Tell me where they are and maybe I'll let you keep a shred of dignity as you die."

Eli leaned forward as far as the handcuffs would allow. "Hey, it's news to me. If some prophets got away with their lives, then praise Jah. I don't know where they are."

She stepped back and rested her chin on her fingertips. "This morning, you told my husband that if Baal won the day tomorrow, that you and 'all the prophets of Jah with you' would turn yourselves in. You know where they are." She snickered at Eli's reaction. "Yes, I keep an eye *and* an ear on Ahab. I know every little thing he does or says and all of his pathetically grandiose plans, including your little 'contest' tomorrow, which I'm sorry to say, you won't be able to attend."

She took another step back, as if removing a barrier of protection between the prophet of Jah and the priests of Baal. "Instead, I think we should have our own contest right now. Right here. It goes like this: if you can stand up and walk out of here without getting killed, then you win. Otherwise, you tell me what I want to know."

Eli felt the handcuffs' grip loosen. "No good. You've got the home field advantage here."

"Well, I'm afraid life isn't always fair. Luli, show him."

Eli smirked. "Yeah, show me, *Luli*."

He hooked his right foot under the chair's horizontal brace as Luli wrapped his hands around Eli's bald head—one palm over each ear—and began to squeeze. Bright spots popped up in his vision almost instantly. Luli's golden amulet, a small likeness of Baal, dangled in Eli's face, tickling his bloody cheek.

The handcuffs fell to the floor with a clang.

Eli grabbed the amulet and yanked down, wrenching the priest off his feet. At the same time, he launched his right hand up into Luli's face, crushing cartilage with the meat of his palm. Luli crumpled to the ground and Eli lurched forward, kicking sharply and sending the metal chair spinning up toward El-Baal's head. It slammed solidly into the bridge of his nose, squirting blood from both nostrils in force and throwing him back several feet, where he landed on his back, his skull slapping the concrete floor.

The two younger priests fumbled in their jackets, dumbfounded, hands grasping for guns. Eli covered the distance between them in an instant. The bigger of the two was the first to clear his weapon. Before he could fire, he felt his hand bent roughly backward. His wrist gave way with a loud *pop* and the gun fired, sending the last priest down with a scream as the bullet ripped through his thigh—a messy wound. Eli smashed his forehead into the heavy's temple, sending him to the ground unarmed and seeing stars.

As the dazed men struggled to collect themselves, Eli grabbed a chunk of Isabel's hair and jerked her close. Two more priests rushed into the room, having heard the gunshot from outside. Eli cocked the gun and shoved it hard into the queen's temple.

"Drop. Them." Several guns clacked to the floor. "Now kick them over to me. Good. All of you, over to the wall and down on your stomachs." While the bloodied men obeyed, Eli scooped up the rest of their guns, awkwardly, careful to keep his grip on Isabel. He snapped one into his shoulder holster and tossed the rest out the window.

Noticing his car parked below, he demanded, "Which of you heathens has my keys?"

"I have them," Isabel blurted.

"That's good, Princess, because we're going for a ride." He addressed the prostrate priests. "Any of you guys decide to follow me, I shoot her and then I shoot you. If you think I'm bluffing, just test me."

Eli burst out the door into the parking lot, queen in tow. The landscape was an industrial wasteland, cracked concrete stretching out to infinity in every direction, marked by deserted warehouses and burned-out factories wearing rusted barbed wire fences. Three black sedans and Eli's Rekev were parked neatly side by side.

The sight of the Shomron skyline poking up in the distance gave Eli his bearings. He tried the driver's door of his car. It was unlocked.

He shot Isabel a disappointed look.

"You know, when *I* kidnap people, I at least have the decency to lock their cars." He shoved her in behind the wheel, and growled, "Move over—you're not driving."

שׁוֹפָר בְּאֶפְרָיִם
a trumpet in ephraim

The Wreck churned down 30th Street toward the towering downtown skyscrapers. Eli leaned back in the driver's seat, a black cigarette perched between his lips, driving with one hand and gesticulating wildly with the other.

He was mid-rant. ". . . I mean, especially if I parked it in *that kind* of neighborhood. Anybody could have just opened the door and taken my stereo! And you see those clothes in the back? That's *all* my clothes. Seriously. Sure, to you that's no big deal. You've got a mansion and servants and everything. You can afford to leave your cars unlocked in *gangland*."

He turned a hard left then right, moving to a parallel street, before continuing his tirade.

"Really, how much effort does it take to lock a car? It takes, at most, two seconds. It's just . . . you're just . . . you're *inconsiderate* is what you are!"

He glanced in the rearview mirror. No one following him. No chopper overhead either. But he knew his luck wouldn't hold out indefinitely.

"I really would not want to be in your shoes. Not now and especially not tomorrow. Put your seatbelt on."

She didn't.

They entered a densely populated neighborhood packed with rows of neglected homes, many of which were burned out and boarded up. Isabel stared out her window, chewing at a flawlessly manicured nail.

"Admiring your handiwork?" Eli asked.

She scoffed. "You brought the drought, not me."

"You don't really believe that. If there's a curse on this land, it's the curse you brought down from Tsidon. Jah spelled out the blessings and cursings for his people hundreds of years before I was born. You lit the fuse on this one, and it's going to blow up in your face."

The queen scoffed again, loudly, overselling it. Eli tried to out-do her with a sarcastic *hmmph*. Both held their tongues for a few minutes, sulking.

Isabel finally broke the silence. "How did you get out of the handcuffs?"

"That's why you're so quiet over there?" He snorted a laugh. "You're trying to figure out how I got out of the handcuffs. You'll wrack your brain over that, but the fact that it *hasn't rained in three and a half years* doesn't bother you at all." She studied the floor. "Three and a half years that began, coincidentally, with me telling you it won't rain until I give the word. Talk about intentionally blind."

Isabel spoke slowly. "Our prophets said that Jah is an inland god. They said the storms can't rest on the land until we've crushed him." She emphatically added, "You must have dislocated your thumb and forced your hand through. I've heard of people doing that."

"*Inland god?*" Eli shook his head in amusement. "Yeah, an inland god who parts the sea and floods the whole earth. Wow. You are in for quite a surprise tomorrow. You and Ahab both. I have a feeling you're not long for this world."

Fear edged into her voice. "Look, I don't know where you're taking me, but we can work something out, okay?"

"I've already worked it all out with the king. Don't worry your pretty little head about it. It's time you realized that Ahab has been anointed to rule Ephraim; you haven't."

"Anointed? By who?"

"By Jah."

"Oh, what a hypocrite you are," she said, disgusted. "So far today, you've insulted, assaulted, choked, and threatened Ahab, but I'm the one who needs to remember that he's God's pick to be king."

"Hey, every government needs checks and balances. That's where I come in."

"Ah. If you say so, Zimri."

Eli raised an eyebrow. "*Zimri*? I see we've been boning up on our Ephraimite history. And that's an obscure one, too—Zimri ruled for, what, a week?"

"And then he began driving around in a disgusting old car and kidnapping world leaders."

"I'm nothing like Zimri. He wanted power. I only want—"

"Zimri!"

"I'm not even going to—"

"Zimri."

"Are you done? You're being childish. Besides, if anyone's to blame for my beef with the king, it's you. If it weren't for you, Ahab might have turned out an entirely different kind of man. With some solid advisors and a godly wife, who knows what he might have accomplished."

"Without me, he'd be nothing," she spat. "Ahab is a worm, a simpleton." She looked over at Eli, an idea forming. "He's not powerful, confident, like you."

Eli sensed the change in her tone and threw a glance in her direction. "You've got to be kidding me."

She held up a hand. "No, hear me out. We could get him out of the way. It would be so easy. If it came down to it, almost everyone would side with me over Ahab. They love me. And you certainly have your share of admirers."

"You are a depraved lady."

She smiled maliciously. "I know. But think about it. Your god and my god—you and I—ruling together. You could make it rain tomorrow and then we could build this nation back up until it was stronger than in the days of Shlomo. I've done my homework on him, too. You know he had an alliance with Tsidon."

"It was different back then. He ruled a united kingdom."

"We could unite it. The south is weaker than Ephraim right now. The timing is perfect. And I think we'd be good at *uniting*, don't you?" Eli let her suggestive tone slide, kept driving.

She pushed on. "Anyone who hates me loves you. Between us, we would have the support of everyone." Her mouth hung half open as the implications dawned on her.

A disgusted amazement expanded in Eli's stomach. He pretended he wasn't enticed by her, that he'd never thought of it himself. As if he wasn't glued to the screen whenever Isabel spoke, drawn like a fly to so much forbidden fruit.

He went on the offensive. "You'd do it, wouldn't you? In a heartbeat. You'd betray the man who made you queen in the first place."

"He didn't make me anything. I made him. And I could make you into something too."

Eli guffawed.

"Not that you would need the kind of help that Ahab does. But there would be . . . other benefits as well." She shifted in her seat to face Eli, her back to the door. Her legs fell open and her skirt slid up, revealing the satin and lace beneath. Eli looked at her, down and then back up. Temptation passed through him for a fraction of a second.

Then he slammed on the brakes.

Isabel was thrown into the dashboard and bounced back onto the seat hard as the car ground to a stop. Eli was out of the car in an instant and around to the passenger side. Isabel, a bit shook up but unhurt, tried too late to hit the lock before Eli yanked the door open and pulled her out onto the sidewalk by her arm.

"*Now* she locks the door," he quipped. She stared back at him, frozen in terror. "Don't give me that look; I told you to put your seatbelt on, remember?"

He flipped open his cell phone, punched a button, and shoved it to his ear. "Hey, it's me. Patch me through to the king's private line." Pause. "Just do it."

He waited a moment for Ahab to pick up and greeted him enthusiastically. "Hey, your highness! Guess who? . . . No, everything's fine . . . It's still on . . . Yeah, as planned. You have my word." He rolled his eyes at Isabel and made a gabbing motion with his hand. "No, this is awkward, but I'm calling because—how do I put this?— I *have your wife* . . . No, trust me, you can keep her. If you want to send someone to pick her up, you'll find her at the corner of 30th and Sirach. And I'd hurry. This isn't the best neighborhood. Yes . . . yes, I'm serious. Very serious. Okay, see you tomorrow, Chief."

Eli stowed his phone and then, very deliberately, pushed down the lock on the passenger door.

"You see? It's that easy."

Isabel glowered as he slammed the door and returned to the driver side.

"30th and Sirach is three miles from here," she said.

"Yeah," he laughed. "Better start walking."

In an instant, her demeanor changed. She let loose with a barrage of curses, capping it with, "I swear to Baal, I'm going to make you suffer in ways you've never even imagined! You will burn and scream and long for death but I won't let you have it until I've seen enough!"

A soft *tsk, tsk* escaped Eli's lips. "Such hostility. You know what you need? A good night's sleep. Maybe a bubble bath and some cucumbers on your eyes. Tomorrow's a big day."

"You're not going to live to see tomorrow, you insignificant tick," she vowed. "There will be no 'showdown of the gods,' and I'll get a good night's sleep because I've seen you choke on your last breath!"

Eli feigned consideration. "No, I think we should stick with the original plan." He started to duck into the car, but paused. "You know, you really could be attractive if you found a way to downplay your devil-worshiping, mass-murdering side."

He slammed on the gas and left Isabel choking on his exhaust.

"This is unacceptable!" Brent Rose teetered on the verge of tears as he studied his reflection in the dressing room mirror. "I can't wear pastels. I don't *do* pastels!"

Standing behind him, his unappreciated wardrobe assistant studied the floor. He was used to accepting the brunt of the news anchor's tantrums.

Brent railed on, "I've *never* done pastels! In eight years at Channel 7, have you ever known me to wear an article of pastel clothing? Even once?"

His assistant calmly replied, "Uh, sir, you wore a salmon shirt last night and you said that you wanted to—"

"Shut up! Shhh! Shut up! This is simply not going to work. I look like a clown. I have the second highest ratings in the city—I am not a clown!"

"Sir, I really don't think you look like a clown. You look very nice."

"*Nice?* I look like a campy, mint green clown." With mock joy, he shouted, "Look at me! I'm a minty green clown!" His over-gelled hair gripped his head firmly as he flailed. "This is not going to work. Get me something else immediately."

Asaph, Channel 7's news director, poked his head into the dressing room. "Is there a problem in here, Brent? You're late on the set."

"I look like an idiot. I need a new outfit," he replied.

"Brent, we're on in thirteen minutes. There's no time to put together a whole new outfit." His assistant nonchalantly moved to block the view of the backup outfit, another experiment in pastels.

Brent sat and stated incredulously, "Well, then. I just won't go out there. I simply refuse."

Asaph wanted a drink. Or to hit his star reporter in the face with a cinder block. He rubbed his knuckles against his temples. "I really don't see the problem, Brent. You liked the outfit half an hour ago."

His assistant chimed in helpfully, "And you really look great, too. It's—"

"No. No. No! I look like a magician. A gay magician."

Asaph slowly started backing out the door into the hallway. "No, you look handsome. You look like a star. Trust me. Now let's get a move on, okay?" He slid out the door and walked briskly down the hall, glancing at his watch. Eleven minutes.

Rayeh, the graphics guy, sidled up next to him. "Boss, there's a problem with these images for the six o'clock." He had a hard time matching Asaph's stride, heading down the narrow hallway to Studio A.

"What now?"

He handed Asaph a printout of a police sketch, front view and profile. "These are supposed to be Eli Tishbi."

Asaph snatched it from him. "Yeah. He shaved his head, shaved his beard. Why is that hard to believe?"

"It just doesn't look like him. Are you sure these didn't get mixed up?"

"They're the right sketches. Came from Justice and Conduct an hour ago." He handed the sheet back.

Rayeh surveyed the pictures for a moment. "It's a crappy drawing, then. Beard or no, it doesn't look anything like him. I saw Eli once. His eyes are way darker than this. He's scary."

They arrived at the studio. The news desk was lit up with a dozen mounted spotlights. The grips and techs were all in place. The only thing missing was Brent Rose.

And a decent lead story. Asaph sighed. On days like this, he just wanted to run a half hour of the words "No news is good news" scrolling across the screen. Only, no news is bad news in the middle of a drought.

"Alright, Rayeh, get in position and let's make sure the logo doesn't look like it's growing out of Susan's elbow tonight, okay? Rayeh?"

Rayeh was frozen, staring at the door. Everyone was staring at the door.

Eli-Jah Tishbi had just walked into the room.

A rent-a-cop rushed in after him, fake fur collar flopping on his not-quite-official jacket.

"Sir, that area is restricted. You can't—" His objections evaporated at the sight of Eli's pistol.

Every eye was on Eli as he walked down the stairs, into the middle of the studio, and asked the room, "You guys want a really *good* story?"

The Channel 7 theme music played as Brent Rose—in all his pastel glory—and his sidekick Susan Taylor beamed at the camera and rearranged blank sheets of paper.

"Good evening. I'm Brent Rose and Channel 7 Action News is just ahead."

"And I'm Susan Taylor. Our top story tonight, a Channel 7 exclusive: Eli Tishbi is indeed back in Shomron and he's . . . welcome?" Asaph cringed. *Last-minute rewrites. Oh, well. An interview with the most elusive man alive is worth some bad copy.*

Brent awkwardly countered, "That's right, Susan. We have confirmed with several of King Ahab's top officials that the manhunt has been called off and the reward money for Tishbi's death or capture has been cancelled. The reason for this may surprise and shock you. Coming up: the secret behind Eli Tishbi's new lease on life and an exclusive Channel 7 interview with the man himself. Stay tuned."

"Troubler of Ephraim!" Isabel threw her half-full wineglass at the big-screen TV. She sat on a velvet loveseat in the executive mansion's lavish sitting room. "No more freedom of the press. I want our people approving everything. Take care of it, Luli."

Luli nodded and muted the television. "Yes, ma'am. I've never liked that Brent Rose anyway. Reminds me of a cartoon."

He and El-Baal stood against the wall, looking the worse for wear, both sporting black eyes and gauze-packed noses.

Isabel shot him a look of disgust. "This is not funny. Don't you see what just happened? Eli has tied our hands. Now we have to allow this stupid charade to take place tomorrow. If we don't, we'll look like cowards and Baal a weakling!" She buried her face in her hands. "Promise me this will turn out in our favor."

"It will," Luli answered confidently. "Jah is a vulnerable god. He has weaknesses."

"Like what?"

"Mercy. He's not ruthless like Baal. This leaves him quite exposed."

Isabel turned on him. "He did not seem so exposed this afternoon."

Luli gazed at his feet in shame.

"Why were you two so powerless against Eli today? I was nearly killed because of your incompetence. Six of you, all armed, and still Eli dragged me down the stairs and out the door. I'm starting to think I'd be better off using the Shomrey-Melek."

El-Baal stepped away from the wall and quietly seethed, "Perhaps Baal wasn't powerless. Perhaps he saw your lack of loyalty and chose not to protect you."

"What . . . ?"

El-Baal stepped to the loveseat. "When will you learn, Isabel? You can't hide things from us. Baal reveals all." He sat down beside her. His speech was angry but controlled. "What were you thinking offering Jah a position beside Baal? Are you *trying* to lose his favor?"

"Y-you said Baal is not a jealous god. You said he doesn't mind if we pay tribute to other deities."

"Any god but Jah. He *hates* Jah."

Confusion surfaced on her face.

"Why do you think your father sent you here to marry this spineless Ahab? Did you think it was merely political? There is more priest than king in your father. He always has Baal's will in the forefront of his mind."

Isabel listened attentively.

"He saw in your coming here a final solution to the problem of Jah. Through you, we can snuff the name from the earth. Your influence on Ahab is enormous and, when your son becomes king, we will have complete control of Ephraim. We can *turn* this people. We'll make them servants of Baal for eternity."

Luli smiled and added, "And as for the Southern Kingdom, Jehudah will fall in the same way. Your daughter Athaliah will make a perfect wife for their weakling king. We will control the thrones of both of Jah's kingdoms. Indeed, El-Baal has already begun the negotiations."

Placing his hand on her knee, El-Baal leaned in an inch from her face. She could smell his aftershave. "But you, child, have risked everything today with your treachery. So don't ask me to guarantee victory tomorrow. Perhaps Baal will overlook your blasphemy and perhaps not."

Isabel panicked. "We can fix it. We can fix it. If we kill Eli tonight—in secret—we can make it look like he fled. I'll call LOCUST in. He can't have gotten far from that television studio. They'll hunt him down and just make him disappear! The people will assume he didn't have the nerve to show up. Then we declare Baal the winner by default. Yes. This can work to our advantage. We can declare tomorrow a national holiday, when we celebrate Jah's defeat at the hand of Baal. And when we—"

El-Baal slapped her across the face. "Wake up. If we kill Eli, the drought continues. But if we meet him tomorrow—even if we defeat him—it will rain. Jah is a god who keeps his word. He's pathetic. We can humiliate him and rid ourselves of this problem all at once. These events were set in motion long ago by powers far greater than ourselves. We've been building toward tomorrow for decades. We have to let it happen."

"But Baal is angry with me. You said so yourself. He may allow us to lose."

El-Baal grinned. "There are ways of re-gaining his favor. Call your husband and tell him we'll be picking him up in a couple of hours." He kissed her on the forehead. "Don't worry. Baal is the True God. If nothing else, you can trust in that."

Sitting back in the loveseat, he picked up the remote and turned the sound back on. The interview was underway.

Eli sat behind the news desk next to Brent Rose, who kept nervously eyeing the handgun hanging beneath the prophet's left arm.

"Now, Eli, you've been at odds with this regime for quite some time. You've been banished for repeatedly disturbing the peace and, more recently, Ahab has offered ten million shekels for your capture for failing to pay tribute to Baal. Why do you think he's suddenly so open to this meeting tomorrow?"

"Because it hasn't rained in three and a half years. Ahab knows that he himself brought this drought on our land and he's looking for a way to make it right. Even if it means swallowing his pride. Might be the first smart move he's made as king."

Brent leaned forward melodramatically. "So, you're suggesting that King Ahab himself is responsible for the drought?"

"I'm not *suggesting* anything. It was all Ahab. He's allowed these goyim to brainwash him. Under Ahab's leadership, our country has turned its back on Jah and embraced Baal as god. We've built altars and high places in his honor and desecrated the land that Jah gave us. And if we don't turn back to him, this drought will look like a fun-filled picnic at the lake, complete with really good potato salad and complimentary puppies, compared to what comes next."

"So, what exactly is the purpose of tomorrow's . . . uh . . . contest?"

Eli looked right into the camera. "Tomorrow is a day of decision. We've been unwilling to make up our minds about who we, as a nation, want to serve. Tomorrow, we will see what Baal is made of. And then we will see Jah in all his glory and we will decide which god deserves our loyalty. The time for riding the fence is over." He stood up and walked off the set.

Susan took over. "Once again, the event is scheduled to take place tomorrow morning at eight o'clock at Mount Karmel Stadium in downtown Shomron. Children under sixteen will not be admitted. Admission is free and the public is welcome, but Mount Karmel only seats sixty thousand, so arrive early."

baal

Reporters from five networks, as well as a half dozen local channels, swarmed to the Channel 7 headquarters where they found the place locked up tight, lights off. But Eli had to be inside, they reasoned, and so they would wait right there at the door of their competitor's studio for seconds. Why should one channel get all the goods?

The painfully modern building, situated in the comparatively wealthy East Shomron business district, was a bit of an eyesore, but seemed to lend itself to the gathering of media personalities. A sampling of news vans had parked on the small, dead lawn and, hovering around them, cameramen, correspondents, and technical personnel waited. And waited.

Restless and bored as they were, the professional attitude was fast devolving:

" . . . been two hours since the interview ended. He ever coming out?"

" . . . starting to get dark. We're waiting another half hour and then . . . "

" . . . sure he didn't slip out the back door? I don't think there's an underground . . . "

" . . . hate that Brent Rose guy. Sure, I'd win awards too if I gave the king an open forum every time he . . . "

" . . . wasn't really Eli. It was an actor. Eli's four inches taller than that guy . . . "

" . . . really, *really* hate Brent Rose. I mean, with a passion!"

A young female reporter from Channel 14 was doing a live feed near the entrance. "We're waiting for Eli Tishbi to exit the building. Hopefully he'll have some additional comments for us. As you know, Tishbi has been a brutally candid critic of King Ahab and even more so of the queen. Apparently, he sees her Tsidonian heritage and the institution of the Baalist party here in Ephraim as evidence that the regime is compromising with—" She put a finger to her earpiece. "We've just received word that Mr. Tishbi will be coming out momentarily."

At once, the front door flew wide and a bald figure sprinted from the building, past the camera crews, and down the street, trench coat billowing behind him. The throng of reporters struggled to gather their equipment and give chase. Less than half were able to go mobile in time, shifting cameras and mics en route. Their target turned down Commerce and chugged along the center line of the street. A small crowd followed fifty paces behind. Gradually, his head start began to shrink.

He was winded.

The more physically fit of the TV crews caught up to him just as he collapsed in the middle of an intersection, huffing and wheezing. Cameras flashed and whirred. Reporters shouted questions and shoved microphones in his face.

The excitement quickly died down as they realized that the man was crying. And that he was wearing a trench coat over a pastel shirt and tie. And that he was not Eli Tishbi.

"My beautiful hair," Brent Rose sobbed. "Keep him away from me!"

Eli walked through the back door of the Channel 7 building and out into the evening, a smirk planted on his face. There was not a soul around, save a few homeless men slouched against a liquor store, preoccupied with the contents of their bottles. Eli's light coat was inside-out, complimented by a fedora that didn't quite fit him. Street lights flickered on with a buzz as he passed beneath them. After half a block, he disappeared down some steps into a westbound UrbanRail station.

The train was two minutes out.

Ahab's father, Omri, had ordered the construction of Shomron's underground train system in the early years of his reign, basing it on the one in Damesq. Short, light, automated trains just three cars long came fast and frequent, twenty-four hours a day. On the longest north-south stretch, the Ebal-Gerizim line got up to 115 miles per hour. The transportation was affordable and convenient. There had never been an accident resulting in a fatality. And Transit Patrol kept most stations free of loiterers and troublemakers.

Projects like UrbanRail were the reason that Omri had maintained a high approval rating, even while he wed Ephraim to her one-time enemy, Tsidon. Ahab's father had possessed a certain finesse that was glaringly absent in Ahab himself—which explained his own low approval. That and the drought.

Finesse made no difference to Eli—only wisdom and faithfulness mattered. And as far as he was concerned, if Omri's line became a dynasty, Ephraim was through.

The train zipped into the station and hissed to a stop. Three commuters bustled past Eli without a second glance and ascended the stairs to the street.

Eli took one more cautious look around and boarded the train.

A thin black limo waited impatiently on the long circle drive of the executive mansion, sandwiched between two massive armored cars. Several Shomrey-Melek in dark business suits brandished shotguns and kept watch in all directions, on their guard even within the impregnable walls of the king's official residence.

For all the jabs from the late-night comedians, Joab took great pride in his security force. Even as he found their role and authority systematically usurped by the priests of Baal, he did his best to keep the Shomrey-Melek disciplined and committed to their mission, as if no one was looking over their shoulder. He forced the thought of goyim interlopers from his mind—he couldn't concentrate on any task when the anger started building up. As if on cue, Luli and El-Baal emerged from the side of the house, escorting the king and queen to the small convoy.

Ahab was more than a little irritated. "I don't understand why this is necessary. I wish you guys would make up your minds. One minute Baal is some unstoppable force, crushing all who oppose him, all-mighty, all-consuming—and now we need to do some ritual to build his confidence. This is so ridiculous. David never worried about Jah's self esteem."

They reached the limo. Luli helped Ahab into the car with a shove. Isabel followed him, and then the two high priests. The royal couple arranged themselves in one leather seat, El-Baal and Luli facing them in another.

Joab ordered his agents back to the armored cars. As one, the convoy pulled out through the gate and away from the mansion.

Ahab pointed at Luli and fumed, "El-Baal, I'm warning you. Control him before—uh—" El-Baal pulled out a long, shining dagger with a long and wickedly jagged blade and gently placed it against Ahab's neck.

"Shut up," he commanded. "Tonight is only necessary because you've both been less than loyal to Baal. He is not at all pleased with your accommodating attitudes toward Eli and his god. Baal has sucked the life out of people—left them writhing in years of agony—for less. He is not patient. He will not suffer long with you. He does not forget transgressions. So shut your mouth and do exactly as you're told and *maybe* tomorrow won't be unspeakably horrible for you, you pathetic piece of window dressing."

Very deliberately, he moved the blade to Ahab's cheek. Ahab could only stare back in disbelief as El-Baal made a deep, three-inch long cut down the side of his terrified face. Luli grabbed a handful of the king's hair and, pushing at the wound with a small glass vial, collected a few ounces of blood, before capping the vial and placing it in his coat pocket.

Ahab stared out the side window in shock, pushing his sleeve against the seeping wound, paralyzed by fear. Next to him, his wife gazed out the opposite window, a ruthlessly amused smile on her face.

The Kishon Heights Housing Projects sprawled five city blocks. They weren't on any cop's beat. In fact, rumor was that even the army was unwilling to enter the projects unless they absolutely had to, and then in force. As a result, drug trafficking, prostitution, and gambling flourished, unfettered by any pretense of law enforcement.

At the corner of Division and Gaza, six new units had been erected only two years earlier under Obadijah's housing initiative, thrown up by construction crews demanding heavily armed protection and overtime for all work done after ten in the morning. They went up in three weeks and now, two years later, were already candidates for condemnation. Windows broken. Gang graffiti over every surface. Garbage strewn across the dirt yards.

Except for Unit 33.

Everyone in the projects knew to keep clear of that particular building. The walls were spotless, the windows barred, and there were always two men with absolutely no sense of humor guarding the front door, heavily armed and on-edge. Tonight, that number was tripled. Security was always beefed up when Jehu had a meeting.

On the second floor, in apartment 210, Obadijah sat at the head of a table that could easily have accommodated fifteen. Tonight it settled for two.

The apartment had been converted into something of a boardroom. A couple of computers sat against the far wall, humming away. Several large maps hung on another wall next to a large dry erase board. The kitchenette was stocked with office supplies and a small stash of bottled water.

Across from Obadijah sat Jehu, a compactly muscular man in his late twenties. His shoulder-length hair, as black as his T-shirt, was pulled back tightly in a rubber band.

Obadijah was running down a checklist. "How are you for water?"

"We're getting by," Jehu replied in his usual clipped fashion.

He hated having to hoard it. All around them were people who could barely afford to stay hydrated. They turned to crime and prostitution or got desperate and drank urine or gutter water and became horribly ill.

Obadijah narrowed his eyes. "I know you want to help everyone in the projects, Jehu, but *my* first responsibility is to the prophets in this building. Make sure you don't spread it too thin."

"Yeah. We've got enough."

"What about Jah-El? How's he doing?"

"As well as could be expected. He's getting chemo under an assumed name down at Horeb General."

Obadijah loosened his tie and carefully rolled up the sleeves of his burgundy shirt. "Look man, this situation will get touchy tomorrow. Depending on how this thing turns out, I think it might be smart to get you guys out of here tonight."

"Not an option. We stay."

"Listen to me," Obadijah pleaded. "The latest opinion polls show that the public overwhelmingly believes Baal to be the one true god, that Jah is an antique, and that those of us who still serve him are *intolerant* and should be exiled or even executed in the interest of progress."

Jehu was unmoved. "That's some thick irony."

"Yeah, it's thick alright. Look, whatever the outcome tomorrow, there could be a backlash against followers of Jah. Now, I did my best to make this place look like a regular housing unit, but if someone had my number and they really started digging, it wouldn't be too hard to figure out what's going on here." He pulled a sheet of paper from a battered green file folder and slid it to Jehu. "I got a message from Eli tonight; Isabel's on to us. She knows that there are more prophets somewhere in the city. I think we need to cut our losses and get you people as far away from here as possible."

Jehu scanned the e-mail and handed it back to Obadijah. "If we leave tonight and you've suddenly got an empty building on your hands, someone *will* notice. And then you're a dead man. Besides, you remove us from this neighborhood and the whole place goes to hell. I can't let that happen. We're armed. We're organized. We're networked. And if the worst should go down, I can have everyone out of here, moving in different directions, within five minutes. If it comes to that, we will simply disappear."

"LOCUST comes up here, you'll *disappear* all right. There won't be time to run. You're my responsibility. Jah's orders. I've got my own demons; I don't need all of your deaths on my conscience."

"There's a hundred of us. I'm pretty sure we could handle LOCUST."

"No. You couldn't. Believe me."

Jehu frowned. "You do claim to be a prophet, right? Have a little faith."

Obadijah rustled some papers around for a moment. "I don't know." He put the folders back in his briefcase and slid his jacket on. "I hate this. Nobody asked us about any of it." He slammed the briefcase shut and headed to the door.

"Just two weeks to prepare would have been enough." Under his breath he added, "But Eli doesn't seem to work on anyone's timeline but his own."

Jehu eyed him suspiciously. "But he's not working on his own timeline. He's working on Jah's."

"Yeah, probably." He hovered by the door.

"Is there something I should know here?"

"Look, you've never even met Eli. You don't know how he can be. He's . . . " Obadijah searched for the right word, then realized it didn't exist. "I mean, I just can't figure out why every time I hear from Jah, he's perfectly rational. Yet every time he talks to Eli, he's got some insane stunt for him to perform."

Jehu shrugged. "Maybe he knows you wouldn't do the crazy stuff. Or maybe he figures that you won't question him at every turn. Anyway, I guess we'll find out tomorrow, won't we?"

"Yeah, I guess we will."

The convoy came to a stop in front of the Ministry of Justice and Conduct. Joab got out first, followed by the rest of the Shomrey-Melek, shotguns at the ready. They established a perimeter around the limousine before Isabel and Ahab exited the vehicle, followed by the high priests.

El-Baal pointed at the agent nearest him. "You. What's your name?"

"Enoch, sir."

"Enoch, you come with us. The rest of you men, stay put."

Joab moved to block his path. "If the king's going in there, then I am too."

El-Baal sneered. "We only need one little commando tonight and I'd rather have Enoch here than you; no offense. He's got a better attitude. Now step aside." Over his shoulder, he added, "Come along, Enoch."

Enoch stood frozen, unsure of what to do. "Sir?"

Joab kept his shotgun barrel down, pointed at the sidewalk, just inches in front of El-Baal's feet. He glanced at Ahab.

"What happened to your face, sir?"

Ahab didn't answer.

"Sir, I highly recommend that I accompany you into the J and C headquarters, whether additional agents are coming or not."

"We don't have time for this," El-Baal spat. Grabbing Enoch by the arm, he moved to walk around the agent.

Joab clicked off the safety and raised the gun, aiming it at the high priest's chest.

El-Baal glared back defiantly. "I would advise against that, Jah-lover," he gritted.

"What would you like me to do, your highness?" Joab asked anxiously.

Ahab was unsure. He looked sidelong at Isabel, whose expression told him what *she* would have him do, then to Luli, who slowly rolled the vile of blood back and forth between his thumb and middle finger.

"Wait down here, Joab. We'll call you if we need you," Ahab finally stammered.

"Very well." He lowered the gun and stepped out of their path. The five filed past Joab, through a gate in the ten-foot fence, and toward the eight-story building.

The headquarters resembled a police station, stacked on top of a fort, surrounded by a park, all enclosed in razor wire. A huge sculpture of Baal stood in the courtyard, illuminated by half a dozen spotlights. A large metal sign mounted over the entrance identified the building with an official-looking insignia: Baal holding the world in one hand and a sword in the other.

 Luli and El-Baal led the way into the building where two more priests stood on either side of the door, acting as sentries. They buzzed off the magnetic lock and nodded to El-Baal as he entered. One of them stopped Enoch, who was taking up the rear.

"You'll have to check your weapons here."

Enoch looked at Ahab with obvious concern. The king gestured for him to obey. Uneasily, he handed over his shotgun and sidearm.

Crippling taxes, along with a steady stream of funding from Tsidon, allowed Isabel's men to keep the facility always on the cutting edge of technology. Security doors, requiring card access, blocked off every hallway and the more sensitive areas were outfitted with retinal scan equipment. In the middle of the lobby, a smaller statue of Baal continually spilled water from its hands, like raindrops from his fingertips, in an elaborate indoor fountain. Enoch resisted the urge to run to the fountain and gulp down some of the precious water.

Despite the hour, a full staff was present. Several priests gave orders to throngs of business-attired employees.

El-Baal's little field trip picked up more people as he led them down a corridor, to a large elevator, into which they just barely fit. He swiped an ID card through a slot and pushed the top floor button. Smoothly and quickly, the elevator ascended to the eighth floor.

As the doors opened, Enoch's jaw dropped. This floor—comprised of one enormous room—was far different from the others. Illuminated only by candles and the stars and light pollution that spilled in through the massive central skylight, there was nothing high-tech about this place at all.

This was the Temple of Baal.

Dark-skinned men in white hooded tunics—prophets of Baal—moved around the room, lighting candles and incense. Ten more priests stood near a large stone table at the temple's center, sharpening knives and muttering chants under their breath. Panic shot through Enoch, starting in the base of his skull and spreading quickly down his spine. He glanced back at the elevator door, now closed.

El-Baal put an arm around him and smiled. "What a lovely night, don't you think?"

Eli shared the train car with three others. The homeless man across from him was asleep, hunched over awkwardly, his head resting against the metal hand bar. Eli shot a quick look at the other two, who were obviously stoned and posed no threat of recognizing him. He sat back, relaxing a little, and took off Brent Rose's hat. He decided that, in the interest of his prophetic reputation, he'd better send it back to him.

For now, however, he didn't know exactly where he should be going. There were always holes in Jah's instructions—gaps, sometimes long ones, in which he had to fill the time with whatever he thought best.

A speaker six inches from his ear crackled, "This stop, Janoah Avenue. Next stop, Sokoh North." The train braked with a loud hiss and the doors slid open. As he passed the homeless man, Eli reached down and gently moved his head from off the metal bar. He placed his last few bills in the fedora, and put it on the sleeping man's head. He was sure Mr. Rose would approve.

Eli stepped onto the platform of the mostly deserted rail station and bounded up the stairs and out onto the sidewalk. Sokoh was a wealthy street, lined with tall, shining apartment buildings. Few people were out and about.

As he cleared the last two stairs, Eli was suddenly slammed to his knees by an invisible force. The opulent district before him disintegrated before his eyes and, for a moment, there was just black.

Very slowly, his vision focused on the slums that were growing in its place. Crumbling buildings rose up out of the ground around him. A burned out car sat on blocks to his right. To his left, a trash can had been knocked over, spilling its contents into the road, where flies buzzed from trash to trash.

It was hot. Eli guessed a hundred and twenty, a hundred and thirty, who knows. The sun was impossibly huge, taking up most of the sky. Eli looked around.

What is this dump?

Then he spotted El-Baal, standing in the middle of the street, holding a gun to a teenage boy's head. The kid whimpered, tears and snot flowing, and begged for his life. El-Baal just smiled and fired a shot that blew the top off the kid's skull and blasted him to the street. The lifeless body landed on a pile of corpses, sending ripples through them like a pebble in a still pond.

The dead bodies shifted, morphed. Clothing became hair. Dead, empty faces slowly turned into deeply painted eyes. *Isabel*. She laughed and laughed like a little kid who had just thought of something clever and couldn't wait to tell everyone. Her face was splattered red. Eli looked down to her hands. They were full of thick, red blood, pouring down from her fingers like rain, pattering to the ground.

She was sitting on the back of a dragon. A hideous red beast with a long row of tall, razor-sharp horns. Eli felt the hot, sulfurous breath surging from the creature's nostrils, as its forked tongue darted in and out of its mouth. Rage began to pulse through the prophet's body. This was Baal—the real Baal.

The idols, now common in Ephraim, were an eclectic lot, usually in human form but not always. Baal had many different titles: Baal-Zaphon, Baal-Peor, Baal-Zebub, Bel. Devotees often thought of them as entirely different gods, each with his own sphere of influence. But Eli knew better. Those were just masks. The slithering creature before him was the force behind them all.

Isabel ran her hand down the dragon's scaly neck in a thoroughly sensual motion. In her other hand, she held aloft a goblet overflowing with a thick, red liquid. Eli knew what it was; she was drunk on the blood of Jah's holy ones. As she took another long sip, blood spilling down her chin, he noticed a number written on her hand. He tried to add it up—it should have been simple—but for some reason he couldn't do the math.

The sun grew even larger, relentlessly expanding until it filled the entire sky with red and yellow flames, which began to churn, moving around clockwise over the earth. Eli's heart pounded in his chest. As before, a fireball grew and pulsated in the eye of this hurricane of flame. Eli closed his eyes. He was sweating through his clothes, drenched. Even with eyes clamped tight, he saw flowers and trees wilting and dying, collapsing to the cracked pavement.

Then it went dark. In an instant, the temperature dropped fifty degrees. He looked back up at the sky. The fire was gone, replaced by towering black thunderheads.

The temperature was still dropping. He could smell the rain coming.

All at once, Eli saw a thousand faucets gushing water, hoses spitting, fire hydrants shooting it into the air. And then he heard the unmistakable sound of a revolver being cocked.

Sokoh Avenue slammed back into place. The apartment buildings, the stairs, the entrance to the UrbanRail. He was still on his knees, trying desperately to catch his breath and reorient himself.

"Don't make a sound, Mr. Wine-and-Oil. Just give me the cash and it better be a lot."

Eli turned his head slightly and found himself looking sidelong down the barrel of a gun.

"Don't look at me!" The man was gaunt and dirty, dressed in ragged clothes. He rocked nervously back and forth. "Just hand it over nice and slow and we'll both be on our merry ways."

Eli had his breathing back under command. "You're out of luck, my friend. I don't have a shekel."

The man kicked Eli solidly between the shoulder blades with surprising might, knocking him to his hands and knees.

"Don't give me that crap. What're you doing on Sokoh if you don't have any money?" he demanded.

"I don't know; what are *you* doing on Sokoh if you don't have any money?"

The man leaned in, treating Eli to his foul breath, and pushed the gun up against the back of his bald head. The ring of cold metal sent a shiver down his back.

"I'm going to tell you one more time. Give me your money. Now"

Eli turned to face him, easily swatting the gun from his hand. It clattered to the concrete steps. In the same motion, he landed a hard kick into the man's abdomen, propelling him down a few stairs into the concrete wall with a *fwump*. Eli scooped up the small revolver, bounded down the five steps, and pinned the man to the wall by his collar.

"What's the matter with you? Huh? That's not *nice*," Eli lectured. "Putting a gun to a perfect stranger's head. Your mother taught you better than that, didn't she, Kohath?"

The man stared back in disbelief. It had been years since anyone had addressed him by his given name.

Recognition oozed over Kohath's face, alarm right on its heels. "Oh man, I know who you are! Awww, no. I screwed up. I'm dead." He steeled himself. "Well, go ahead and kill me. A bullet in the head is nice and quick."

Annoyed, Eli said, "Kill you? I'm not going to kill you! What's the *matter* with you?"

"What's the matter . . . ?! Oh man, that's just perf . . . I'm *dehydrated!* I haven't had any water in two days. The lines are too long and even if you can wait, you have to bribe your way to the front or people just keep getting in ahead of you. I need some money or I'm going to die!"

Eli let go of his collar and lowered the gun.

Tears streamed down Kohath's sunken cheeks. "What did I do to make Jah so mad at me? I've never bowed my knee to Baal. I don't even *own* an Ishtar pole. You know him, right? So you tell me, Eli: why does he hate me so much?"

"He doesn't hate you. He's . . . " Eli tried to pin his thoughts to words. "He's punishing the entire nation. His pledge is to us as a whole and, as a whole, we've turned from him."

"He's punishing all of us, huh? Well, you look pretty comfortable, buddy. He providing for you pretty well?"

"In ways," Eli replied. "But I'd trade places with you in a second. Trust me—you wouldn't want to be me. Be happy with the yoke you've been given."

"That's easy for you to say. You're a man with options. You pray and it stops raining. I suppose you could pray again and end the drought any time you wanted. You ever think about that? How many lives could you have saved today? Yesterday? This month?!"

Eli had no answer.

Kohath sniffed back some tears. "I'm sorry. I'm talking nonsense. I'm just so desperate right now, I just—" He started sobbing uncontrollably.

Eli toyed with the idea of putting a hand on his shoulder, but thought better of it. "It's almost over," he reassured. "Just hold on."

Kohath stopped crying abruptly and wiped his eyes and nose with a filthy sleeve. "I can't hold on anymore. Shoot me."

"Nope. Sorry."

"Then give me my gun back. I'll do it myself."

Eli eased the hammer back into place. "I'll make you a deal. Try this: Go home and fill up your bathtub with water." He stopped and thought for a moment. "Clean it out first. Really. *Then* fill it up. All the way to the top. Before that water runs out, it will rain."

An angry, desperate laugh came up from deep inside Kohath. "My faucet's been dry for two years, genius. You see, they've got this 'drought' on."

"Humor me," said Eli. "Go home and try it. If there's no water, *then* kill yourself." He slapped the revolver back into Kohath's hand and walked up onto the street. He reached into his pocket and pulled out a scrap of paper that read, *144 Sokoh North Apt 77.*

The Temple of Baal glowed with the light of five hundred candles. The priests were squeezed in thick around the stone table like ants around a melting gumdrop. They had removed their jackets and were in the process of wrestling with Enoch, trying to hold him down long enough to fasten his wrists and ankles with leather straps anchored at the table's four corners. The room was filled with shouts and grunts. Enoch produced a particularly unnerving wail as he labored to fight off the room full of men.

He was doing a decent job of resisting, considering the odds. He thrashed and kicked with an adrenaline-fueled strength, occasionally freeing an arm and landing a desperate punch or elbow on one of the black-clad priests. El-Baal stood outside of the fray, softly encouraging Enoch to give up.

"I'll never bow to you devil-worshiping goyim!" He kicked Luli in the face, re-breaking his already bruised and lacerated nose.

Five priests jumped on Enoch's legs all at once, weighing them down long enough for Luli to buckle them into the restraints. They then piled on his torso, smothering him until he had no strength left, and secured his wrists as well. He was spread out now, completely vulnerable.

Enoch looked up at Ahab, tears striping his cheeks. "Your Highness, help me! What are they doing? I've been loyal! I'm loyal! I'd never betray you!"

Ahab swallowed hard and turned his back to Enoch. The other priests parted for El-Baal, who sidled up to the table, holding the same knife with which he'd opened Ahab's face in the limo. The room suddenly went silent as El-Baal cut Enoch's shirt down the front, exposing his brown chest. The only sound was Enoch's panicked breathing.

El-Baal closed his eyes and proclaimed, "Lord Baal, we come to this sacred place, seeking your favor." He lifted his hands up toward the skylight. "We have wronged you Baal, and you demand an act of ruthlessness as proof of our dedication. Tonight, we give to you this Treachery

Offering—a trusted friend of the king. He will serve to seal this king and this land to you."

The priests all placed their hands on Enoch, who had again begun to thrash with all his might. El-Baal continued, "We dedicate this land to you. Its king is your loyal subject." Luli grabbed Ahab by the back of the neck and forced him to turn and face the table. Ahab was sweating profusely and shaking.

Luli pushed the small vial of blood into the king's palm and demanded, "Do you dedicate yourself to the service of Baal and commit all that you own and control to his benefit?"

Ahab tried his hardest not to look at Enoch's face. "Uh, yeh—uh, yes."

El-Baal looked at the king with contempt. "Then seal the offering with your blood." Enoch closed his eyes tightly as Ahab removed the cap from the vial and dribbled his blood on the agent's face and chest.

"We dedicate this people to you, Baal. Their queen is your loyal subject," El-Baal said, handing the long, jagged knife to Isabel.

"I dedicate myself to the service of Baal," she recited for the hundredth time, "and commit all that I own and control to his benefit." She expertly cut the tip of her finger and ran it along Enoch's forehead, leaving a trail of blood. "I seal this Treachery Offering with my blood."

All of the priests pushed up their sleeves, revealing long, straight scars zig-zagging their arms. As one, they droned, "We serve only Baal. We forsake all other gods." They produced similar knives and each made a long fresh slash on both of his arms, then sheathed their blades and stretched their hands up toward the skylight. Blood covered their arms, soaking their bunched sleeves. They shouted their allegiance to Baal over and over, louder and louder.

Suddenly, they stopped. El-Baal raised his large dagger above his head, gripping it with both fists. With a look of ecstasy, he declared, "Baal is God."

Ahab's face contorted as he watched the priest punch the knife into Enoch's chest with a hollow *thud*. He fell to the floor and vomited.

El-Baal gave him a contemptuous kick. "Get up."

אבדיה
obadijah

The elevator doors parted with a ding on the seventh floor of Beth David Plaza. Obadijah walked briskly down the hall to his apartment, yawning violently. It was after 2 AM and all he could think about was sleep. Tomorrow would be an especially early morning and both of his bosses—human and divine—would insist that he be there on time. In a series of automatic motions, he slipped a key into the lock, pushed the door open, flipped on the light, and reached for the burglar alarm.

He froze. The console hung away from the wall, revealing several wires cut and spliced together. Instantly awake, he reached down to his ankle holster and pulled out a small pistol. Cautiously, he made his way into the bedroom. Light came in through the half-closed blinds and bounced around the room. He held the gun out at arm's length, tracing the bedroom from corner to corner.

Finding no one, he slowly made his way down the hallway, and into the spacious living room. Two small lamps were on, casting long shadows across the carpet. He scanned the room, studying the backs of two tall chairs and a leather couch.

Adrenaline pumped through him as his eyes locked on the silhouette of a man's head barely peaking up over the top of the sofa. Silently, he made his way up behind the couch, aimed the gun, and chambered a round.

"Put your hands on your head while you still have one," he growled—his best imitation of someone who wasn't scared to death.

"What is it with people pointing guns at my *head* today?" Eli threw up his hands in exasperation. "Do you have any idea how unsettling that is?"

A long, annoyed—yet relieved—sigh hissed out of Obadijah. He flipped the safety back on and tossed the gun to an end table on his way around to confront his friend, who was sitting calmly on the couch, a thick book open on his lap and a mug of coffee next to him.

Obadijah blew a gasket. "What are you thinking?"

Eli looked into the coffee cup. "I helped myself to some java. I didn't think it was a big deal."

"Why, *why* would you come here?"

"I needed a place to lay low and get some sleep." He added dryly, "Good to know I'm always welcome."

Obadijah began to pace. "Oh, man. Oh, man. This is not good."

"What's caught in your armor?"

"Okay, let's review the facts here! Number one," he held a finger an inch from Eli's nose. "Everyone knows that I have a reputation for being a 'Jah-sympathizer.' Number two: you came to *me* first when you returned to Shomron. Number three: Isabel is a paranoid, psychotic witch who never really liked me to begin with!" He clamped his hands together. "Add these things up and what do you get?"

Eli took a long drink from his coffee and looked up at Obadijah, semi-interested.

"They've been out there, keeping an eye on my place ever since you came back! I see them whenever I come and go!"

Eli nodded. "Oh, you mean the goyim in the blue surveillance van across the street. Yeah, I was hoping to just slip past, but they made me at the door."

Obadijah stared at him, alarmed, for a moment before scrambling to the window and peering down at the street. "Where are they now?"

"Sheol." Eli set the mug down and turned back to the book in his lap.

With a defeated moan, Obadijah flopped down in a leather chair and cradled his head in his hands. "You idiot. When they're not there tomorrow morning, I'm screwed."

Eli slammed the book shut. "Tomorrow, it's not going to matter anymore. The people of Ephraim will see the power of Jah and if Ahab doesn't put things back in order, he'll be replaced. Either way, what Isabel and her pallid pals think will be moot. Super-moot. This is the last night you have to worry about Isabel 'discovering' that you serve the One True God." He was judging his friend and he didn't care. "Tomorrow starts a whole new era. Jah will show the people his unmistakable glory. There will be repentance. There will be tears. There will be judgment. Oh, and don't forget to pack a slicker, my friend, because there will be rain."

"And what if there isn't?" Obadijah stood up and swiped at the air. "I mean, I don't want to sound like a scoffer or anything, but people have been praying for rain for three and a half years and it doesn't look like Jah's listening."

"What's happened to you?" Eli looked at him suspiciously. "That harlot has gotten her hooks into you, hasn't she?"

"No, I believe in him. You know I do," Obadijah said. He looked around the room for the right words. "But this is reality, Eli. And sometimes, reality doesn't work out the way we want it to."

Eli shook his head. "Just go to bed. You'll be convinced tomorrow."

A few minutes after 4 AM, Obadijah's body began to shake. His eyes were clamped tightly shut as he squeezed two fistfuls of bed sheet. And yet, he wasn't sleeping, and this wasn't a dream. He was sitting on a curb between a pile of trash and the shell of a car in a poor and shabby neighborhood. The sun was impossibly huge, a giant canopy, leaving only a shallow ring of blue sky above the horizon in every direction.

The air was dry, and hotter than he'd ever experienced. Each breath seemed to burn his lungs and infuse them with a mist of angry dust. The only thought he could manage was that he didn't want to be there. He took off his jacket and tie and unbuttoned his shirt, fanning it against his chest. Dust and sand swirled up in a gust of wind and clung to Obadijah's sticky face and neck.

His eyes felt as dry as the dust creeping into them and they stung with each blink. He tried to cry out to Jah, but found that his lips would not part—they were cemented together by dirt, grit, and dried sweat. He focused all of his strength into his jaw and cranked the muscles. His mouth stuck fast. In desperation, he grabbed his lower jaw with both hands and yanked down, forcing his mouth open inch by painful inch. His lips clung to each other with a fierce grip before cracking and bleeding their way apart.

Obadijah pulled himself to his knees and stared up at the sky. Whatever Jah was telling him, he was pretty sure it was not a happy omen. After all, if it were good news, he'd probably be telling Eli. Cheerful homecomings, optimism, and long-awaited rain were Eli's lot. Obadijah was in charge of watching over the suffering of those left behind. He hated himself for being so angry with his God. Tears streamed down his face, turning the dust to mud and mixing with the blood on his mouth and chin.

Despair enveloped him.

Eli perched on the edge of the couch, staring at the muted television and cleaning a disassembled gun with a small rag and rod. His face was emotionless as he robotically swabbed and oiled the pistol, never tearing his eyes from the news archive on the screen.

It was footage of a multiple execution in a vast outdoor stadium. The place was packed. Vendors sold food and candy. People cheered and waved at the camera. *Hi, Mom!* In the middle of it all stood a line of twenty men, shoulder-to-shoulder, their mouths gagged, their hands bound behind their backs. Their unmasked eyes were wild with fear. Standing opposite them were twenty gunmen, each armed with a large rifle.

The picture cut to Isabel and Ahab sitting in a box seat, El-Baal and Luli seated on either side of them. Isabel was speaking into a microphone. She appeared to be holding back laughter—almost ecstatic. Next to her, Ahab shifted uncomfortably. Noticing the cameras, he tried to steel his jaw and look regal.

Obadijah's tears stopped rolling as he sensed a change in the atmosphere. He looked up to the sky, which was beginning to darken. It occurred to him all at once that he was so thirsty he'd drink anything. He'd gulp down the foulest sewer water if someone offered it to him cold.

Then he felt it. Rain was coming. A certain smell, like wet cedar, that always preceded rain, found its way through the dust and heat and into Obadijah's nostrils. He closed his eyes and opened his mouth wider. He could hear the beginnings of thunder.

Rain is coming. He's going to quench my thirst.

Blood flowed from his mouth, down his neck, staining his shirt a brown-red. He waited, mouth open, for the torrents of rain to come flooding down.

Suddenly the sound of rushing water filled the air at a hundred decibels. Obadijah's eyes flew wide. The world had taken on an orange tint. Fire was swirling around the sky, burning and roaring. Faster and faster. He looked down at himself. The blood and mud were gone. He was no longer hot. No longer sweaty. No longer thirsty. A smile slowly spread across his lips.

On the television, the prisoners were being executed one at a time—each gunman shooting the man opposite him in turn. Avoiding the head and heart, they aimed for the right side of the chest, causing their victims to fall to the ground and writhe in pain, gasping for breath. With each shot, the crowd went wild.

The bedroom door slammed open and Obadijah came crashing out. He stumbled into the living room and stood a few feet behind Eli, trying to re-orient himself to the reality of his apartment in the middle of the night.

Eli didn't take his eyes off the screen for even a second. "I told you," he said flatly.

Obadijah walked around to the couch once again and sat down next to his friend. He studied the television for a minute, confused by the word "Live" in the corner of the picture. Only one of the condemned men on the screen was still alive. A stocky priest of Baal, hair slicked back, swaggered up to him. They were face to face, only an inch separating them. The picture jostled as the cameraman moved in as close as possible.

Quietly, the priest demanded, "Renounce him." He slid a jagged knife under the gag and cut it loose.

The man met his gaze fearlessly. "Never." A few jeers wafted in from the stands.

Wham. The burly priest slammed a rock into the side of the man's head, sending him to the ground, dazed. The priest wound up and launched the stone at him, hitting him in the chest. Blood gushed from a gash above his ear. Another rock struck him in the abdomen. Then one in the face. The rest of the gunmen slung their rifles over their shoulders and mercilessly hurled stones at the fallen man again and again even after he'd stopped moving, slowly burying him.

Obadijah rose and quickly walked to the television. The screen went green as he ejected a small video disc from a slot in the front.

"What, you carry this around with you?"

Eli continued to stare at the green screen. "That Brent Rose guy burned a copy for me. I really like him."

"This is sick. What good could possibly come from watching this? You can't fix this, Eli. It's done."

"Micaijah was my friend." His voice cracked.

Obadijah tossed the disc to him. "He was my friend too. But you're just going to hollow yourself out if you keep watching this over and over and thinking about it all the time!" His eyes met Eli's. "Ahab is still Jah's anointed. It doesn't make sense to fill yourself up with hatred for the king. He may still repent. He's not a completely evil man. Just weak. Like all of us, he needs strength."

Eli finished reassembling the gun and locked the slide back.

"Eli? You ignoring me now?"

"To hell with him. I hope he doesn't repent." He shoved a full, oiled clip into the gun and pushed down the safety, shooting the slide back into place with a loud *ratchet*. "I want nothing but to kill him."

"That is not for you to decide."

Silence.

"Come on, man! You don't have to keep it all together with me. Any time I try to talk to you about *you*, you either make a big joke out of it or you just shut down. I'm right here. Talk to me."

Eli held up the disc. "How could Jah possibly forgive him for this?"

"If he couldn't, then he'd be just like Baal. Is that the kind of god you want?"

Eli studied his reflection in the disc for a few seconds before quietly answering, "No."

Obadijah tilted Eli's head up and looked him in the eye. "Jah is the one who loves in freedom. You know he'll do what's right and what's just. He always does." He changed the subject. "Look, I have to leave in three hours. I'm riding to the stadium with the king and queen. If I were you, I'd get a little sleep and then disappear before relief shows up for our friends across the street."

"I'll be gone before sunup." He tossed the disc toward the wicker trash can in the corner. It went wide. "I was going to ask you: can I borrow some money? A couple thousand shekels?"

"Yeah, no problem. I'll leave it on the table by the door."

"Oh, and a suit. I need to borrow one of your fancy suits."

"Sure, man. Help yourself," he laughed. "I'm not worried about this anymore. Jah will take care of it. Don't you lose your edge now."

Eli slept very little that night. His dreams once again brought him to the temple room in the foreign land. The king and the Prophet of Jah stood in the background and watched as the two priests of Baal went about preparing the altar with ritual precision. Wordlessly, they stacked thick cuts of raw meat next to the idol on the stone surface, their beaded beards clacking together as they worked. Dozens of assistants, dressed in similar clerical garb, continually brought the meat in through the single entrance and handed it to the two priests. The pile was soon eighteen inches tall. Blood rolled down the altar from the raw flesh and pooled at the base of the idol.

The older of the priests added two large jugs of what looked like wine next to the meat. When he was satisfied with their placement, he stepped back and surveyed the altar from a different angle. Their assistants backed out of the room, heads bowed. The two men prostrated themselves before the altar.

Eli couldn't help but notice that they were smiling.

karmel

Eli burst out the door of the Trembling Cup Café, grandé coffee in hand, and bounded cheerfully into the early morning sun. Inhaling deeply, he smiled at the clean morning air before lighting up a cigarette and filling his lungs with black smoke. His head was freshly shaven and he wore a gray pinstripe suit. Despite only ninety minutes of sleep, he felt sharp and alert.

He stepped to the curb just as a tow truck slowed to a stop in front of the coffee shop, Eli's car secured to the crane. The driver nodded at him and hopped out onto the street. He was a big, tough-looking guy, boasting five o'clock shadow at six o'clock in the morning.

"You the guy who called?" he asked Eli without a trace of recognition.

"Yeah. Did anyone follow you?"

"Nah," the driver assured him. "Just give me a minute and I'll have you ready to go, Mr. Jones."

"Did you take the route I asked?"

"Yeah, don't worry about it." He began to lower the car to the ground.

"Hold on a minute." Eli walked over and inspected the bottom of the car, running his hands over the transmission box.

"What you lookin' for?"

"Explosives."

"You paranoid or something?"

"Extremely." Satisfied, Eli backed away and let the driver expertly lower the car to the street.

"You're *sure* no one followed you?"

He nodded. "There's no way. The whole place was deserted. I think all the reporters in the city are covering that thing down at the stadium."

Eli nodded and handed the driver a few bills. "An extra thousand, like we agreed."

The driver handed back the money and smiled. "This one's on the house. Just do me a favor and make 'em all look really stupid today, okay *Mr. Jones*?" He slapped Eli on the shoulder and climbed back into the truck.

Jah's prophet took a long drag on his cigarette and slowly let it out as he watched the tow truck disappear.

Mount Karmel Stadium was an enormous open-air venue, in a sense the hub of downtown Shomron. Office buildings and trendy restaurants boxed it in and elevated freeways snaked around it. A huge color television screen above the main entrance announced the event: "Jah vs. Baal" in gaudy, flashing, animated text.

The entrance was mobbed with people, forming a shoving, jostling pseudo-line, five men thick. Thousands were continuously shuffling in to the already overcrowded facility. Walk-through metal detectors had been set up just inside and the tedious process of searches and pat-downs kept the crowd outside continually pressing with little effect.

Oversized barricades blocked all street access to the facility. Shomrey-Melek, with the help of several hundred armed troops from Justice and Conduct, kept order amid the honking, yelling, and pushing. Slowly, Eli pulled his car up to a barricade and laid on his horn. The man standing guard gestured *stay put* and held a brief conversation via radio before moving the barricade and directing Eli to pull around to the rear of the stadium.

Halfway around, two Shomrey-Melek agents met him on foot and waved him over to a loading dock. The one fondling his shotgun ordered, "Please exit the vehicle" and then announced, "Eli is here, sir," into a two-way radio.

Eli got out of the car and obeyed the command to remove his coat. The agents frisked him thoroughly, and traced his limbs with a hand-held metal detector, turning up only a chrome cigarette lighter. They had just finished the search when Joab strode up, an agent on either side.

"Good morning, Eli," he said with a hint of a smile. "We were starting to worry that you wouldn't show."

"Wouldn't miss this for all the ivory in Tyre."

Joab motioned to a flight of stairs leading into the facility. "You can leave your vehicle with my men. We'll escort you to the field through the back here—avoid the press that way."

Eli shook his head. "No way. I bring my car in with me. I got a tip there's going to be a real nasty rainstorm this afternoon and I'd like the option of leaving in a hurry."

Joab's face fell. "So, we're going to play this game again."

"Look, you know El-Baal better than I do. Do you really think these goyim will let me come back here and pick up my car from the valet if Baal loses today? They'll try to kill me without hesitating. So cut me some slack, eh?"

Joab frowned.

"Tell me I'm wrong."

"Don't worry about the priests of Baal. My men and I can handle them."

"You know, Joab, five years ago that would have been good enough for me. Not anymore."

The captain sighed. "How do I know you don't have a bomb in the trunk?"

"That's a Baalist trick—not my M.O. But hey, if it will make you feel better, search it."

Ten minutes later, Joab was satisfied that the car was clean. The nitrous tank gave him pause, but after testing it out, he let it slide.

"You know those are illegal, right?" Joab chided, handing over the keys.

Eli held out his wrists. "You gonna book me now or after the game?"

"I think the head of the king's protection forces can probably overlook a misdemeanor. But really, those things aren't safe. You get broad-sided and you're prophet flambé."

"Hey, everybody dies. Right?"

Joab shrugged and ordered one of the loading bays opened. The door came down slowly with a hydraulic hiss, unfolding into a ramp.

"You can park in the access tunnel, Eli. You better get going." Against his better judgment he added, "I sure hope you know what you're doing."

"You don't need to worry about me. The question is, are *you* prepared for whatever might happen today?"

"I'm prepared to do whatever the king commands."

Eli shook his head sadly. "I just can't figure you out. How does someone who once served Jah with such zeal turn one-eighty on him for a snake like Ahab?"

"I still serve Jah," Joab countered, anger edging into his voice. "I serve him by protecting his anointed. It's almost eight; you'd better go. And please, try not to get killed."

"Don't worry about me, Joab. I'm larger than life."

Eli slid back into his car and pulled slowly up the ramp and into the stadium. He rolled down the length of the tunnel at just a few miles per hour, suddenly dreading what might await him in the arena. A couple hundred feet from the entrance, he put it in park.

Spinning around in his seat, he yanked up on the headrest and reached up underneath, feeling around for the release. It clicked, and the headrest came free, bringing behind it a cutout of upholstery, a block of yellow foam, and finally his shoulder holster—a gun and three clips snapped in place. He carefully blew some foam from the vent and wiped some more from the grip.

Eli hated guns almost as much as he loved them. To believe the political cartoons, he was a trigger-happy maniac who would just as soon shoot you as look at you. But in truth, a gun was just a tool to Eli. If Jah told him to build houses, he'd carry a hammer. He didn't pick the assignments—he just rolled with them, obeyed without hesitation. If that made him trigger-happy, then so be it.

When Jah speaks, there's no time to analyze every order.

Eli reminded himself of this truth on a regular basis. After all, Shamuel didn't hesitate to put a slug in King Agog's head. Ehud received the word of Jah and buried a blade in Eglon's fat gut. No questions. Sure, there were prophets whose whole job was standing on a soapbox, announcing a message of repentance or hope to all who would listen. But that wasn't usually what Jah asked of Eli.

Eli made big scenes. That was his talent. Agent of grace, agent of judgment. No choice—enforce the covenant. Some day the Anointed One would come. Some day, all the handguns could be doorstops. But today, a heathen queen had dragged the Kingdom of Ephraim into idolatry and today, Eli was ready to carry out his calling.

He got out of the car, donned gun and overcoat, and made for the light at the end of the tunnel.

The reaction from the stands was enormous and mixed as Eli walked onto the field. The booing and heckling outnumbered the cheers but couldn't quite drown them out. The stadium was far beyond capacity, every seat filled and every aisle packed. Eli noted that the general mood was jovial. Vendors made the rounds, selling souvenirs— plastic Baal amulets and commemorative *Contest of the Gods* merchandise.

Scattered throughout the stands were large signs rooting for the away team. "Baal is God" was the most popular. Others were more clever: "Jah is an Antique" and "Jah, Right" among them. A small cluster of brave dissenters held smaller signs challenging, "Baal Lies; Where's the Rain?" and "I'm *Tyred* of Baal." They weren't drawing much attention to themselves just yet. But they were hopeful.

The field itself was covered with dark gravel. At its center was the Altar of Baal: an enormous ziggurat, fifty feet squared at its base and pyramiding up to a platform adorned with a gleaming aluminum statue of Baal as tall as two men. At the statue's feet was a large granite killing surface, stained a dark brown.

The altar was the center of activity on the field. All 450 prophets of Baal were present, each in spotless white tunic, hood concealing most of his face, and a single dagger girded to his simple belt. A handful of black-clad priests barked orders, inspected the prophets and their work, and continually checked back in with the two high priests via radio.

El-Baal and Luli were up in the Executive Box, sitting in comfortable chairs next to the royal couple. Obadijah leaned nervously against the window and drummed his fingers against the bulletproof glass. He checked his watch for the fifth time in as many minutes. 7:58.

Twenty yards away, in the press box, reporters made their last minute sound checks and some applied makeup. Brent Rose straightened his wig. They all knew this could be the biggest event they would ever cover. The new restrictions would make it a fairly one-sided story, but that didn't stop each of them from looking for an angle.

Directly above them, on the roof of the press box, a priest of Baal lay on his stomach, a sniper rifle stretched out in front of him, resting on a tripod. He peered through the scope, pointing here and there, picking out imaginary targets. Two Shomrey-Melek agents sat on the concrete roof next to him, endlessly shifting and readjusting on the uncomfortable surface.

The sniper shot them a look of disgust. "You men aren't needed up here. Go down to the main level and work crowd control with the rest of the boy scouts."

The silver-haired agent replied apologetically, "With all due respect, sir, we were told to remain here with you throughout the event."

"Told by who? Get down there before I have you flogged!"

"I'm afraid I can't comply, sir. Our orders come from the king himself."

The priest scoffed. His eyes lingered on the two agents for a moment before returning to his scope.

"The *king*, huh?" He swiveled the gun to his right and took a bead on Ahab leaning back obliviously in his chair. "You think you're important? You're not. If you get in my way or if you get on my nerves, I'll send you down the quick way."

Similar conversations were being played out at four other locations atop the stadium, where four other snipers lay in position, each accompanied by two Shomrey-Melek.

The enormous clock on the stadium wall flipped over to 8:00. Time to begin.

A ruddy, charismatic man in a tuxedo bounded up to a microphone in the center of the field and announced, "Ladies and gentlemen, welcome to Mount Karmel Stadium! I'm Dan Bethel and this," he paused dramatically, "is the contest of the gods!"

The crowd cheered with one voice. The emcee paused for half a minute and gestured humbly as if the applause were for him. When it had died down, he continued, "This morning, you will witness a showdown of epic proportions. Our god Baal and the still beloved—if outdated—god Jah will be put to the test for the right to be called the One True God!" Again, he paused for the crowd to quiet. "Please put your head in your hands as Ephraim's

Minster of Justice and Conduct, Baal-Adonay, brings us the invocation prayer."

A stocky priest with slicked-back, almost-white hair and slits for eyes trudged up and removed the microphone from its ornate carved stand. He and Eli made eye contact. Eli had never seen Baal-Adonay in person, but he had memorized that face on the television screen.

It was Baal-Adonay who had cast the first stone at Micaijah. On this very field, no less. Eli felt the old hate filling him up again.

The priest found an excuse to break away from Eli's gaze, announcing, "Cover your face." Throughout the auditorium, people lowered their heads into their hands.

Eli didn't move.

"Lord Baal," began Baal-Adonay, "we come to this proving ground, seeking your favor. We have dedicated this land to you. Its king and queen and all the people are your loyal subjects. You are mighty, Baal. You crush those who oppose you. You destroy all who offend you. You do not forgive or forget. Prove your might today. And if anyone here is not completely dedicated to you, then your wrath and more be upon us if we do not destroy them all before this day is over. Baal is God."

Eli spat and swaggered over to Bethel who was gingerly replacing the microphone.

"Thank you, minister," fawned the emcee. "We will now cast lots to determine the nature of the contest." With an intentionally smooth flip of the hand, he released two nine-sided dice onto a small stone table. When they had settled, he squeezed out an apologetic smile and murmured, "The lot has fallen to Prophet Tishbi. What will be the exact nature of the contest?"

Plucking the microphone from in front of the emcee, Eli unloaded the scenario. "Well, Danny-boy, I think we'll do it like this: Prepare two bulls for sacrifice. Let the priests and prophets of Baal choose one for themselves, cut it into pieces, and arrange the pieces on the altar. They can even pile as much wood under it as they want, but they *can't light the fire.* I will prepare the other bull. Then they will call on their lord and I will call on my Lord. Whoever answers with fire—he is the One True God."

Dan Bethel's eyes shifted uneasily from Eli to the priest. "Rev. Minister," he asked, a forced grin plastered to his face, "is this acceptable?"

"Oh, I can't wait."

It took half an hour for the Shomrey-Melek to locate two bulls and prepare them for sacrifice. The process was rather involved. First they had to be inspected for defect by men from Levi, The People's priestly tribe. Two Levites were found in Shomron who were loyal to Jah. Another two were found numbered among the prophets of Baal. Once it was certified unblemished, the bull was killed, skinned, and cut into pieces. The fat was placed on top of the cuts of meat as a sacrifice to the respective god. The legs and innards were then scrubbed and placed alongside the rest.

When the bulls were ready, three priests of Baal carried out a thorough inspection of both, made their choice, and began their ritual. They piled the meat into the arms of several willing prophets, staining their white robes a deep crimson. They then carried the hunks of flesh, an armful at a time, to the top of the altar, in a huffing, sweating, forward-leaning human train.

When the last of it had been deposited on the granite platform at Baal's feet, the 450 prophets of Baal surrounded the altar, shoulder-to-shoulder, chest-to-back and, at Baal-Adonay's command, buried their faces in their hands and began to murmur a collective prayer. Standing in a semi-circle outside of the throng of prophets, fifty blonde-haired, black-clad priests of Baal stood tight-lipped, gazing intently at the statue above them.

The audience sat transfixed, silent, everyone waiting to see what Baal would do. Or, failing that, what El-Baal would do. This continued for a minute. Then two. Then ten. The murmur grew in volume and urgency. After twenty minutes, the arc of priests joined in the prayer—all but Baal-Adonay, who picked his way through the crowd, using a short whip to punish those whose prayers were not earnest enough, always with one eye on the top of the altar.

Eli took all of this in with a detached amusement. When he tired of standing, he plopped down on the ground and lit a cigarette. There, smoking and chuckling to himself, he played the spectator—a man without a care in the world.

By 9:15, Baal's priests and prophets had lost their grip on the audience. Those who had brought dissenting signs displayed them and, after one brave soul dared to duck down and shout, "What's taking him?" the place erupted in a mixture of heckling, laughing, and a righteous defense of the as-of-yet absent god.

A few of Baal's more devout followers were allowed to congregate on a corner of the field to join the prayer for intervention by fire. Still, no fire came. Baal-Adonay ordered priest and prophet alike to his knees. As one, they prostrated themselves, foreheads to gravel, exposing their backs even more readily to the stocky high priest's displaced anger.

In the Executive Box, Luli and El-Baal sat and watched intently. They hadn't spoken a word since the prayer began. Luli occasionally cleared his throat or snorted, presumably hoping to find the right combination of stimuli to elicit a cosmic rain of fire from the heavens. El-Baal just perched motionless on the front half-inch of his seat, expecting a response from above at any moment. To his right, Isabel and Ahab slumped in their plush seats, now wearing their alleged lack of faith on their faces, while Obadijah remained at the window, drumming away the minutes with his fingers.

On the field, Baal-Adonay suddenly whipped his head back and howled, "Baal is God" from the bottom of his lungs, causing all 450 prophets to flinch. He grabbed the nearest two by the collars and pulled them to their feet. The others followed suit. Heads tipped back; they shouted themselves hoarse. "Baal is God! Baal is God!" Some in the audience took this as a sign that an answer was imminent. Excitement was rekindled in the crowd. Many joined in the mantra. *Baal is God. Baal is God.* Eli lay back, hands interlocked behind his head, and stared up into the hazy, smoggy orange sky.

Ten o'clock rolled around and voices started to give way. Some of the priests rested their lungs and throats and the rest took this as permission for a short break. Baal-Adonay begrudgingly allowed it.

Some laughter floated down from the upper deck.

A woman in the front row shouted encouragement.

As they all savored the moment of respite, a petite prophet made his way from the innermost ring of the group and approached the minister.

Fanning himself with his sweat-soaked tunic, he probatively asked, "Sir, forgive my weakness, but is there any way we could get just a swallow of water?" The only reply was a dead stare. "I-I just fear that some in my order are becoming dehydrated and a small drink would revitalize them." The stare focused into a smoldering glare, under which the prophet shifted uneasily for a moment before slightly bowing and offering an apologetic, "Never mind, Sir. We'll be fine," and backing away.

"Wait. Come back here," the priest barked. The smaller man obeyed. Baal-Adonay pinched a smile at him and slipped an arm around his shoulders. "I understand how you must be feeling. Really, I do. And I can appreciate your discomfort. Why don't you wet your whistle on this?"

The arm tightened around his neck and yanked the prophet off his feet, onto his back. Baal-Adonay reigned blows upon the dazed, prone figure, stomping the life out of him with his heavy black boots while cursing him in Baal's name. A blood-curdling shout resonated from deep within the priest as he delivered the final crushing stomp. Without warning, he sprung forward and slammed into the prophets in front of him, knocking several over, sending others sprawling into the row ahead of them like dominos.

He dove deep into the sea of men, slamming his head, elbows, and chest in every direction. The other priests on the perimeter followed his lead and soon they were all thrashing and moshing in a churning mass of arms and legs.

This spectacle elicited solemn nods and derisive laughs from the crowd in equal numbers. The faithful who had gathered on the field to petition Baal looked on with a hint of embarrassment for just a minute before awkwardly wrapping up the prayer and filing back to their seats.

El-Baal and Obadijah had now switched places in the Executive Box. The high priest stood against the window, watching the events unfold below with a growing concern. He concentrated, willing the sacrifice to catch fire. Having already brought the request to Baal, he dared not bother him again with prayer. He glanced at his watch: 10:48.

Behind him, Luli rested his face in his hands, studying the floor through splayed fingers. He was trying not to think about anything at all.

Obadijah had settled in a leather recliner, where he relaxed and worked on a vegetable plate, less than interested in the violent slam dance underway below.

Off in a corner, Ahab held a hushed cell phone conversation.

By eleven, the tactics had changed yet again. Baal-Adonay stood on a small platform halfway up the altar, directing the men below like the conductor of a symphony. They were arranged west of the altar in a pentacle formation. They beat their breasts and repeated a prayer, one line at a time, offering to do the vilest of things for Baal if he would only provide a flame.

The offers got more absurd as the ritual wore on. The leader's body language was beginning to betray a sense of hopelessness. Seeing this, Eli decided to offer some encouragement. Pulling himself to his feet, he strolled over to the base of the altar, snatching Dan Bethel's wireless microphone on the way.

"Louder! Shout louder!" he coaxed, his voice booming throughout the stadium. "Come on, you can do it! He's never going to hear you if you don't pick it up a little bit." They did their best to ignore him, beating their breasts all the harder.

The giant screen abruptly cut from Eli's rant to a close-up of several priests. Still, the audio continued to find its way through the stadium's sound system.

"What's wrong? Where is he? I thought he was God! There's no way you could have been mistaken about that, right? Maybe he's sleeping. If you get a little more volume, you might wake him up." His voice cracked with laughter. "Wait, wait. *Maybe* he's on the toilet! It's that Tsidonian food, right? Even those ruthless, all-powerful devil-gods can get the runs from time to time. I'm sure he'll be here in just a minute. Really. Don't lose faith!" Someone found the right knob and Eli's voice was cut off with a squeal.

The chants continued, now with Eli as their subject: If Baal would provide the fire, they'd use it to burn Eli alive for blasphemy. They'd burn his parents and his dog. They'd bring the fire to his birthplace and burn it to the ground. Et cetera, et cetera.

Their threats echoing all around him, Eli threw his hands up in a "What're you gonna do?" gesture and moved back to the sidelines, chuckling. Much of the crowd laughed with him.

This reaction threw Baal-Adonay, who looked around frantically with a combination of rage and confusion.

Deciding to raise the stakes yet again, he removed his black jacket and pushed up the sleeves of the shirt beneath. The fabric bunched and released a river of sweat that traveled down his arms, rolling through the many narrow tracks of long, straight scars.

As one, the prophets and priests below followed his example, revealing similar scars. They all pulled out daggers from within the folds of their cloaks—the priests' long and jagged, the prophets' short and stubby—all gleaming and razor-sharp. The arena was again silent.

In unison, each man positioned his dagger against his left forearm, skillfully avoiding major nerves and arteries. Banshee screams filled the stadium as five hundred men pushed in and pulled down, splitting skin and blood vessels, sending blood flowing freely down their arms. The human star went from white to pink almost at once.

They jumped up and down, their left arms extended in the air, blood flipping in short bursts from each wound. "Baal is God," they screamed. "All is Baal!" El-Baal watched the ritual from above, heart pounding, eyes wide, an almost sexual excitement gathering in his stomach. It was close—a breaking point. Something was about to spill the scales to one side. He sensed the presence of great power building.

Below, Baal's servants were cutting their right arms to match the left. Shrieks of pain and ecstasy rose as the bloody bodies churned on. The crowd's reaction was loud but indiscernible. All the while, the meat sat atop the altar, long-since rancid and covered with flies—still no spark, no flame, no combustion.

Eli got up again and scanned the ground around him. Quickly, he found what he was looking for. Amidst the gravel were some rather large stones—twelve in particular—strewn around the outer edge of the field. He set about gathering them. They were scattered over the space of fifty yards, but one by one, he lugged them to the spot where he had been sitting and watching. He carefully set each stone on the pile, which—with the fitting of each new rock—took on more and more the form of an altar. Between placing stones, he worked with a small shovel supplied by Joab, to dig a shallow trench around the whole thing.

Boredom had again overtaken the spectators. Those who tried to leave found out quickly that it would not be allowed. The signs lay abandoned. Some appeared traumatized as they stared down, disillusioned, at the pathetic priests and prophets. But most just casually talked with those around them. What did it matter? Ahab was in charge. Which meant that Isabel was in charge. Which meant that Baal was going nowhere, whether he was real or not.

As Eli positioned the final stone on the altar, now about four feet tall, it began to dawn on the priests of Baal just what he was doing and what it meant. Collectively, they received a second wind, their adrenal glands squeezing out the last few drops of desperation.

They screamed without form or liturgy to their god, tasting blood from their vocal chords. Some raked their fingernails down their faces, ripping flesh. Some beat their breasts so hard they knocked the wind from their lungs. Eli sat on the ground, back to the altar, trying to cram himself into the little sliver of shade, and looked on. He didn't find it funny anymore. Rather, he felt like he was about to vomit. Ephraim worshiping a devil. A jewel packed in manure.

At 12:00, after four hours of begging, pleading, promising, and bleeding, there was nothing left to offer Baal. Loss of blood, lack of food, and dehydration had taken their toll and, as one person, the prophets and priests of Baal quit their shouting. Each man hunched over, gasping for every scratchy breath, staring at the ground in disbelief.

Eli jumped to his feet. Time to finish this. Time to send Baal back to hell.

He strutted up to Dan Bethel and again removed the microphone from his chubby hands. By the time he reached the center of the field, Eli had the undivided attention of each person in the stands.

Jah's prophet was in his element. There were idols and idolaters to be exposed, humiliated. Eli was the man for the job. He studied the spent prophets and priests for a minute before inquiring, "Why'd you stop? You were getting somewhere. I could feel it!"

The five hundred men stared their hatred back. Eli's laughter was joined by a low and growing rumble from the audience.

He waited a beat, until the silence got awkward. Turning to the crowd, he asked "Now are you ready to see the real God?"

A thick cheer was the response.

Eli continued, "People of Ephraim, how long will you waver between two opinions? If Jah is God, then follow him alone. If Baal is god, then follow him. You can't have it both ways! Jah demands your allegiance! Hasn't he earned it?

כרמל

"He brought our ancestors out of slavery in Mitzrayim. He gave us this land and provides for us. But you have abandoned his commands and worshiped Baal." His voice edged with angry passion. "You've allowed goyim to come here and infect our nation! I am the only one of Jah's prophets left, but Baal has four hundred and fifty! Still, they couldn't get Baal to produce even a single spark. You've let them knock down Jah's altar, but today I have rebuilt it.

"Now watch closely and make your choice. Jah isn't like Baal. If you will reject your idols today and turn back to Jah, he will accept you and forgive you and bless you." Eli steadied himself and put all his breath behind the words. "And it will *rain today!*"

The cheers from the people hit Eli like a brick wall of sound, and strengthened him.

Tossing the mic to the ground, he signaled to four Shomrey-Melek agents. The first brought in the meat on a small wooden palette and carefully positioned it on the altar. The other three agents each brought Eli a bucket of water as large as a man could lift. The thirsty crowd's cheers multiplied at the sight of the precious water. Eli lifted the first bucket to his lips and took a long drink.

Then the cheers turned to confusion as he poured thousands of shekels worth of crystal clear water over the meat, down the altar, and into the foot-deep trench that surrounded it. He repeated the process with the other two buckets.

Dan Bethel, obeying orders radioed from El-Baal, drew close to the altar, sniffing the liquid. Detecting no odor, he lit a match and dropped it into the trench. As it hit the water, the flame disappeared with a *tsst*.

Eli ordered the emcee, "Tell them."

"It's water," he confirmed into the microphone. Eli motioned for Bethel to get lost and then knelt before the altar. The rocks were shiny and slick, glistening in the noon sun. The prophet looked down into his reflection in the half-filled trench.

He quickly inventoried his spirit for doubt and, finding none, whispered a prayer. "O Jah, God of Avraham, Yitzhak, and Ja'acov, let it be known today that you are God and that I, your servant, have done all of this at your command. Hear me, Jah, that these people may know that you alone are God and that you have turned their hearts back to you."

For a moment and a half, everything was still and silent. Then slowly, almost indiscernibly, the orange sky began to darken. Thunder rumbled quietly—barely audible, yet shaking the ground. The barometric pressure was undulating rapidly, as if to stir up any panic that might be stuck like plaque within the crowd. The people in the stands looked on in horror as the thunder grew louder and the sky redder. They began to weep. They clung to each other, prayed.

A sudden, deafening clap of thunder and the sky erupted into flame. Horizon to horizon, the atmosphere was burning. Blue, red, and orange flame swirled around the sky, slow at first and then picking up speed, the eye of the storm directly above the altar.

The sound of rushing water filled the city. Those who could move at all recoiled in horror, screamed, hid behind their seats. Ninety degrees became a hundred and then one-ten in the span of a few seconds. The spiraling blaze grew larger at its center—a bulb of flame growing and pulsing with increasing speed like a beating heart. Eli slowly rose to his feet in the orange light, a gaping smile on his face as he watched the fireball expand.

With a bone-rattling explosion, a column of fire shot down from the heavens and smashed into the stone altar. The meat was consumed in less than a second, then the water, which boiled and evaporated. The wood turned directly to ash and blew away. Finally, the rocks melted into a bubbling, molten mess. Burning debris from the initial explosion fluttered down around the altar.

The column of fire evaporated and the thick smell of chemical flame sunk to the ground. The flames above faded away quicker than they had appeared, leaving a blue, cloudless sky.

Those in the stands experimentally lifted their heads.

Eli reached into his coat and produced a pack of smokes, his expression beyond smug as he retrieved the last one, ignited the cardboard box on a piece of burning palette, and lit the black cigarette between his lips.

Order vanished from the stands in the moments that followed. There was weeping and praying. There was laughter and celebration. But mostly there was rage.

When the sky had lit up, the prophets and priests of Baal had been too exhausted to respond beyond going fetal and covering their heads. But they were quickened by the realization that they themselves were the object of the anger in the stadium. The people in the stands jeered the priests and hurled things down on them—drinks and greasy concession foods. They crushed their Baal talismans and threw their souvenirs and amulets onto the field.

In the Executive Box, Obadijah couldn't hide his smile. Everyone else looked dead serious. Or just dead. El-Baal spoke quietly into his two-way radio. "Take him out. Now."

"Finally," breathed the sniper stretched out on the press box. He clicked off his safety and centered the smoking, gloating prophet in his crosshairs. The *click-click* of a handgun being cocked snatched his attention away from his target. He looked to his right, directly up the barrel of the silver-haired agent's pistol.

"*What?*" the priest demanded. "Get that gun out of my face. That's an order!"

Emotionless, the agent answered, "I've already received my orders. You lost." Two large caliber slugs bisected the agent's head. Shots rang out around the upper perimeter of the stadium as the Shomrey-Melek, under orders from King Ahab, executed the four sniper-priests.

Down on the field, the angry spectators rushed over the wall and down toward Baal's earthly representatives, easily overtaking the tired and bleeding men. Those fans who had earlier supported Baal tossed their signs onto the waning flame on the altar, building it back into a huge bonfire.

The confrontation between the prophets and the people escalated quickly into a dirty battle. The prophets unsheathed their daggers and lashed out at the human tide in an attempt to drive them back. The unarmed horde took casualties, but inevitably overpowered Baal's servants by sheer numbers, scattering the black-clad priests and white-robed prophets.

The priests were the first to run.

Eli found himself caught between the action and the altar of Jah. For a moment he just stood and smoked, watching the battle unfold, until a half dozen priests of Baal fled in his direction. Spotting him, they swarmed. The prophet of the True God drew his gun and quickly dispatched each one with a well-aimed shot to the head. His voice rose above the sounds of the fray, "Grab the prophets of Baal. Don't let one escape!"

Another wave of prophets and priests rushed Eli. Again he raised his gun and dropped the five closest, stopping their advance cold. The rest drew their own side arms, but were dragged into the mob before they could get a shot off.

As it reached Eli, the surging mob changed direction again without warning. And, before he knew it, he found himself pushed up against the altar of Baal, where a pocket of heathen prophets were holding their own. Eli retreated up the ziggurat, unsteadily moving backwards up the incline and shooting the two prophets who dared to pursue him. He discharged the empty clip from his gun, shoved a fresh one in, and released the slide back into place.

Pausing at the platform from which Baal-Adonay had directed the morning's ritual, he inventoried the situation. The prophets of Baal were dead. The few priests who remained were even now being overpowered. The idol was defeated.

In victory, Eli climbed to the top of Baal's altar and stood on the pile of rancid meat. He kicked the statue of the pagan god as hard as he could. It whined and bent down to a 45-degree angle. He kicked it again just as hard. The bolts holding it in place snapped and shot out in three directions. The statue broke free and slid down the pyramid to the waiting crowd below. Gleefully, they crushed it under foot.

Safe in his plush box, but with diminishing security, El-Baal looked even whiter than usual. He addressed everyone in the room with an air of uncontested authority: "We're getting out of here. Come on," and herded them out the door.

From atop the altar, Eli could see the whole stadium. Near the far exit, he spotted Baal-Adonay, who was almost home free. A safe distance from the angry crowd and a trail of bleeding bodies in his wake, he ran for an exit with surprising lightness for a man of his girth. Eli took a long drag on his cigarette, threw the butt to the ground, and took careful aim with his pistol. The shot caught the stocky priest between the shoulder blades, sending him sliding to the ground, as dead as the gravel that covered him. Smoke churned from Eli's nose, mouth, and gun.

Every eye was on him. A chant grew from the people below. "Jah is God! Jah is God!"

Eli descended the altar. At its base, he silenced them with a hand and addressed them. "Anyone can *say* that Jah is God. Live like it."

They listened with an earnestness that comes only from conviction and penitence. With a hint of a smile, he added, "And since none of you seems to have remembered an umbrella, I think you should all head home."

They cried and sniffed. Some hugged and offered comforting words. It wasn't Eli's scene.

Without fanfare, he turned and walked back toward the tunnel and his waiting car. The crowd parted for him even as it began moving toward the main exit. Joab's men had regrouped and were doing their best to re-establish some sort of post-carnage order. As he walked, Eli flipped open his phone and punched a speed-dial button.

Without anyone noticing, the sky had grown dark gray with massive thunderhead clouds.

קישון
kishon

Beneath Mount Karmel, in the VIP parking structure, the eight surviving priests of Baal escorted Ahab, Isabel, and Obadijah to a silver limousine. El-Baal fired orders to each priest in turn.

"You, take the limo and get the king and queen as far from here as possible. You two are in the chopper. You ride with me and Luli. You two, follow us."

Isabel was beside herself. "Where are you going?"

El-Baal smiled. "We're going to kill Eli."

Luli balked. "We've got full military clearance here. Why don't we hold off until we can get the Shamayim fleet in for air support? Or better yet, a few LOCUST squads from Tsidon? This old chopper is worthless."

"No," El-Baal answered flatly. "No time. They take this bird. He's not going to disappear on us again." With a sudden tripling of volume, he added, *And somebody find out what in Baal's name happened to my snipers!*

The queen wiped tears on her silk sleeve and then kissed the high priest hard on the mouth, clearly not a first kiss. Ahab looked away for an awkward moment.

Between sobs, she said, "Bring me back his head and his hands."

A scrawny priest opened the limo door for Ahab, Isabel, and Obadiah. He then slid behind the wheel and the car squealed off. In the back seat, Obadijah's phone rang. He answered it impatiently and handed it to the king.

"Sir, it's for you."

Ahab pressed the phone to his ear and barked, "Joab, we need a Shomrey-Melek escort. Meet us at rendezvous point D, we'll be there in—"

"Guess again, Your Highness," came Eli's voice. As he talked, he was walking briskly down the tunnel to his car, which he found blocked by a thick-necked Shomrey-Melek agent armed with a shotgun. "Hang on a second, Ahab." He locked a steely look on the agent. "Move. Now."

The agent swallowed hard and gripped the gun harder. "I'm sorry, sir. The king requires your presence at the compound tonight. You have to come with me."

Eli sighed. He stowed his phone and, grabbing the shotgun with both hands, slammed it into the agent's forehead, dropping him to the ground.

"You'll get over it," he threw over his shoulder as he tossed the gun onto the passenger seat and climbed in after it. The Wreck came to life with a deep roar. He popped it into reverse and punched the gas.

Retrieving the phone from his pocket, he asked, "You still there? Good. Now listen. You've been given another chance. I wouldn't have done it this way, but whatever. As far as I can tell, you did the right thing today. There's just one final test."

The Wreck reached the end of the tunnel at forty miles per hour, sending the door exploding off the loading bay. The car flew out backwards, sprayed sparks off the concrete, and with a mist of brake fluid squealed a hundred and eighty degrees. High on the moment, Eli stood on the accelerator and shot off down the road.

"Here it is," he continued. "Put a short leash on Isabel. She's done enough damage to Ephraim. She can't be allowed to have any power. None. Take control of your kingdom. Tear down the monuments to Baal. Turn back to Jah and see what he will do. If you're willing to do that, everyone will follow. Even me." He accelerated onto an entrance ramp and merged with the freeway.

Ahab was beginning to sweat as he listened to Eli's demands. "I don't know if I can do this. Look, I want to. I want to do the right thing, but it might be too late for that kind of—"

"You can do it," Eli reassured. "Dig down into your marrow and see if there's a real leader in there somewhere. I honestly don't see it, but someone I trust is sure it's there."

The king of Ephraim steeled his jaw. "Okay. I will."

"Good to hear. And because you've stepped up to the plate like a champ today, things are going to get easier here in about five minutes. How's that sound?"

"I don't . . . get it."

Eli laughed. "It's going to rain, Your Highness! Am I a man of my word or what? Now, tell your little driver there to go fast and find some shelter. This is going to be one hell of a storm."

"Will do." He was surprised by the lack of animosity he felt toward the prophet. "And Eli, thank you."

At the sound of Eli's name, Isabel leaped on her husband, clawing for the phone. "Give it to me!" She wrenched the mobile from his hands. She wanted to scream every curse she knew, but her mind froze and all she managed to get out was, "You!"

Eli sniggered. "What can I do for you, Princess? You want me to buy you a one-way ticket back home?"

Isabel's voice was soft but razor sharp. "I swear you will pay for this with your life. Baal's wrath be upon me and more if you don't become like one of the prophets of Baal whom you have slaughtered today!"

"Yeah, where have I heard that before?" A clap of thunder and a flash of lightning caught them both off guard. The clouds burst. Rain came down in buckets. Eli could barely see the road in front of him.

"Listen, you kids be good, mmmkay?" he said. "I'm hanging up now."

He snapped the phone closed and turned the windshield wipers to high. He wasn't sure where he was going. No word from Jah as to what would come next. Retirement sounded pretty good. Sure, he was only thirty-three, but prophets had a shorter shelf life than most. Maybe he'd head for the hill country for a while and just lay low. Even the Kerith Ravine Inn sounded like a nice change of scenery. He wondered if his old room was available.

Whatever he decided, he was almost home free. Just ahead was the Megiddo, a three-mile long suspension bridge that spanned the Kishon Valley. Once that was behind him, it would be easy to fall off the radar, to disappear in the little roads, trails, and villages beyond. He'd done it a dozen times before.

In the rearview mirror, through the deluge, the lights of downtown Shomron were eerily beautiful. It was a bittersweet thought that he might never be back. From this distance it was so peaceful. The rain had apparently driven everyone inside. There were only two cars behind him and he saw none ahead. All the better to conceal his escape.

A sharp crunch jarred him from his thoughts of rest and he felt himself abruptly slammed into the steering column. Cranking his head, he saw El-Baal behind the wheel of a black Susah sedan. Luli sat in the passenger seat and Eli could see at least one other priest in the back. They rammed him again, harder this time, and then pulled up on his left, windows down, guns extended, their headlights dodging through the raindrops.

Eli ducked and swerved, skidding on the wet pavement as several bullets cut through the driver side window and out through the windshield. He steadied the vehicle and yanked the wheel to the left, connecting solidly with the sedan and sending it spinning.

As El-Baal righted the car and made up the space between them, Eli smashed out what was left of his driver's window with his elbow and sent a half-dozen rounds in the high priests' direction. The two cars exchanged bullets, but the wind and rain made it nearly impossible to see, let alone aim. And Eli was not left-handed.

He felt the car begin to hydroplane and turned his attention back to driving. From behind the veil of rain, two more priests pulled up to Eli's right in an identical car, less than a foot between them. The driver, an owl-eyed man pushing sixty, smiled and waved, brandishing a machine gun.

The three vehicles crossed onto the Megiddo Bridge like a photo finish. Eli sent a couple rounds toward El-Baal at his left and with his right scooped the shotgun off the seat. His knees held the steering wheel steady while he punched the barrel of the shotgun up to the passenger window and let fly a volley of buckshot, blowing the windows out of both cars and ripping a hole in the older driver.

Dropping the shotgun, Eli flipped on the nitrous and roared out from between the goyim. The dead driver's weight pulled his car sharply out in front of the high priests. The impact of the collision sent El-Baal's car spinning into the three-foot tall concrete median. Both driver side tires tore open and the engine sputtered out. The other sedan went sliding into the guardrail, flipped it, and disappeared into Kishon Valley.

Eli smiled at his rearview mirror and turned off the nitrous. He'd lost track, but hoped that the car at the bottom of the valley contained El-Baal and Luli. With them out of the picture, Ahab might actually follow through on his promise. Stupid pagans. Would they never learn?

His smile disappeared as the dull *whup-whup-whup* of a chopper echoed from down in the valley. Eli's heart fell at the sight of the helicopter slowly rising up like a leviathan next to the bridge. The back of the chopper was wide open. A gunner sat behind a mounted Matzor machine gun, squinting through the rain. An expletive formed in Eli's mind and emerged from his mouth. With or without the nitrous, it was clear that the chopper could keep pace. He threw his head down between his knees as a few dozen rounds ripped through the car.

A second burst came and Eli alternately slammed on the brakes and punched the gas in an attempt to throw the gunner off his aim and gain a window to regroup.

By the kindness of Jah he hadn't been hit.

Eli chambered a round in the shotgun and swerved toward the chopper. He popped up just long enough to fire wildly out the passenger side in the direction of the gunner. The lucky shot smacked into the chopper's domed windshield, leaving a hundred little dimples right in front of the pilot's shocked face. The chopper dipped back down into the valley. Eli cocked the shotgun again and stepped harder on the gas.

A few seconds later, the chopper thundered back into sight, spewing round after round at the bullet-riddled car. Eli grabbed the lever on his seat and threw it back to a full recline, shouting a prayer in his mind. Flat on his back, he desperately poked the shotgun out the window and fired another blind shot. It didn't find the target, but the spooked pilot brought the chopper back down into the valley all the same, buying Eli another brief respite.

His car honeycombed with bullet holes, steam pouring from under the hood, Eli slammed on the brakes and cranked the wheel right, aiming the headlights off the side of the bridge. He flipped the nitrous back on and the sick sound of the engine got louder and sicker. Pressing the brake down with both feet, Eli mashed the butt of the shotgun against the accelerator and wedged the barrel between the seats. The engine revved louder. He couldn't even hear the chopper anymore as he opened the driver's door and put one foot on the ground. For that matter, he could barely hear the engine over the ringing in his ears — the blast from the shotgun in close quarters had taken its toll.

The car began to shake as the needle on the RPM gauge buried itself in the red. Eli stared straight ahead. Sweat and rain poured down his face.

The blades of the helicopter emerged from the valley, almost in slow motion. Eli removed his foot from the brake and calmly stepped away from the car, which lurched forward, tires squealing. It crashed through the safety rail and careened ten feet through the air, passing through the opening in the chopper and taking the mounted machine gun and its operator with it down to the bottom of the rocky valley.

The gutted helicopter quivered in mid air, the pilot fighting for control, and then bumped into the bridge with a crunch. Four long strides and Eli was standing in the back of the chopper. He poked his gun to the top of the pilot's helmet and fired two shots. The priest squeezed the stick and spasmed.

The aircraft turned hard counter-clockwise and tipped over onto the bridge, throwing Eli to the wet concrete, then landing all around him, caging him in on all sides. Two of the rotor blades crushed themselves into the bridge and snapped off, flying into the night. Eli hugged the severed end of the guardrail and covered his head as the helicopter's remaining rotor blades shoved the aircraft back up into the sky, where it convulsed and spiraled down into the Kishon Valley, burying itself in the rocks, and throwing a ball of fire back up toward the bridge.

The prophet slowly pulled himself to his feet, soaked through and a little torn up, but alive. The thunder and lightning had intensified, giving the world a strobe light effect. More than a bit disoriented, Eli wondered if it made more sense to push ahead on foot or to leg it back to Shomron for a car. He picked his pistol up off the ground where it had landed. The slide was locked back on an empty clip. He ejected the spent cartridge and loaded his last thirteen bullets.

A ride off this bridge would be nice, he thought in Jah's direction.

קישון

Right on cue, the headlights of a small blue car illuminated him, drawing his hand up by reflex to shield his eyes. The old man behind the wheel pulled up to Eli and rolled down the window.

"Are you nuts? Get in!" he shouted. "You'll die out here in this storm!" Less than surprised, Eli made his way around the front of the car, feeling sluggish and bruised. Yeah, retirement was sounding better every moment.

He paused before the car and looked down at his side, lain open by his fall to the bridge. Illuminated by the high beams, he could see that he was leaking slowly onto his once-crisp white shirt. His mortality snapped to the surface of his mind as it did on occasion.

Everybody dies.

Instantly, his legs were taken from beneath him and he found himself smashed up against the old man's windshield. A bubblegum pink SUV had rammed the car from behind, sending it skidding forward. The old man and Eli stared at each other as the windshield wipers passed between them once. Then twice.

Eli rolled off the hood and charged off down the road away from the civilian, his side seeping. The commandeered SUV separated itself from the little car and followed, closing the distance between them quickly.

Eli stopped, spun, and raised the Maqil .60. He couldn't see their faces, but he knew El-Baal and Luli were inside. Pausing a moment to let them get closer, he could see the silhouette of a third person behind them.

"Say hi to Baal for me."

The headlights flared on, blinding Eli. In the glare he fired three shots, trying to space them evenly across the windshield of the approaching vehicle.

The three priests had grabbed the floor at the sight of the prophet's gun and hung below the dash until the shots had stopped. Not feeling the *crump* of a car-body collision, they came up for air. Eli was gone. The SUV fishtailed on the slick pavement, struck the concrete median, and clanged onto its side, grinding to a stop with a grand finale of tiny fireworks.

Hanging from the passenger seat by his safety belt, Luli could see Eli on the far side of the median, running back toward Shomron. He rolled down the window of the capsized vehicle and pulled himself out. El-Baal declined Luli's offer of help and made his own way from the driver's seat, up the console, and out into the rain. Impatiently he reached down to lift the third priest, Phelles, who was not moving.

"I think my ribs are cracked. And my shoulder is . . . Ah!" He winced in pain as he tried to reach up to El-Baal. "I need a doctor." The two high priests stared hollowly back down at him. "I can't get out," he added, a mixture of apology and defiance.

El-Baal drew his gun and pointed it down into the vehicle. "Yes. You can."

The injured priest took Luli's hand and, with terrific pain, emerged from the SUV, moaning and gasping. El-Baal had already jumped the median and was pursuing Eli on foot.

"Move!" he barked back at the others. "He cannot escape!"

The rain and fog had thickened, making Eli invisible to his pursuers, despite only a twenty-yard lead. El-Baal pushed his body all the harder. Veins bulged in his neck and water shot up from his feet in hard jets with each stride. He was overtaking the Jah-lover and could almost make out his form in the streetlights, muted by the downpour. Luli and Phelles trailed thirty paces behind him.

Eli's lungs were on fire. He prayed for strength, his body tapped out. Just ahead, the bridge ended and beyond that lay the city he had meant to leave behind. He could feel the high priests of Baal on his back. As he cleared the bridge, his eyes fell on a glowing sign: a red and white *1A* that marked the beginning of the A-Line UrbanRail. He was down the stairs and over the turnstile in an instant.

El-Baal's stomach folded in on itself as he ran out of bridge and found himself looking down Omri Avenue at several dozen possible avenues of escape. Eli would disappear again—he knew it. The rain continued to beat down relentlessly, limiting visibility to about fifty feet. He considered whispering a prayer to Baal, but thought better of it. Clearly, he wasn't in the best of standing with his lord. How else could he explain the events at Karmel? He planted both feet and opened his senses wide for any sign of Eli. He smelled cooking grease and alcohol wafting out from a bar where a crowd had sought refuge from the rain and a place to celebrate Jah's victory.

The downpour eased for just a second and the priest saw his quarry disappear into the rail station. His stomach unclenched and a smile spread across his face. Luli stumbled to a stop at his right a moment before Phelles arrived at the edge of the bridge, hugging his chest. El-Baal uncurled a thin finger in the direction of the staircase. "He's down there. Let's go."

The three men drew their guns and double-checked their safeties, descending shoulder-to-shoulder down the steps into the rail station. They jumped the turnstiles and rounded the corner to the platform, where a train sat— three cars, doors open.

The station seemed to El-Baal like a still image. Despite the rain outside, the air down here was cool, dry, and stagnant. A handful of people were either seated or finding seats, but no sign of Eli. El-Baal motioned for Luli and Phelles to check the last two cars. He raced to the first himself and swung around the open door, gun extended. A couple of teenagers dropped their magazines and slowly raised their hands. No Eli. He dropped to one knee and scanned the length of the car beneath the seats. With a curse, he stood up, kicked the hand bar with all his might and stepped back on to the platform.

Luli was emerging from the middle car with the same results. He looked back at El-Baal and threw up his hands weakly. El-Baal's eyes shifted to the last car, where Phelles, who had acquired an exaggerated limp in protest, had just reached the door. Leaning against the train car and still hugging his side, he popped his head in for a look.

A distorted *ding-dong* sounded from the speaker above, followed by a hydraulic spit from below. Phelles withdrew his head and shrugged apathetically at his superior. "He's not here."

An angry sob burst out from between El-Baal's lips as he overturned a trashcan. The doors were closing. Eli had slipped through their fingers yet again. Wanting to cry but not knowing how, he just closed his eyes as tightly as he could and hated Jah with every ounce of strength in his body.

As the train doors were coming together, Eli swung out from under a seat, grabbed the golden idol hanging around Phelles's neck, and yanked him to the car. The doors closed on the leather cord, slapping the priest up against the glass. Only a window between them, he was face-to-face with Eli, who twisted the amulet and pulled even harder. Phelles's gun clattered to the ground and he slapped the door with his palms.

The commotion jerked El-Baal from his rage and self-pity. The train was beginning to move now, dragging Phelles across the platform. His face flattened against the window, he punched the glass, clawed at the strap around his neck, and shrieked.

El-Baal raised his gun. "Both of them," he growled and fired a three-round-burst that buried itself in Phelles's back. Luli's shots were also stopped by the priest's body as the train disappeared into the tunnel.

As they reached full speed, Eli gave the gold amulet one last yank, popping it from the leather lanyard and sending the priest's body bouncing to the track below. He dropped the little likeness of the heathen god to the floor of the car and crushed it under his heel.

Back in the station, the two priests referred to a large illuminated map of the UrbanRail system mounted on the grimy wall. Luli pointed to the next station on the route: Kishon Valley East. There was a curve in the track — that would slow the train down. If they could find a fast enough car, they could make it.

The rain had let up a bit just before sunset.

Night settled in under a pattering of steady drizzle as Ahab's limo—now flanked by two armored cars—neared the royal compound at Naboth's Vineyard. Ahab was asleep, balled up under a fleece blanket. Obadijah was lost in thought, eyes trained on the sunroof, but not registering anything outside. Isabel stared out the side window, reassessing her life.

She wasn't sure what it meant that Jah had produced both fire and rain, while Baal remained silent. What *could* it mean to her? Her options were very limited. She was the daughter of the King of Tsidon, Supreme Priest of Baal. Faith in Him was not an option; it was a given. If her current doubts ever became known to her father—and she irrationally feared that he already knew—she would likely find herself spread-eagle, buckled down to a granite table while black-clad priests and white-robed prophets sharpened knives. Baal loved treachery offerings and there was none higher than one's own children.

No, losing faith in Baal was not an option.

She wasn't sure how or even if she could strike back against Jah, but she knew she couldn't join him. Besides, that would mean acknowledging that Eli had won, which was also out of the question. She despised him more than she would have thought possible even a day earlier when he left her on a corner in Lowtown. Her vision swam with pure hate when she thought about his smugness at the stadium, how the first thing he had done after Karmel was to call and gloat.

Something dawned on her all at once. A memory, which gave birth to an epiphany. She turned and stared at Obadijah.

He felt her eyes on him and awoke from his trance. "What?" he asked, uneasy.

A smile tugged at the corner of her mouth. "How did Eli know your cell number?"

"This stop, Kishon Valley West. Next stop, Kishon Heights," crackled the UrbanRail's loudspeaker. The train squeaked and hissed to a halt. This station was the mirror image of its Omri Avenue counterpart. The doors slid open, issuing a few people who chatted their way around the corner and up to the street. No one was waiting to board and, for a minute, the platform was deserted.

Then Eli tentatively emerged from between two cars and hopped to the platform. His eyes skipped across the station. Smiling inwardly, he tightened his tie, straightened his coat, and made for the exit. Yet another successful disappearing act by the Amazing Eli. *I'll be in town all week, tip well.* He only needed a place to dry off and sew himself back together.

The crack of a gunshot echoed through the station and stopped Eli mid-step. He looked down at his chest to see a crimson circle growing on his white shirt. He could hear the air being sucked wetly from his chest as his baffled eyes met El-Baal's. The high priest stood at the bottom of the stairs, smoking gun in hand and sadistic ecstasy plastered on his face. Eli fell hard to his knees, his breaths short and raspy. He looked up in utter confusion at the two men closing in on him. This was unscripted.

He reached into his coat and halfheartedly drew his gun. Luli easily slapped it from his hand, sending it sliding loudly down the platform. He then dragged Eli to his feet by the collar and pressed a pistol to his temple.

Eli laughed an amused, painful laugh.

El-Baal laughed with him for a moment, an inch from his face, his eyes crueler than ever. His laughter trailed off and he quietly said, "I can't even imagine what you find humorous about this situation."

This struck Eli as hilarious and, between alternating winces and bursts of hysterical laughter, he managed, "You're not a very good loser, are you?"

The smile disappeared from El-Baal's face. "Shut up," he commanded.

Eli coughed and leaned back against Luli. He formed a weak, antagonistic smile. "Oh yeah. Sorry, *El-Bosheth*. I guess Baal is really the loser today. Too scared to even show up."

"Shut up!" El-Baal slammed a fist into Eli's cheekbone, eliciting an overwhelmed groan from the prophet. The *ding-dong* sounded above them. Eli's heavy eyes searched the station, disoriented. El-Baal hit him again while Luli held him up by the shoulders of his coat.

"How's that feel?" El-Baal demanded. "Where's your bragging now? Where's your god now? Huh?!"

He punched him again in the face and then in the chest, right on top of the bullet wound. Eli screamed. The high priest hit him in the same spot again. And again.

With a hiss, the doors closed and the automated train pulled away, down the track and out of sight. This once again jarred El-Baal from his rage. He took a step back from Eli, an idea forming. He breathed in and out slowly, calming himself. He then very deliberately removed his soaked black coat, rolled up his left sleeve and with his long, curved dagger, cut his arm deeply. In a trancelike tone, he droned, "Lord Baal, we come to this place of retribution, seeking your favor."

With a sudden burst of energy, Eli slammed the back of his head into Luli's nose. Blood exploded against Luli's face and began to ooze down to his chin. Still he kept the injured prophet secured in a tight chokehold. Luli smashed the butt of his pistol into Eli's temple, then his ear. Eli slumped, dead weight once again. His breathing was shallower and his vision little more than whites and blacks. Luli's eyes grew wild as El-Baal continued the ritual.

"We have shown weakness and so you demand an act of ruthlessness as proof of our dedication. Tonight we bring to you this Vengeance Offering – a hated enemy of Baal. He will serve to seal our souls to you." He sheathed the dagger and rubbed the blood around on his arm in an almost playful manner. "We dedicate ourselves to you. We are your loyal subjects, Baal. We commit all that we own and control to your benefit."

Another train thundered into the station and came to a stop. The priests paused, irritated but willing to wait out the unwelcome interruption. They wanted this to be perfect, a memory they could return to again and again as they lay in bed, drifting off to sleep.

The train's doors rolled open and a group of half-drunk men stepped to the platform. The men looked at Eli and then to El-Baal, to Luli, and back to Eli before it dawned on them what was happening. A big, burly guy burst out from the group and pulled a hunting knife from his boot.

"Let him go, you freak," he commanded, stepping toward El-Baal. Luli let loose a barrage of bullets, cutting them all down.

El Baal sneered. "Infidels. Traitors. Where was I?"

"The blood," Luli answered.

"Oh, yes. We seal this vengeance offering with our blood." He rubbed his bloody hand on the top of Eli's head. Luli pushed his own bloodied face against Eli's cheek, leaving a red smear. El-Baal drew his pistol and pointed it an inch from Eli's right eye. Luli craned his head off to the side as far as his neck would allow.

Both high priests were flushed and pink. El-Baal looked into Eli's glassy eyes and was relieved to find some recognition. He smiled at the servant of Jah, now defeated, and, with certainty, declared, "Baal is God."

"Haven't you heard?" The two priests wheeled to see Jehu standing on the platform next to them, a long-barreled revolver in his thick hand. "Baal is dead."

The gunshot reduced El-Baal's head by half and sent him flopping to the concrete floor. Jehu stepped behind him as he fell and aimed the revolver at the narrow space between Luli's eyes.

Luli quivered and pushed the barrel of his own gun against Eli's head "I-I'll kill him," he stuttered. "I swear!" He stepped back into the train, dragging his human shield, now barely breathing.

קישון

Jehu chuckled. "Luli, Luli, Luli. You should see the look on your face right now." He adopted a mocking tone. *"How did he get here? How'd he know where to find us?"* His booming laugh filled the small station. "Oh, that's so priceless." The *ding-dong* sounded again from the blown speaker overhead. "Well, you're gonna love this part: Jah told me where to find you. He told me that you and your little girlfriend would be right where you stood. He told me you'd have Eli with you.

"But most importantly . . . " He paused and took a step toward the train. " . . . he told me that you . . . " Veins and tendons shifted below Jehu's brown skin as he re-centered his aim. " . . . would be out . . . " A loud *chak-chak-chak* echoed through the station as Jehu drew back the hammer. " . . . of bullets."

Luli's eyes flew wide. Brakes hissed.

A defeated click sounded from his empty gun.

The sliding doors of the train car came together.

Jehu fired.

The bullet shattered glass, connected with Luli's head, and left a fist-sized hole in its wake. Luli's body teetered for a moment, then crashed to the floor, pulling Eli down on top of him.

The train was pulling away. Jehu sprinted to its side, smashing his fist against the window of the last car, spider- webbing the glass. Too late. The train disappeared. Jehu looked down into the black void of the tunnel and prayed for Eli.

Ahab flopped from his left side to his right and tried to untangle himself from the Egyptian cotton sheets. Next to him, Isabel sighed loudly. The two rarely shared a bed, but the compound at Naboth's Vineyard was short on living space and had been remodeled during a brief spell of amicability. They had arrived after midnight and Ahab had almost volunteered to sleep on the sofa, but decided against it, as that would have meant speaking to her—a thought that did not appeal to him.

He was terrified of her to begin with, but the looming prospect of obeying Eli's orders and asserting himself had him even more on edge. The memory of his wife entangled with El-Baal only heightened his tension. Not that he blamed her for the infidelity. Ahab would have had an affair himself—a dozen of them if he weren't so embarrassingly afraid of his wife. He had certainly had opportunity.

But El-Baal? The Tsidonian, almost ten years her senior, had known Isabel since she was a child. When she arrived in Ephraim for the wedding, he was part of the package. After thinking about it most of the night, Ahab had deemed it unlikely that this intimacy had begun since their arrival. He felt like the victim of a long and elaborate con, forced to sleep with the perpetrator. The very real possibility that the high priest was dead caused the knot in the king's guts to loosen a bit.

He got up and felt his way to the medicine cabinet for some sleeping pills. The bathroom was barely illuminated by a small nightlight, lending everything a warm orange glow. To his disappointment, the cabinet was empty save some aspirin and an assortment of Isabel's lotions and salves. He grunted to himself and swung the door closed.

142

Ahab's heart dropped. The breath was sucked out of him and replaced with a familiar dread. In the mirror—looking him squarely in the face—was his dead father. He closed his eyes for a moment and when he opened them, saw only his own reflection. He hurriedly fumbled his way back to bed, where the queen had finally drifted off to sleep, and lay down next to her. His heart was still pounding. He pulled the sheet up to his chin for protection and closed his eyes, willing himself to fall asleep.

But his eyelids proved no barrier and he found himself again looking into the face of his father, Omri, floating in the blackness. He opened his eyes to escape, but there was Omri still, hovering somewhere between the bed and the ceiling.

This was far from the first time Omri had appeared to Ahab since his death twenty years prior. At least once a year, during times of particular ineptitude on Ahab's part, he would find himself the subject of his dead father's judgmental gaze. It no longer struck him as unusual, though still plenty unpleasant. There was always a dull but constant dread lurking in the back of his mind in anticipation of his father's next appearance.

Of course, Ahab knew it wasn't really Omri who visited him during the oppressive hours of the night. The foul breath and elongated limbs gave him away. It was Baal who haunted him. Occasionally, during these apparitions, the god even seemed to lose his focus for just a moment and his serpentine face would half emerge from behind the late king's visage.

If it was meant to frighten Ahab, it worked.

In life, Omri had been a self-made man. He joined the army young and quickly climbed the chain of command.

143

Before his thirtieth birthday, he was in charge of all of Ephraim's fighting men. When the political assassinations began, Omri had vowed to stay out of it. After all, his loyalty was to the kingdom, not any particular man. In a quarter century, four men sat on the throne, three of them murdered and succeeded by their killers. The shortest reign was seven days.

This political free-for-all ended, however, when Zimri, a low-ranking agent of the Shomrey-Melek, killed his sovereign and declared himself the new monarch. Having had enough, the military looked to Omri to restore order to the nation and dignity to the office. He put himself immediately and completely to the task.

Tirzah was the capitol in those days and Omri saturated the city with his men, declared martial law, and brought the fight to Zimri's front door. The self-proclaimed king barricaded himself inside his mansion. In the end, Zimri burned the house down around him, perishing in the flames, rather than face Omri.

As king, Omri had left nothing to chance. He quickly moved the capitol from Tirzah to Shomron, building it up from almost nothing. After gaining the allegiance of the Shomrey-Melek, he crushed any and all rivals to the throne, killing whole families without mercy. In the twelve years he reigned, King Omri reclaimed several dozen cities that had been captured during Ephraim's unrest. He also capitulated to the Baalist party, first relaxing, then overturning the idolatry laws—a move that had lost him the support of the fast-waning conservative Jahwist party, but gained him a broader popularity and reinforced his reputation as a king who was on the throne to stay. There

קישון

were few people in Ephraim who did not consider Omri to be either the best or worst king the nation had ever known.

When he died suddenly, leaving the kingdom in the hands of his young, untested son, Omri's shadow became Ahab's permanent home. Most political analysts agreed, at least privately, that had Omri not pre-arranged the marriage with Isabel—thus forming an alliance with Tsidon—Ahab would have been picked off inside a week and replaced by someone more fit to lead.

Indeed, Ahab was a disappointment to everyone—particularly himself. He didn't have the presence that his father commanded. His own attempts at conquest against neighboring Aram had continually led to stalemate. So his bride easily took the reins from his hands. Under Isabel's direction, tolerance of Baalism became an endorsement and then a requirement, causing Ahab's approval rating to dip at times into the single digits.

Ahab was quite simply a so-so king. And mediocrity was less than useless in light of the legacy his father had left. Baal was well aware of this sense of inadequacy, Ahab assumed, and used it to manipulate him. If the king toyed with the idea of granting amnesty to Jah's prophets, there was Omri, haunting his dreams or appearing suddenly in the dark. When he and Joab spoke well into the night as they did on occasion, discussing ways to restore the glory to the kingdom, he would try to reverse his schedule in the days that followed, sleeping during the day and busying himself during the dark hours, because he was terrified of what the night would bring if he found himself alone.

What kept Ahab on edge was the ongoing escalation of Omri's appearance. As soon as Ahab grew more or less used to his dead father's presence, the next apparition

145

would be all the more horrifying. He'd gone from an exact likeness to a sallow, elongated version to a half-rotten corpse.

Just two days earlier, Joab had pushed for a change in policy, shortening the leash on Baal's troops after the massacre at the Executive Offices. Ahab had compromised, signing the "Non-Lethal Response" bill. That night, the king's dreams had been filled with a gray-skinned Omri, cheeks rotted out to expose his upper teeth, beckoning Ahab to join him in his grave.

Ahab's attention was jerked back to the current apparition by the hint of a forked tongue flickering out of Omri's mouth and back in. The king cringed. He had never dared address the phantom and certainly wasn't going to start tonight. He got up again and made his way to the small adjoining study, sliding the door shut behind him.

He picked up the phone and dialed the number of a dormitory room at an elite boarding school in Tyre of Tsidon. It rang twice before a young voice answered.

"Hello?"

"Ahazijah?"

"No, hold on a second." Ahab heard a muffled exchange and the crackle of the phone being passed around. This went on for a full minute. The same voice returned. "Who's this?"

Annoyance dusted with indignation filled Ahab's words. "This is King Ahab of Ephraim. Please put Ahazijah on."

The young voice announced, "It's your dad." Ahab heard a spattering of laughs and jeers from the dorm room. A moment later, his son was on the line.

"Hi Dad." Ahazijah was out of breath and chewing as he spoke.

"Why are you still up? It's late."

"It's not that late, Dad." Another volley of laughter. "Anyway, why'd you call if it's so late? I can't talk on the phone in my sleep, can I?"

Ahab tried to adopt an authoritative, fatherly tone. An Omri tone. "Don't get cocky with me, young man. A future king needs his sleep and a future king needs to perform well academically."

Ahab had been a C student.

"How do *you* know?" Ahazijah laughed. "Are you a future king?" Ahab said nothing. "I saw you on the news today, you know. What the *hell* was that?"

The king's face felt suddenly hot. That quick, the roles had reversed. "I don't know. It was . . . grownup stuff."

"I *am* grown up." The boy was insulted. Ahab tried to remember if his son was fifteen or sixteen. Before he could decide, Ahazijah demanded, "Why'd you agree to a contest anyway? You don't have to choose one god. Don't you know anything?"

Beads of sweat budded on Ahab's forehead and upper lip.

"You can worship any god you want. A true leader bows at every altar."

A sharp adrenaline spike prickled up Ahab's back and down to his fingertips. "It's not that simple," he said. "Believe me."

"Yes it is." His son raised his voice. "Mom taught me this stuff when I was like five years old. Baal isn't a jealous god. You can worship others. She knows a lot more than you about this stuff. Besides, we have all kinds of chapel services here: Molech, Ishtar, Marduk—"

"But not Jah."

Ahazijah thought for a moment. "No, not him. But that's because he's weak. We could worship him if we wanted to."

"No. Believe me, it's dangerous."

His son scoffed. "You're scared. You're scared of the lovey-dovey inland god!" He began to taunt his father. "I'm going to pray to him."

"Ahaz, please . . . "

"Right when I hang up, I'm gonna pray to him. And I'm going to ask him what it felt like to show you up in front of the whole world." He expelled a short burst of laughter that hurt Ahab's ear. "Ya know what? I think he's my hero. I think he's my new favorite god."

Hair stood up on the back of Ahab's neck. He knew better than to look behind him. He could hear the slithering of the apparition. "Son, just trust me," he pleaded. "That's not a good idea."

Ahazijah changed the subject. "I heard that Ben Hadad re-captured Ramoth Gilead again tonight. Bravo, Dad! What're you gonna do about that?"

This was not something Ahab wanted to hear. Ben Hadad was the king of Aram, which lay north and east of Ephraim. During the years of unrest, Aram had occupied a dozen of Ephraim's border towns. Early in his career, Omri had re-taken them all in one massive campaign. But beginning the day of Omri's death, Ben Hadad had slowly started moving his troops back across the border.

Ahab's counter-offensives were ill-conceived and usually more flash than bang. When he did manage to drive the Arameans back, it was always very temporary. Ramoth Gilead alone had changed hands six times. Seven if his son was right. And if his son was right, then a teenager had heard about it on TV before the king had been briefed on the matter.

Ahab wished he hadn't called. "You let me worry about that, son. You'll have plenty of time to fight Aram when you take over the throne. That's why you need to study hard now"

"My civics teacher says that Ben Hadad is making an idiot out of you."

Ahab was incensed. "What's his name?"

"Mr. Belel. He said he's not afraid to say that kind of stuff because soon Ephraim will be a Tsidonian colony."

"Does he know you're the prince? What a stupid thing to say! Your father is the king of Ephraim—"

"And my grandfather's the king of Tsidon! What do I care? Look, Dad. I gotta go."

A *click* sounded from the receiver. Ahab placed the phone on the cradle and looked over his shoulder tentatively. Omri's face was decomposing and regenerating every couple seconds.

It was going to be a long night.

צרפת

zarephath

Eli didn't die.

When the bullet ripped into his chest, the world went slow-motion, surreal, like the physical plane had been mixed with a prophetic vision. His lungs felt scarred. His heart got heavy. It beat weakly with a *squish-squish* every few seconds. He was sure this was the end. Mission accomplished. Time to join his fathers.

It seemed to confirm his thoughts when a man he'd never seen before walked right up behind El-Baal and blew his head off with that hand cannon. *What a going-away present*, he thought. *To see those devil-worshiping goyim sent to Sheol.*

Only Eli kept on breathing. He felt even heavier, clumsier as he was dragged into the train. The hole in his chest was making kissing noises and the world was growing darker by the second. When the mystery man killed Luli too, Eli heard the bullet rip past his ear at a snails pace. The two men had fallen to the ground together, but Eli never landed.

He kept falling.

Looking up, he saw a light. A beautiful, glowing white orb. There was always a light drawing people toward the end of a tunnel in those dubious near-death stories in the tabloids. Eli had never understood what could be so compelling about a simple light that it would warrant telling and re-telling, but when he felt the warmth of this light on his face, it made perfect sense. He would have gladly walked toward *this* light if he could. But Eli was in a pit, not a tunnel. And he was being pulled down away from the glowing ball.

He fell until the light was just a dot far above him, a pinhole in the blackness. Then it disappeared altogether. He didn't know if he was still falling. He hadn't felt any drop in his stomach to begin with and without a visual reference, up and down lost their meaning.

He tried to speak. Nothing came out. He was still and quiet for what could have been a few seconds or a few days. Time had lost its grip on him. He began to wonder if this was eternity. He could think of worse things if it was. There was a certain peace about it, albeit an incomplete peace.

Finally, a diffused glow slowly illuminated a scene before him. He was no longer falling. Once again he found himself watching the strange temple room in the foreign land. There was still a pile of meat on the altar next to Baal. The bearded king stood back by the wall, arms folded, amusement written on his face. The Prophet of Jah was sprinkling—what were those, ashes?—across the floor of the room. Systematically, he made his way, wall to wall, covering every square inch. He muttered as he sprinkled. His voice was muffled and Eli strained to hear him.

What is he saying? It sounded like chanting. Eli frowned inwardly. Why would he be chanting? A horrible thought dawned on him. Was this some pagan ritual? The statue of Baal seemed to be smiling at him now. His long twisted limbs were almost indiscernibly moving. What was a man of Jah doing in a place like this to begin with? Why was he chanting and sprinkling ashes? Eli hated the thought of

Jah's faithful turning from the Truth and bowing the knee to Baal. He told his eyes to close, but the Prophet kept sprinkling, his lips kept moving, and he kept drawing closer and closer until his face filled Eli's field of vision.

That's when Eli realized he wasn't chanting. He was chuckling. Having carpeted the entire floor with ashes, he tiptoed over to where the king stood by the door. Surveying his work, he laughed out loud for a moment. Then the two men left the room and the door slammed shut, leaving Eli once again in darkness.

Apparently the ashes were funny.

Eli didn't get it.

At once a new scene materialized. It was a filthy hospital room. He wanted to understand the first dream before he encountered a new one. He willed the temple to come back. He wanted to get the joke about the ashes.

But the hospital remained. Fluorescent lights flickered above. The floor had a patina of dirt mixed with blood and other assorted byproducts of childbirth. Lying in a rusted and rickety hospital bed, a young woman was in the throes of labor. Her hair was long and black and her skin as dark as Eli's. She breathed heavily and issued a guttural response to each contraction. A nurse stood next to the bed in bloodstained scrubs, offering instructions and encouragement.

Neither woman noticed the dragon crouched at the foot of the bed. Eli felt bile bubble at the back of his throat at the sight and sulfurous stink of Baal. His form was small—so small that he fit in the tight space between the bed and the commode. The ten horns on his head stood straight up, glinting in the greenish light. His mouth was open two hundred-seventy degrees and viscous saliva dripped from his razor-sharp teeth.

The baby began to emerge, the nurse cradling its head. The dragon shook with anticipation. With each push of the young woman, the beast craned its neck further. As the birth was completed, the dragon's claws clenched and, with an obscene thrust, he snapped for the infant boy. His jaws clapped together, missing their target.

The baby was gone. The nurse had clutched him to her chest, spread a broad pair of wings, and launched into the air, passing through the ceiling as if it were not there. The dragon stared up in disbelief for a minute or two, angry grunts vibrating from his quivering throat. His eyes narrowed and his breathing quickened. He redirected his rage at the woman and leapt for her, but the bed was empty. The dragon roared and bounded out into the hallway. The doctors and patients and orderlies took no notice of him. The woman was nowhere to be found. The dragon was growing with each passing moment and now took up the entire hall.

He crashed out the front door into the balmy night. There was no sign of mother or child. The dragon continued to grow. He was as tall as two men now. His nostrils picked up the woman's scent and he began to track her. He followed a dirt highway for a few miles, running with catlike speed, passing cars and trucks, deeper and deeper into the desert. The air was dusty out here. His nostrils dried up and filled with grit. He couldn't keep the scent.

A powerful gust of wind brought a wall of sand from beyond the horizon. The dragon slid a translucent membrane over his eyes and curled up in a ball. A million grains of sand cut into him like so many knives.

Eli then saw the place where Jah had hidden the woman. She was in a deep cave cut sharply from the side of a rock face surrounded by miles of desert in every direction. She was safe there for the moment. Eli waited and watched while the moments became hours, then days, then months. For a time, times, and half a time, the malakim—Jah's heavenly messengers—brought her meat and water. Three and a half years the woman remained in the cave; forty-two dry months, sweltering but safe.

Eli could have watched the woman forever, but there the dream ended. Real-world physical sensations, particularly pain, returned to him. He drew his eyelids up slowly. A sharp, dirty light pierced his retinas. It seemed vulgar compared to the warm glowing ball that had illuminated his dreams. He groaned. His chest ached like fury. His heart was still *squish-squishing*, sending a pounding pain through his head with each beat. He smelled garbage, mildew, and sweat. His eyes searched around, rolling in their sockets.

He was still in the train. The doors were wide open and there, framed perfectly between them, stood a young woman, backlit and beautiful. She had light skin and chocolate brown hair that reached to her shoulders. Her eyes were wide and her tiny mouth formed an *O* as she looked down at Eli.

He tried to muster a charming smile. It was a failed project. He twisted uncomfortably on the ground.

What was he lying on? It was soft, but lumpy and moist.

Oh, yeah. Luli.

Ahab made his way down the hall, clad in a velvet robe, his slippers shuffling along the Tyrian purple carpet. As he rounded a corner, two Shomrey-Melek agents standing guard snapped to attention. Ahab thought he noticed a new sense of pride and professionalism among those who had accompanied him back to Naboth's Vineyard. He wasn't sure if it had more to do with the day's events at Karmel or the absence of Baal's priests. Either way, he liked it. It reminded him of being a real king, something of which he'd tasted very little firsthand.

Just inside the compound's main entrance stood Joab and a hulking agent whose neck Ahab estimated to be the same circumference as his own thigh. Both men straightened upon seeing the king. Yes, Ahab was sure they hadn't puffed out their chests like this yesterday.

The rain had started again and it made a pleasant patter on the portico roof. Ahab closed his eyes and drank in the sound for a moment. Very deliberately, he said, "I've waited one thousand, two-hundred and sixty days to hear that."

Joab smiled and nodded slowly. The other agent announced that he was leaving to check the perimeter of the compound. This was standard; whenever Ahab came by after hours to talk with Joab, everyone else was to make themselves useful elsewhere.

The king and his captain stood in a comfortable silence for a few minutes.

Joab spoke first. "Quite a day."

Ahab half-laughed through his nose at the understatement. "Yeah." He was bad at small talk. "I talked to Eli on the way out here, you know."

"I know."

"I wonder if you'd let me into your office?"

Joab crinkled his brow. "What do you need, sir? If you need a drink, I can get that, but I don't keep anything in my office anymore."

"No, your *other* office."

A grin broke out on Joab's face. "Certainly, sir. This way." He led Ahab briskly down a narrow hall to a metal door, dressed with a DANGER: HIGH VOLTAGE sign. Joab punched a code into a keypad. A green light blinked on followed by a *click* and the door swung open.

Joab had to duck to get in. Ahab didn't. The smell of matches filled the air as Joab lit seven small oil lamps affixed to a single reservoir. The flames flickered and quivered, illuminating the room with an ever-changing light. The place was small, maybe six feet squared, with concrete walls. A bolster pillow sat on the floor just in front of a small wooden bookstand. There were three volumes stacked next to it: a copy of the *Torah*—the instructions that Jah had given Moshe; a gold foil, leather-bound collection of the prophets of Jah from the crossing of the river up until just twenty years ago; and a tattered old edition of the *Mishkilim*—the poems of their great king, David.

Ahab had known about this room for years and had warned his friend what would likely happen if El-Baal ever stumbled upon it. But Joab always laughed it off. It sometimes seemed liked the captain was actually eager to force a confrontation between El-Baal's men and the Shomrey-Melek.

As Joab ducked back out into the hall, Ahab said, "Make sure nobody comes in here, okay?"

Joab nodded. "Don't worry. I won't let her in, Your Highness." The door clicked shut behind him.

The king was alone. There in the dim light, he knew that his son was right. He was afraid of Jah. But talking to Joab always gave him courage—at least for the moment.

He gracelessly knelt on the purple cushion and opened the book of sacred poetry. He began to flip, looking for an out. Eli had given him clear instructions and, for the first time ever, his instinct was not to do the opposite. He wanted what Eli promised. He wanted to surrender in his long fight against Jah's prophet. And he was almost certain that he wanted to be reconciled with the God who had showered blessings in the form of rain on Ephraim that afternoon.

But it was complicated. Isabel had led him down certain paths that would be difficult to backtrack. Blood had been spilled. He'd made promises to Baal and received favors in return. And, considering who they had locked up in the brig, he had some very difficult decisions ahead of him. If Jah could give him a painless solution to this mess, he was more than ready to listen.

Ahab continued thumbing the old pages, no real destination in mind. Suddenly, his hand froze. His eyes were drawn immediately to the words

> *Jah is my light and my deliverance.*
> *Of whom must I be afraid?*
> *Jah is a bunker for my life. Who should I dread?*

Ahab closed his eyes. The tension ball that had been squeezing his mind as long as he could remember was melting away. A peace began to spread over him. It was a feeling he'd never experienced directly, only in whiffs and glimpses. This was the beginning of something that could change everything.

The king knew that somehow what was happening here could be even bigger than what had happened at Karmel.

The Kishon Heights UrbanRail station had the same floor plan as all the others. What set it apart was the gang graffiti covering every surface and the trash covering the platform. Two bums slept against a vending machine that lay on its side, smashed open and picked clean. In the shadows, a small pack of rats grazed through a few foil wrappers.

A lone woman sat on a bench waiting for the train. She wore an old print skirt, a green blouse, and a knit cap. All were soaked as was the bag of groceries at her feet. An old transistor radio on the bench next to her tinily reproduced the words of an ecstatic deejay.

"The market jumped 800% today between one o'clock and close. If you don't know why, come on out from the bomb shelter!" He paused for a zany sound effect. "The drought is over! The recession is over! The depression is over! Torrential rainfall is expected to continue throughout the night and the forecast calls for rain every day this week. Water service has been restored to approximately fifty thousand homes today and authorities estimate that within the month, the remainder will—" She clicked off the radio.

Too late, too late, too late. The words played a continuous loop in her mind. Her fingers made slow circles against her temples, the same habit that had prompted her mother to continually warn, "Zarephath, honey, you're going to break out if you keep touching your face." This only encouraged her to keep it up. Especially since she hated being addressed by her full name. The prediction never came true, though. She was twenty-nine now and her skin remained perfect as always.

She decided to leave the radio behind. Let a homeless man keep it. She certainly wouldn't need it anymore. The train was approaching—she could hear it—so she collected her bag of groceries, hugged it to her chest and moved out onto the platform. This filthy place was one she was not going to miss. The train groaned to a stop and three sets of doors opened in unison.

Zara froze. Lying in the middle of the train floor were two men. One was very dead. The other lay on top of him, injured and bleeding, sucking short, shallow breaths. The groceries thudded to the ground.

"Oh my God," she whispered. The prophet lifted his head sluggishly and regarded her with dazed eyes.

"Mr. Tishbi!" She was at his side in an instant. "I'm going to get you to a hospital. You'll be okay."

Eli opened his mouth to speak. The only thing that came out was a bubble of blood, which popped audibly.

Zara tugged on his shirt, trying to lift him. "We need to get you off the train. I'll call an ambulance."

Eli rasped, "No. No hospital . . . on my way home now. Finished my job."

She shushed him. "Nonsense. You're going to be all right! I'll get you to a doctor."

"Forget it." A weak cough brought more blood to his chin. "They'll kill me if they find me. I don't know how many more . . ." His eyes went glassy. The *ding-dong* sounded above.

"Can you walk?" she asked.

He stared at nothing.

"Eli, do you think you can walk?"

"I blew up the helicopter."

She hesitated. "Okay. I'll take that as a *yes*."

Ahab felt safe. He could sense that Baal was not present in this place. Not right now. And he felt a soft tapping on his soul. He'd heard about the great kings of ages past who had Jah's spirit with them and how it empowered them to do incredible things. But those were just myths, he'd convinced himself. Just an attempt to justify an outdated religious exclusivism.

Ahab stopped thinking and listened.

The words were audible, as clear as they had been twelve hours earlier: *"How long will you waver between two opinions? If Jah is God, then follow him alone. If Baal is god, then follow him. You can't have it both ways! Jah demands your allegiance! Hasn't he earned it? He brought our ancestors out of slavery in Mitzrayim. He gave us this land and provides for us. But you have abandoned his commands and worshiped idols. Jah isn't like Baal. If you will reject Baal today and turn back to Jah, he will accept you and forgive you and bless you."*

The king was surprised to find himself flipping now though the book of the prophets. He didn't know where he was headed, but his hands seemed to. They stopped flipping and his finger ran down the page, coming to rest at a block quote in the middle of a narrative. The words of Jehoshua Nun.

If serving Jah seems evil to you, then chose today whom you will serve: the gods your fathers served on the other side of the river or the gods of the goyim in whose land you now dwell? As for me and my house, we will serve Jah."

Ahab got it. And it scared him. He thought of Isabel's judging eyes, how quickly she would shut him down if he tried to defect now. He thought about Enoch on the granite table grunting and thrashing about. Jah was asking for too much.

I won't choose, he thought. *I refuse. They'll just have to learn to get along like grownups.* Maybe Ahazijah was right about that too. Maybe you *can* serve both. Maybe Jah could protect him from Baal. Maybe Jah could keep Omri in the grave where he belonged. Yes, he was beginning to think he'd found the answer.

He closed the *Prophets,* opened the *Torah,* and read some more. "You shall have no molten gods. You will die, pleading, screaming, the blood of your children in your nostrils, you traitorous weakling . . . "

He stopped short. These words didn't belong here. A rattlesnake sound drifted from above the bookstand. Ahab's stomach dropped. He looked up to see Omri's face, rotten almost beyond recognition. Behind the putrid flesh, he saw yellow dragon eyes. Three horns emerged from the cracked skin of his forehead.

צרפת

Ahab stared into the emotionless eyes. "I'm sorry," he whispered. Baal opened Omri's mouth and roared.

The king overturned the bookstand, frantically scrambling back out into the hall. He could still feel Baal's hot breath on his face and smell its sulfur stink. His heartbeats were running into each other. He began to hyperventilate.

That was a stupid idea.

Nadab Circle was Zarephath's stop. She rode the train such a short distance twice a week because, while this stretch of rail wasn't exactly safe, the alternative was walking through the Kishon Heights Housing Projects. She'd rather pay the thirty-five shekels for a token and pass beneath them.

When the train came to a stop, there were three teenage boys and a girl waiting to board. To them, Eli and Zara looked like a couple who had partied too hard in celebration of the rain. Eli wore Luli's black sport coat—buttoned to his chin to conceal the blood-soaked shirt beneath—and Zara's knit cap, pulled down to his eyes. She held his arm around her shoulder and helped him walk onto the platform.

The four youths boarded the train and gathered around a large object on the floor, covered over with a tan tarp. One of them reached down and pulled away what turned out to be a bloody trench coat, revealing Luli's corpse. In unison, they snapped their attention to Zarephath, eyes wide.

She shrugged, "It's not mine," and helped Eli up the stairs.

Eli was drifting. Several times, he felt like he might regain consciousness, but it kept eluding him. He had dreams. Everyday dreams. No meaning, no prophecy, just stuff about his parents, his friends, his car. Man, he was going to miss that car.

He wanted to return to the temple room in the strange land, find out what was so funny about the ashes, but he couldn't make it appear.

He sensed that at least one night had come and gone before he finally came to. The process of fighting his eyes open and dealing with the harsh light was becoming commonplace. His vision was a blur, coming slowly into focus, one level of detail at a time. He was in bed. He looked to his left—a wall of faux wood paneling. He looked to his right.

"Gyaaaaa!" He jolted awake. A little kid, maybe four years old, was sitting on the side of the bed, staring at him—hand stuck in his mouth, drool cascading down his arm, his huge eyes analyzing. He was skinny as a rail with ears that looked like outstretched wings on a seagull.

Eli wasn't into kids. He recovered quickly, tried to smile, and said, "Hi there, pal!"

The kid hopped off the bed and trotted out the door. A moment later he returned, followed by Zarephath. She sat where the boy had been and handed Eli a plastic cup of water.

"Here, Mr. Tishbi. Drink this." He accepted it gladly. "Our faucet just came back on yesterday morning," she was explaining. "The TV said we should still boil it, so I did. Is it cold enough, Mr. Tishbi?"

Eli loved her slight Tsidonian accent. He slowly sat up with a little effort. The bed was tiny. *Probably the kid's,* he thought. He was shirtless, marked by a good amount of stubble all over his head and face, blanket pulled up to his waist.

"It's fine," he said after a long gulp. "And you can just call me Eli."

"Okay, Eli. My name is Zara." She giggled, nervous. "How do you feel?"

"You know what? I feel great! How long have I been here?" He shifted and popped his knuckles.

She adopted a motherly tone. "Take it slow. You've been asleep for thirty-six hours."

The prophet stretched and cracked his neck. Life was returning to his body. "Slow? Why? I feel better than I ever have!" His words came in rapid-fire bursts. "I've got people to see, things to do. But first, how about some breakfast? Need some coffee. Breakfast with coffee."

He hopped out of bed, felt that he was naked, and was back under the covers instantly. "What—what'd you . . . ?"

"I didn't do anything. The doctor was here to see you and *he* took your clothes off." She fought the smile that wanted to form. "They were all bloody anyway. You can wear some of my husband's clothes when you get up. They should fit you just fine."

He nodded. Remembering his wound, he looked down to see a large, ugly scar on his chest, but not a trace of blood or scab. "Whoa," is all he could say.

"That's exactly what Dr. Manasseh said. He wanted to bring you to the hospital but I told him how you were dead-set against the idea."

Looking to his lesser wounds, he found that the split in his side had been stitched together and was mostly healed. The rest were just sore, minor annoyances. The doctor had done good work.

"I'll have to thank him later. And your husband too. Where is he? I'd like to meet him."

"He's dead." She was no longer smiling but not overly solemn. "Dehydration, two years ago."

"Sorry." And he didn't just mean, *My condolences.*

Zara smiled. "At least I still have my son. This is Hiram."

Eli gave it another try, extending his hand and offering, "Good to meet you, buddy." Hiram stared back blankly. "Cute kid. Listen, I'm starving. Have you two eaten anything today?"

She shook her head slowly. "We haven't eaten more than a few bites in quite some time. All my money has been going to keep us hydrated. There hasn't been much left for food."

"But it's been a couple days, right? Things haven't gotten any better?"

She shrugged. "A rebounding economy doesn't help when you're broke and jobless. When I found you, I had just spent my last hundred shekels on some groceries. I was going to cook a last meal for Hiram and me so we could die with full stomachs."

Eli let out a low whistle. "Kind of bleak."

"That's funny to you."

"There's something I want to show you, Zara. But let me get dressed first."

"Sure. Come on, Hiram. Let's go outside." She took the boy's hand. On the way out, she indicated a cedar wardrobe. "The clothes are in here. You're welcome to whatever you can use. They've just been sitting in there collecting dust."

"Thanks."

She hesitated a beat and then asked, "Tell me, why did you want to meet my husband?"

"I wanted to thank him."

"Why thank him? I'm the one who saved your life." She gave him a sly smile and then she was out the door.

Half an hour later, Eli emerged from the ten-story apartment building. Zara was waiting on the steps, Hiram in her lap. The neighborhood was rundown, but seemed less so this morning. It was a cool seventy degrees. The sun shone. A few clouds drifted through the blue sky, building up for another rain. A backlog of water continuously lumbered down the gutters, tinkling into the storm sewer, a sound that no one could imagine ever getting old. And the street was alive with people out enjoying the weather.

Eli was showered, his face clean-shaven. He wore a button-up shirt and tie, pressed slacks, and a light gray trench coat.

Zara squelched a laugh, then let it out when he announced, "I think your husband had incredible taste in clothing. Some kind of professional, I take it?"

"He was a lawyer. Mostly rights and freedoms, back when people used to talk about such things. He always said he had to look sharp when he brought grievances against the government."

"I know exactly what he meant. Sounds like he and I were in the same business more or less. Not a very popular line of work these days."

"It cost him plenty. They blackballed him when the drought came. Water Rationing said he wasn't a registered citizen and every aid agency we went to gave us the run-around. We never had enough for the three of us, but he hid it from me. He'd give it all to Hiram and me and then pretend he was drinking too."

Some kids recognized Eli and shouted a greeting.

Zara raised her eyebrows. "Your fans?"

"That's a new one." He sat down next to her.

"They love you. A lot of people are saying that they always have. And that they hated Baal all along. They just needed you to knock his teeth in for them."

"That's ridiculous. Baal is nothing. If they didn't want to bow their knee, they didn't have to. But that doesn't matter anymore. What matters is how they live going forward, now that they've seen and they know."

"You've got to be wondering about me. I mean, I'm not sure if it's a compliment or an insult that you haven't asked. Or maybe you just already know. Prophet and all." She leaned back on her elbows, stretched out on the steps.

"What, that you're Tsidonian?"

"*Obviously* I'm Tsidonian. You don't need an oracle to see that."

"And I don't need an oracle to see that you once worshiped Baal but left him behind when you left Tsidon."

He let his eyes drift down her figure as if to help his analysis. Her smile told him she didn't buy it. Snapping back to the question at hand, he added, "But then he followed you here, didn't he?"

"You mean Isabel."

"And the ghoul squad and all the new laws. But by then, you were wise to him. Am I right?"

"You know you are."

"Yeah, you don't have the look of someone in his grip. When Baal has his claws in you, it shows."

"Okay, you just lost me. Is Baal real or is he nothing?"

"Yes," Eli answered, drawing the word out long. He stared off into space, his gaze darkening, mind drifting.

Zara hesitated before breaking the tension with, "You said you wanted to show me something."

He snapped his fingers. "That's right. Would I be correct in assuming that you have a bank account?"

"An empty one."

"Well, let's go have a look at it."

"A *look*."

אֱלִישָׁע
eli-jeshua

They were a quaint picture of domestic bliss to any passer-by, Eli and Zara walking on either side of Hiram, each holding a hand. One would almost expect another 1.5 children to be accompanying them. They were at 44th and Laish, a corner of two pawn shops, a liquor store, and a topless bar, just a few blocks from Zara's apartment. Outside the liquor store, a graffiti-covered kiosk housed a payphone and a Shomron National ATM.

"I usually take the train to a nicer neighborhood to do my banking," Zara explained, "but since you're here, and I don't have any money anyway . . ." She slid her card into the machine and punched her pass code into the keypad.

She chose *Account Balance* and looked at Eli and his smirk while the screen instructed *Please Wait . . . Processing.* The machine spit her card back out, followed by a receipt which read, "Current Balance: ₪700.00."

She opened and closed her mouth twice and, on the third try, managed, "Where did that come from?"

"Jah is providing for you. Now let's get some food. And when you check your account tomorrow, it'll say 700 shekels again. And the next day and the next until you're back on your feet. I know that will be soon."

She grabbed him in a vice-grip hug. "Thank you!"

"Why thank me? It was Jah who saved you."

Eli-Jeshua Shaphat sat in his little office, sweating. He was short but built solidly, and his frame stretched almost from wall to wall. Having been in the retail business most of his life, he was well aware that managers' offices were always small, but this one was quite literally a closet. His father had built the store decades earlier and had prided himself on wasting no space. The shelves out on the sales floor were spaced every five feet, packed with food and medicine—a merchandising nightmare, but everything was visible. The back storeroom was meticulously organized with floor-to-ceiling stock sitting ready to fill any void that might form up front. This was one way in which Eli-Jeshua took after his father.

There had been a number of employees in years past and they had all griped about the owner's fascist sense of order. Now he comprised the entire staff. He kept Shaphat and Son Mercantile open a few hours each morning, but most of his time over the past three years had been spent on his side project—a project that had now come to an end.

His office was plastered with newspaper clippings of his controversial namesake. He'd been collecting them for nearly ten years. He didn't like the word *obsessed*, but he was. He was fifty pounds heavier than the prophet Eli (who was, in turn, six inches taller), but they did share the same hairstyle. Eli-Jeshua buzzed his down with electric clippers every other morning. Unlike Eli Tishbi, he also wore a short, neatly-trimmed goatee and mustache. When he first saw the prophet's new look, he had gone clean-shaven, but not having much of a chin to speak of, he quickly decided that he needed some sort of visual border between his face and neck.

אלישע

His eyes were deep and emotive. Depending on his mood, he was either a teddy bear or a grizzly, the latter coming to the surface at the sight of idolatry and injustice.

Years earlier, when he had begun emulating his hero, growing his hair down his back and his beard down his chest, he had tried to get his friends to call him Eli. It *was* his name after all—he had that going for him. But it never really caught on. They'd already been calling him Jeshua for years. His mother had always called him Eli-Sha, but he'd always thought that sounded like a girl's name.

He rubbed his head from neck to brow and back again—a habit he'd picked up since re-introducing his scalp to the air—and continued poring over the papers before him. As usual, his ends were resisting the idea of meeting.

A harsh buzz broke him from his work. He checked his watch and negotiated his way sideways out the narrow office door, passing an entire wall filled with row after row of unlabeled plastic water bottles. Looking through the peephole, he recognized Jehu, nervously watching his four and eight as he always did, fingers just beneath the surface of his tan jacket. The deadbolt clicked open and Jehu entered.

"Jeshua," he said, nodding. Same bare greeting as always.

"Alone today, huh?"

"Who'm I worried about? The goyim are getting friendly with Baal right about now."

"I wasn't sure I'd even see you this morning."

Jehu shrugged. "It's Sunday. I'm a creature of habit."

"May as well form a new habit now. Nobody needs this stuff anymore." He tipped his head toward the hundreds of bottles. "I don't even know what I'm going to do with what's left. Run a special on not-quite-clear water?"

Jehu got as close to laughing as he ever did. Which is to say, he tipped his head back and half closed his eyes. "Pour it out. It's obsolete. There are other jobs that need our attention now."

"We had it down to a science, though, didn't we?"

"Yeah, we did. But Jah invented science, so let's not try to compete with him. Anyway, you must be ready for a break. I've got to imagine you're sleeping better the past few nights. Bootleggers aren't gonna break in here for your cheese curls and dirt beer."

"Quality merchandise," the shopkeeper corrected with a smile. "Thing is, I really don't want a *break*. No way I can just go back to running the store full time. Not after all this. I'm his—sold out completely. If he still has something for me, anyway. I guess I just need to figure out what, right? Don't suppose you'd ask the prophets to look into that for me."

"He's got a task for you," Jehu assured. "I know that for a fact. But you're going to have to get the details from him yourself. Just keep your ears open and your blinders off—he'll let you know. But first you've got to stop filling your own head with chatter. Drowns him out."

"I suppose you'd know." There was a minute of silence. "You and your guys moving out of the Cave anytime soon? I doubt Izzy would try anything after what happened at Karmel."

"We're taking it slow."

"But, were you there? Eli was amazing. Boom! Boom! BWOOOOM!" He pantomimed a couple gunshots and an explosion from the heavens.

"We watched it on television. Obadijah insisted we keep our distance."

"But when does he think you should come back on the grid?"

"Don't know. I haven't heard from him since Karmel."

"Huh. I thought you met with O every Shabbat."

"I usually do. He didn't show yesterday."

Jeshua frowned. "He's a creature of habit too."

"That's what worries me." He suddenly remembered what he had in his pocket and brought it out. "Speaking of the prophets, they wanted you to have this as a token of thanks for all your work during the drought."

He handed Jeshua a curved gold wedge that just barely filled his hand.

"Thanks." He examined the item briefly. "What is it?"

"That," Jehu proudly answered, "is one of the golden horns from the state idol in Beth-El. You know, calf number two."

"Ohhh, I remember reading about that. Somebody cut a horn off and spray-painted *Ichabod* down its back. Maybe fifty years ago."

Jehu's eyes smiled. "Yeah, that was Jah-El in his early days. Guy's a legend. Young and crazy, all over the TV and in the king's face. A lot like Eli. The horn has been kind of a trophy among the prophets. They pass it down every few years like a rite of passage or something. It's an honor, really."

"So I should build a trophy case?"

"No, just the opposite. Micaijah used it for a toilet-paper holder. You don't even want to know what Adonijah did with it. Be creative."

Eli-Jeshua laughed. If the prophets would bring him in on that, they knew something he didn't.

Yeah, Jah still had work for him to do.

Zara's little kitchen table was full. Chicken, pizza, spaghetti, sandwiches, chips, and a lot more. She, Hiram, and Eli wordlessly wolfed it down. They stopped only to wipe their mouths or smack their lips, feeling like they'd never eat their fill.

After polishing off a peanut butter and jelly, Eli surveyed his options, deciding what to tackle next.

"So, how long did the doctor say I have to rest?" he asked.

"He said a week would be a good idea, but he was just guessing." She was dipping a chicken leg in salad dressing. Eli couldn't decide if that was cute or revolting. "He didn't really know what to make of it, you know? He said you shouldn't be alive, so it was kind of outside his realm of expertise."

Eli put his fork down. "What do you mean?"

"Oh. I didn't tell you." She wasn't sure how to. "The bullet. It . . . went through your heart. Right through it. Dr. Manasseh said he's never even heard of someone surviving that." She spoke quietly, not wanting Hiram—who was more than occupied with a small tower of cookies—to hear. "Your heart healed right up like it was a skinned knee. He listened to it again last night and said it's working perfectly. He called it a miracle."

Eli paled. Then stood and paced. Quietly, he said to himself, "He has something else."

He was making Zara uneasy. "Who?" she asked.

He paced faster. "Jah. He has something else for me to do. That's why I didn't die." Out of nowhere, he punched the wall.

Zara pulled Hiram onto her lap.

Looking straight up, Eli demanded, "What else? I haven't done enough? Huh?" He shifted his head expectantly and opened his eyes wider at to the water-stained ceiling. It didn't answer. Just as abruptly, he was back in the chair, stabbing a falafel ball with his fork.

"Okay. No problem, I'm ready. Let's do this." He stuffed the falafel into his cheek. "You just let me know. One more job before I retire. One last big score." He grabbed a drumstick and dipped it in some ranch. "Maybe I'm stupid, but I thought that *was* the big one."

Eli-Jeshua heard the voice right after Jehu left. The door was creeping closed on its hydraulic arm when a soft whisper floated in from outside. He didn't so much hear it as he just knew it was there, perfectly clear despite the softness and the distance.

"Eli-Sha," it said. A chill spread through the web of nerves in the back of his neck. The door kept closing. When an inch remained, the voice slipped in again, through the crack. "Eli-Sha." For a moment, he thought that it might be Jehu, standing around the corner, messing with him. Then he remembered that Jehu was about as likely to play a practical joke as he was to start an Ahab fan club.

Eli-Sha. It was everywhere now, filling the room. He felt suddenly woozy and plopped into the rolling desk chair at the inventory computer. His mouth was hot like a burning coal. The lights went dim. The hum of the little fridge dropped an octave. What was happening? The monochrome computer monitor in front of him flashed off with a high whine.

He gawked at his dark reflection in the convex screen. Atop his head, a finger-width above his shaved scalp, burned a small orange flame about four inches tall. It just hung in space, burning. He timidly reached up and ran his hand back and forth through it, to no effect. It wasn't hot. It didn't react to wind or even touch, but it was there as sure as he was.

What in the . . . ?

Eli knelt next to Hiram's bed. He'd been listening for orders all day. Nothing. He desperately wanted to know why Jah had kept him around. There was something new and frantic about his need for instructions. He'd been crying a little and he didn't know why. Good thing he was alone.

In the back of his mind, the prophet was well aware of the reason: it was fear that was driving him. Maybe there *wasn't* a next task. Maybe this was retirement. If that was the case, he didn't think he could handle it. Zara he could get used to. That was no problem at all—in fact, he was already getting a little too familiar with her in his thoughts. No, it was the distance that would drive him out of his mind. The distance he felt now. This wasn't like the gaps in Jah's instructions when Eli lay low and waited patiently. This was something else entirely. Jah wasn't just silent now; he was altogether absent.

Eli punched the bed in frustration. He took some deep breaths to center himself then brought his mind back to the temple room. *Find out what's so funny about those ashes. Might be the key.* In his mind, he formed an image of the ornately carved walls as best as he could remember them. He held the image in place, hoping. After a moment, the details began to fill themselves in.

He was there.

The room was dark, barely illuminated by two candles that burned dimly, one on each side of Baal. The eyes of the statue were also glowing. Eli was surprised to find himself a little frightened by the sight.

He felt another presence in the room. And then saw it: the silhouette of a man, growing up out of the floor. When he reached his full height, he stepped aside and another came up behind him. Then five more, each shorter than the last. Eli couldn't really make them out. But he could hear the clacking of their beaded beards and he knew that the priests of Baal were among them. Then he heard the sounds of eating and drinking. It was horrendously loud in his ears. Smacking, gulping, chewing. Disgusting. The eerie sound of children laughing filled in the background.

Eli wanted to leave. Baal's eyes were glowing brighter and he was quite clearly smiling at Eli, his little mouth stretched wide, revealing long, sharp teeth.

Enough of this. Eli fought to open his eyes. It took a minute, but he finally extracted himself from the dream.

Yet, when his eyes opened, he wasn't in Hiram's bedroom. From a dream to a vision, he was on the gravel field at Mount Karmel. Every seat in the stadium was filled with a prophet of Baal. Some were munching popcorn. Some were buying souvenirs from vendors.

In the Executive Box, El-Baal and Luli sat wearing crowns twice as tall as their heads. Their eyes were dead and their faces blood-red, expressionless masks. Eli looked around the field and spotted Baal-Adonay, two dozen paces away. The hole that Eli had put in his back was still there, bigger, continuously belching gray smoke. There was something horribly familiar about the scene.

Behind Baal-Adonay stood a dozen other priests, stones in their hands, rifles slung over their shoulders. Obadijah knelt on the ground in front of them. His eyes were big and sad. He looked up at Eli, begging, pleading. Baal-Adonay heaved a stone that crushed the left side of Obadijah's face. He crumpled to the ground. The other priests joined in, hurling stone after stone.

Eli suddenly realized that he had a gun in his hand— his favorite, the one he'd lost at the Kishon Valley rail station. He racked the slide and picked his target: Baal-Adonay's throat would do nicely. *Bang! Bang! Bang!* The bullets left the gun in slow motion. The priest didn't even notice them as they harmlessly bounced off his Adam's apple. Obadijah was dead now, half-covered with dust and stones. Eli threw the gun at his enemy with all his might. It clattered to the ground six inches from his feet as if he'd dropped it.

אלישע

The priests had finished stoning Obadijah. They now stood in a line, glaring at Eli, their eyes glowing like Baal's and their teeth long and pointed in their smiling mouths. All at once, they rushed him, teeth bared, too-long arms reaching.

Eli screamed.

"What happened? What's wrong?" Zara rushed into the room, concern all over her perfect face. Jarred from the vision, Eli slumped, keeping himself up off the floor with two handfuls of racecar bedspread. He couldn't seem to catch his breath.

All at once, she was hugging him and comforting him and telling him, "It's okay. I'm here." She smelled wonderful, but she brought no comfort to Eli.

"I can't find him," he muttered.

She petted his scalp and spoke softly. "Why don't you just take a break? You're still healing. You need some rest. And some food. I know we had a big breakfast, but it's almost seven now. Why don't we have something to eat, okay? You'll feel better then and you can try some more."

Eli shook his head violently. "I'm going nowhere until I hear from him. I'm not eating. I'm not sleeping. He's going to talk to me."

"Why don't you just—"

"He's *going* to talk to me."

181

Isabel dialed the phone in defiance of the dread filling her up like a poison gas, each push of a button another step down the hall toward the electric chair. She'd successfully avoided her father, her superiors, and her advisors in Tsidon since Baal had lost Ephraim two days earlier. But now she needed their help.

"This is Abigaal," came a voice from the other end. The familiar tone and Tsidonian accent of her friend and official liaison set Isabel at ease.

"Hi. It's me."

"Isabel. It's nice to finally hear from you." Her tone was detached. "Hang on a minute. The king would like to speak with you."

"No! I don't have time to talk to Daddy right now. I need some help."

"Yes, you do. You really, really do."

" Listen, I can make up for it. I know how to find Eli. I just need a favor from you."

"A *favor*."

"I need LOCUST."

Abigaal was unimpressed. "I'm afraid you'll have to make due with the many, many resources we've already given you. We may be able to negotiate more after your next briefing, but—"

The queen burst into tears. "They've killed El-Baal! His body was found in a rail station two days ago, shot in the head. It was Eli. I know it. I haven't got any resources left. My very last priest blew his own brains out this morning. I'm all alone here!"

A hint of compassion softened Abigaal's words. "I'm sorry. But your father has been very specific about this:

אֱלִישָׁע

we're not to send you any more aid until you've come up to see him."

"I can't go back. You know what he'd do. Listen. I can win his favor—Daddy's and Baal's both if you'll just lend me one LOCUST squad. Five men and an aircraft. One day. That's all I'm asking. What's one more time?"

"I'll . . . see what I can do."

Zara opened the flyer and skimmed its contents. SOLEMN ASSEMBLY it read evenly across the top in a smudged "underground newspaper" sort of a font. The page had been folded in half and slipped under the door sometime since lunch, when she had brought a plate to Eli's door, pleading with him to stop and eat. He hadn't, and that was six hours ago. Now she saw Eli's name on the page in her hands.

On Friday last, Prpht. Eli-Jah Tishbi
showed us our grave error at Karmel
There we rejected Baal and there he charged us to follow Jah—
not just in word, but in deed.
For this reason, we the faithful will be gathering together
this Tuesday at City Gate.
Please come for a time of repentance, offering, covenant renewal,
and to petition Jah to send his Anointed One.
Starting at 8:00 AM
(All businesses open)

The bottom of the page identified it as an official communiqué of the Jahwist party. Zara couldn't help but imagine the last three remaining members of the mostly defunct organization huddled in a smoke-filled room putting together this low-tech attempt at resurgence. It made her smile.

Then again, if the leaflet was being slipped under doors all over town, as it seemed, then quite a few new members or returning prodigals must be involved. She didn't think Eli would appreciate the dropping of his name, but the flyer was an excuse to get in there and talk to him. It might even be a way to get him out of the house for a while if she could adequately sell the idea.

She didn't knock this time, just opened the door. The prophet was slumped in the corner, staring into space, clad in a sleeveless undershirt and trousers pushed up to the knees, no socks. He held a toy helicopter in his hands, absentmindedly spinning the rotor with his index finger. He didn't notice her enter.

If it hadn't been for the small circle he continually traced with his finger, she might have thought him dead. He was soaked in sweat. His scalp was dusted with a short crop of spiked hair; his face and neck were sprouting sharp whiskers. Thick, dark rings hung beneath his eyes. Zara moved a little closer, making a bit of noise in the process, hoping to break him out of his torpor. It didn't work.

She leaned in and gently placed her hand on his shoulder. With a sudden spasm that drew a shriek from Zara, Eli flinched and grappled for his gun. Finding nothing there but his armpit, he frantically pushed his way up the wall until he stood right in her face, breathing heavy, eyes wide and crazy.

"What day is it?" he demanded. "What time is it?"

She tried to sound soothing. "It's Monday evening. You've been shut up in here for a day and a half."

Eli whispered, "I missed Shabbat. I didn't even realize." He slammed the heels of his hands into his eyeballs and rubbed hard. The resulting *squish* made Zara wince.

"Eli," she began, but she knew he wasn't listening. He flopped down on Hiram's bed and gazed up at the dinosaur tracks stenciled on the ceiling.

He was sure this is what people meant when they say they've "hit bottom." Drunks always say that—something hopeful. Bottom means you've nowhere to go but up, right? But it wasn't vice or tragedy that had dragged him to this point. Eli barely had a vice to speak of. He hadn't succumbed to drugs or drink. He'd scarcely laid a finger on a woman and that wasn't for lack of opportunity or desire. And he hadn't lost everyone dear to him in a car wreck or a Baalist bombing.

In fact, he could probably count on one hand those who were dear to him to begin with and that would include Zara and Hiram, whom he barely knew. Yet, this was still bottom—because the One that gave his life meaning hadn't been stolen in death, but had chosen to withdraw and leave Eli all alone when he was needed most.

Eli's eyes narrowed as a realization dawned.

"He just used me."

The thought had been lurking in the back of his mind, but it felt strange to say it. Frightening, but freeing.

He said it louder. "He just used me."

Now he was angry.

"It's only been one day," Zara reasoned. "Maybe he just knows you need a break."

"No one will be able to stand against you all the days of your life," he quoted. *"I will never leave you nor abandon you."*

Zara found that she couldn't meet his gaze.

"I had a three and a half year *break*, waiting on Jah. I sat there in the boondocks and smoked and prayed and watched bad television and he never left me even once. Not for a moment and certainly not for a day. I was perfectly content. Not now. The cuffs aren't falling off this time. I've been put out to pasture. That's it." He added again emphatically, "He used me."

She had no idea what to say. "You can . . . " She stopped herself. Did it really make sense to offer? *Why not.* "You can stay here with us. Sleep on the couch for a few weeks until you figure it out. What's the hurry?" She was surprised by how badly she wanted him to stay.

He shook his head almost imperceptibly. "I shouldn't even be here now. People have seen me come and go. Word will spread and then you and the kid'll get dragged into the whole mess." His voice was faint. "I have to stay underground. Even after what happened at Karmel." His face softened and took on what looked to Zara like a bad attempt at self-pity. "I'm like an old paper cup. He got some use out of me. Then he tossed me. Now I'll just blow around in the wind until I finally get crushed."

"That's kind of bleak," she said with a smile, the same words he'd spoken to her the morning before. Eli didn't laugh. She leaned over him, a hand planted on the pillow next to his head. "Just stay. It'll be fine."

"No. It won't. You don't know Isabel. She won't stop as long as she's alive and I'm alive."

"I *do* know Isabel. I know all about her. I lived in Tsidon for twenty-five years. If she's the problem, let's just leave. We'll get out of here. I'm not tied down—where have you always wanted to visit?" Again, she couldn't believe what she was saying. It was funny: being near him made her feel safe, but more than that, it made her feel close to Jah. Even while Eli felt unbearably far from him.

Eli read her. "Ah. You feel a need to stick close to me, don't you? To take care of me. Like if you let me out of your sight or if I got hurt, you'd have a panic attack worse than the time you lost Hiram in the parking lot at Ezra's?"

She just nodded, eyes wide, and pushed some errant hair behind her ear.

"Perfect. Just perfect." He lifted his head off the pillow and threw it back with some force. "That's Jah talking to you. That's his spirit. You nursed me back to health, fed me, gave me a place to lay my head. Makes sense. It'll take a while for the feeling to wear off, but it will."

He produced an unhappy smile. "I can't believe you've got your orders, but I've got nothing. This kingdom's a wash. Jah probably decided to give up on it, pack up and leave. Maybe we *should* go. Track him down, get some straight answers."

Zara remembered the flyer. She handed it to him, feeling silly for it. "Maybe we should go to this," she offered.

He scanned the page and emitted a disappointed chuckle. "Yeah, that's right. Resurrect the political machine and expect changed hearts to grow out of that. They just don't get it."

"Well then, you can help us get it. Everyone will listen to you if you go there." He noticed that she said *us* and not *them*.

"Look at me." He surprised her with a booming laugh. "Do I look like I'm in any condition to be teaching other people how to relate to Jah?"

"They're just going to sing songs and make promises and pray . . . "

"Pray for the Anointed One!" Eli held the flyer up like a dirty magazine discovered by an angry mother. "It's not gonna happen! You don't get it either, do you? I'm supposed to clear the way for him. And if Jah's done using me, then the best I can figure is that Ahab *is* the Anointed One! Wow, the kingdom's in great hands!"

"Now you're just being silly, and you know it. Come for a while. For me."

"No," he stated firmly, and crumpled the flyer for good measure.

She pushed her lower lip out slightly like a pouting child. "Please?"

"Not one mina of me wants to go."

She leaned in closer. "Please?"

"Give me one good reason," he demanded, but his resolve was already breaking.

"I'll be there," she said.

And he knew he didn't stand a chance.

Eli-Sha sat in the cramped apartment above his store, sipping water from a plastic bottle. He had tried, but couldn't get himself to dump the stuff down the drain like

Jehu suggested. It represented too many hours of work. He'd drink them all himself, he decided. They tasted like plastic and chlorine, but at least they wouldn't go to waste.

For about three hours, he'd been sitting on his couch, staring at the television but not really seeing it, trying to decide what to do about his new calling. He'd spent enough time with Jah's prophets to know that no two got their orders in exactly the same way. For some, revelations came in dreams. Others, visions. Rumor had it that Eli-Jah heard an audible voice every morning. Newly commissioned prophets often received Jah's messages second-hand, through an established prophet.

All at once it hit Eli-Sha how stupid he was being. He'd been weighing his options in his mind without so much as asking Jah. He killed the TV and clumped to his knees on the threadbare rug.

"O Jah, God of Avraham, Yitzhak, and Ja'acov, hear me. I am your servant. I will go wherever you ask, do whatever you say. Here I am. Send me. I only ask that you give me an unmistakable sign so that I can do your will without doubt and without question."

He paused. Someone was ascending the stairs to his apartment. The stairway came from around back and was hard to find, so he rarely had unannounced visitors. Yet this one had reached the top of the staircase and was stuffing something under the door.

The sheet of paper was caught by an air current, did two lazy loops through the living room, and came to rest directly in front of Eli-Sha. The headline at the top read SOLEMN ASSEMBLY.

שַׁעַר עִיר
city gate

City Gate was a massive town square situated just north of the financial district. A tourist trap, mostly. Lots of lights. Lots of hip little restaurants, bars, and coffee shops. A few years earlier, the streets had been closed off save to foot traffic, making room for a large open piazza filled with benches and tables where the wares of restaurants and vendors could be enjoyed. A smallish amphitheater rose up at one corner of the square, providing intermittent opportunities for the residents of Shomron to experience some culture.

A band called "Jashar" was cavorting around the stage as Zara and Hiram made their way into City Gate Tuesday morning, Eli straggling a few paces behind. He was dressed in a loose, bright green polo shirt and khaki pants, more hand-me-downs—apparently what the late Mr. Lawyer wore while *not* bringing grievances against the regime. Eli's black hair was growing back in, now four days thick, and he wore a pair of cheap sunglasses that Zara had picked up at a convenience store. She had insisted that he wouldn't be recognized, but Eli still found himself the object of furtive glances and whispers all around as they moved through the crowd.

He quickly found that he could kill all suspicion with a big, disarming smile and friendly wave. He was having a ball watching faces fall as the "Is he or isn't he?" question was put to rest in the negative again and again. Zara kept elbowing him in the ribs and ordering, "Stop that."

The band was playing a heavy version of an old devotional folk tune

The Sun stood still
The Moon stayed its course in the heavens
Until the people had avenged themselves
On their enemies

It had always been one of Eli's favorite songs. But hearing it crooned by the shaggy baritone on stage was doing little for him.

"Nothing to see here," he shot to Zara, and immediately picked up the pace.

As they moved on, they were accosted by several vendors, selling everything from funnel cakes to miniature scrolls of the *Torah*. Eli fought the urge to overturn a few tables. When a ruddy man came running up, hawking T-shirts screened with a picture of a bearded Eli, and promising, "I'll cut you a deal, because you look like da guy," Zara had to physically pull Eli along for fear of him causing a scene.

They passed a group of young men standing in a circle, praying with hands joined, heads crooked toward the ground. Down a ways, there were two rival preachers set up on opposite sides of the piazza, both with their share of gawkers. Eli felt his disenchantment grow as he noticed that the woman with the flame dancing above her head had attracted a much smaller crowd than the man without one.

Zara stopped to listen to an inner-city children's choir singing a rendition of Miriam's Song.

שַׁעַר עִיר

Sing unto Jah,
  For he has triumphed in glory.
The horse and its rider
  He has hurled into the sea.

They spun and slapped tambourines as they belted out the song in perfect harmony. Zara was moved to tears. Eli was surprised to find not only that he was unmoved by these words, but that he had no desire to go back to a time when he would have been affected. The sun had stood still. The armies of Mitzrayim were drowned. Did he believe it was true? Sure, but somehow that seemed irrelevant.

They finished the song and began one about the coming Anointed One. Eli had heard enough. By the time Zara and Hiram caught up to him, he had rounded the corner to the main square. There at the end of a long brick walk was 1 City Gate, an impressive skyscraper fitted with a three-story television screen and news ticker. Eli craned his neck up toward the monitor, disgust etched into his face.

The television was tuned to the Ephraim News Network, which was re-running one of Isabel's speeches from a few years previous. A graphic in the corner identified the day as one set aside to review "Great Moments in Leadership." The headline, "Queen Isabel promises tougher laws in response to stadium riot" continually looped on the news ticker below.

Eli was dumbfounded. "We're not even here."

"Huh?" Zara was starting to wonder what she had seen in him just twelve hours earlier. He rarely made sense.

"None of us are standing here at City Gate right now. As far as the official record is concerned, none of this is even happening."

"But we *are* here."

"No, we're not. If we were here, it would be on the news. But as it is, we're back to business as usual: celebrate that woman Lilith the Unclean and don't even acknowledge that thousands of people are gathered for repentance, albeit in a crass carnival atmosphere."

"Why worry about them?" She flipped a hand up toward the monitor. "You're the one who said it can't happen from the top down. So there's no publicity, big deal. It's grassroots. It's people wanting to turn back to Jah. It's not perfect, but cut them a break."

Eli slowly warmed to the idea. He'd trained himself to always look at the big picture. The national picture. But maybe now he could take some time to think about his own little corner of the canvas. Dealing with his mental and spiritual state could be its own fulltime job lately. A little laugh escaped his mouth and he turned from the big screen to face Zara.

"You're right," he said. And this time the disarming smile was genuine.

They spent the morning listening to music and poetry, eating lentil soup from paper cups, and haggling over the price of a key chain that boasted, "I Saw Eli Burn Baal!" (The cup of soup cost more). Zara swore she would never take it off her key ring despite Eli reminding her that she had not, in fact, been at Karmel and that it was Jah who had "burned Baal." She expected an exhortation filled with righteous anger to follow, but it didn't. Anyway, she explained, she hadn't bought it for the slogan; she just liked the little cartoon of Eli summoning fire from the sky, his eyes huge and his mouth a tiny dot.

Shortly after lunch, Hiram spotted a booth for kids, where a bunch of junior penitents sat at little tables painting pictures of traditional stories. The great flood, the entrusting of the Law to Moshe, the stopping of the Jordan River. It was clear he wouldn't be taking *no* for an answer.

Eli handed over forty shekels to the insufferable woman running the booth while Zara helped Hiram settle in to a place at the table, where he summarily flipped over the picture of Shophet Shimshon destroying the Temple of Dagon and began filling his blank canvas with a fresh scene. They watched him carefully work on the picture for several minutes. Eli was impressed. He wasn't sure what it was the kid was depicting, but it was pretty good for his age.

"What are you painting, Sweetie?" asked Zara.

"It's him," he said, grinning and pointing at Eli, "killing the bad mans!"

Eli and Zara locked eyes. She was touched, if concerned. He just felt like he was going to vomit at any moment. Suddenly lightheaded, he grappled for one of the tiny chairs, needing to sit down. He missed and swiped over a big plastic cup of red paint. It bounced along the table, ejecting its contents onto Hiram's half-painted picture, his shirt, and his face. He began to wail.

Eli felt even worse. "I'm sorry! It was an accident." Hiram's cheeks were striped with tears and red paint. Zara was comforting him and asking the vendor if she had a towel. The response was that Zara would have to clean him up somewhere else and that there were no refunds if he didn't finish his picture.

"I think I should just take off," Eli said. "I'm like a bad omen over here."

"No, don't. It'll just take a minute to clean him off. It's no big deal." She looked down at Hiram and asked, "Do you want Eli to take you inside and help you clean up?" He responded by hugging tight to her thigh, leaving a large red spot on the leg of her jeans. "Okay, I guess the two of us are going to go find out how tough this paint is." She looked at Eli tenderly and said, "Please don't leave."

"All right," he responded.

They made their way up to a long strip of restaurants and bars extending a few hundred feet in both directions from 1 City Gate. Each restaurant had spillover into outdoor seating and each apparently had a long waiting list to get in. For some, this was looking to be their first week in the black since just after the drought began.

Eli opened the door of a little bar called the Waters of Merom Pub. Only after they were all inside did it occur to him just how inappropriate a place it was for a four-year-old boy. *Whatever. Who am I, Father Avraham?*

Zara brought her son into the women's restroom and Eli wandered over to lean on the bar. It took a minute for his eyes to adjust to the dim light. The sunglasses made it harder, but he wasn't willing to part with them. Looking around the place, he decided that if just one of the bars in City Gate would be sparsely occupied, it would be this one.

Every surface in sight was less than clean and the place smelled like canned dog food. All the same, the management was clearly trying too hard to make it a trendy "it" place, with a menu on the bar listing cleverly named appetizers and specialty drinks.

The unpolished bartender wasn't helping sell the image. He scratched his butt as he walked up to Eli, boisterously relocated some phlegm in his sinus cavity, and then asked, "What can I get ya?" with just a bit of contempt.

The smell of alcohol turned Eli's stomach. "I don't suppose you have any coffee drinks."

"Yeah, we've got one. A real gourmet job. It's a single no-whip, no-cream, black, non-decaf blend served in a special brown mug."

His cutting sarcasm brought a laugh from Eli. "I'll take one."

The bartender filled a mug with little care and plopped it down in front of Eli, spilling a good portion of it on the counter. "Enjoy it, yuppie."

Eli did not enjoy it. But coffee was coffee and Zara didn't drink the stuff, so it had been a few days.

"You, uh, you got a light?"

Eli turned to see a doughy young man in his early twenties standing next to him, holding a pack of cigarettes. A pair of large round glasses perched on his chubby nose.

"Eh? Oh. No, I quit."

"I didn't ask if you smoke. I asked if you got a light."

Eli sighed and pulled out his chrome lighter. The doughboy made a grab for it, but Eli fended him off, flipped it open, and held it up for him to light his cigarette. The kid looked with interest at Eli's lighter as he ignited the smoke.

"Never did that for a guy before," Eli commented, a bit unsettled.

The doughboy laughed. "Well, thanks. It's an honor to be your first."

Eli went back to his coffee, which he was pretty sure had been brewed by dipping an old sweat sock filled with dirt into hot water. He wasn't in the mood for conversation, so he turned three-quarters away from the kid.

He didn't take the hint. "You just quit today or something?"

"Heh?"

"Smoking."

"No, a few days ago. Why?"

"Some sort of religious purification thing, right?"

Eli snickered. "Anything but."

"So why'd you quit?"

"I want to live a long, happy, healthy life," Eli answered without a trace of emotion.

"Meh. Everybody dies, right?" The doughboy hovered for a second before asking, "You're, uh, you're not him, are you?"

Oh, great. "I'm not who?"

"You know who."

Eli turned back toward him, the big, cheesy smile on his face.

"I didn't think so." The doughboy mounted a stool next to Eli and ordered a shekar-edom with a twist. "You probably get that a lot, though, huh? I mean, you look a lot like him."

"Yeah, I get that a lot."

"So, I'm curious then. What do you think of the guy?"

Eli frowned. How long could it take to wash some paint off a kid?

"I think he doesn't know where his life is going."

"Yeah, no kidding! I've always said the same thing. People assume these religious nuts have it all together, but I think they're just mega-confused. The only way they can make sense of the world is to make sure everyone thinks the same way they do. It's pathetic."

His drink was placed before him and he downed it with a violent lash of his head and a three-second grimace before continuing, "So that chick who came in here with you—that your girlfriend?"

"I don't know." He really didn't.

"You don't *know*? Aw, come on. She's so hot. Man, I'd—"

He could feel the glare through Eli's shades and the word died in his throat. He stumbled around for a recovery, settling on, "You guys having a good time out there?"

"Yeah, it's all right." *May as well accept that I'm having this conversation*, Eli thought. "What about you?"

"Not likely. I'm just here to gawk, man. This place is Phony Central."

"So you don't think the people out there are really penitent?"

"*Penitent*?"

"Sorry for their sins, ready to turn away from them and return to a righteous life serving Jah."

The doughboy threw his hands up. "Oh, whatever! Saying they're sorry? To who? Mr. Invisible Guy in the sky? It would be funny if it weren't so sad. At least the Baal people realize that they make their god in their own image. These Jah-freaks won't even let anyone draw a picture of him because it makes them nervous."

Eli was done here. He knew the kid's type— Philosophy 101 had him thinking he bore all the answers to the great questions of the universe. Eli had no patience for people that naïve. That smug. That ignorant. Probably educated in the West.

He tried not to, but couldn't help asking, "What do you make of that thing at Karmel? That might be hard to explain if there's no one up there."

The kid let out a long derisive *pffffff*. "People see what they want to see, man."

"I couldn't agree more."

"I mean, I saw the big fireball thing on TV and sure, it looked impressive, but they can do anything with video these days."

"So, there was really no fire at all? Everyone in the stands *imagined* it and the people in power doctored the footage? You gotta wonder who stands to gain from all that."

"I didn't say that, guy. I'm just saying there was no *deus ex shamayim* stepping in and fixing everything like in all the stories. There probably was a *fire*. My theory is that this Eli guy is just a really skilled meteorologist. He rolls back into town when there's a storm system coming, sets something up to attract the lightning and ignite a big pile of fuel. *Fwoom!* There's your god right there! The king and queen couldn't care less *which* god we believe in, so long as we're distracted by some pie-in-the-sky mumbo jumbo and we miss what's really going on."

The doughboy looked around as if to keep information from the uninitiated. "Truth is, there is no god. Everything was generated from nothing and it happened all by itself."

Eli smirked. "Do tell."

"Well, it all started with this goo."

"Goo?"

"Yeah, goo. It was just sort of sitting there bubbling for years and years until one day, it was struck by lightning." The doughboy launched into a fantastical history of the planet.

The would-be lesson faded out as Eli noticed someone familiar at the far end of the bar. The man stood slightly hunched, sweating, checking his watch every few seconds, eyes darting around nervously. He wore a black shirt, black tie, black coat. Eli knew him as a member of Beth-Baal, the original Baalist movement in Ephraim. They had been extremists and terrorists for years, even under Omri, blowing up buildings to make a point that no one could quite decipher.

In Beth-Baal's eyes, the government could never go far enough to the side of serving Tsidon's god. They continually pushed for more. And more. Omri had subjugated them through brute force, torture, and some terror of his own, motivating them to change their position and officially declare that Baal was, in fact, pleased with Ephraim. Still, an isolated attack here or there continued into Ahab's reign, only ending when Isabel truly gave the nation over to the pagan god and his goyim priesthood.

Eli's first impulse was to grab a bottle from behind the counter and send the Baalist to join those goyim priests he loved so much. But then he thought, *Why?* Maybe the man was there to repent. After all, he was of The People too.

Who was Eli to interfere with that? *Besides,* he thought, *I'm not on the payroll anymore. Not my concern.*

Eli's heart jumped as the man scratched his chest, pushing back his long coat for just a moment, and revealing the two large packs of explosives hanging at his sides, one below each arm. Eli took a step back from the bar and pulled off his sunglasses, challenging the man with his eyes. The bomber recognized the prophet and the two men squared off.

The dough boy droned on.

The bomber smiled wickedly, lifted his right hand up next to his face, and slowly pushed his thumb down, depressing the button on a slim detonator. With speed he did not know he possessed, Eli was upon the man. He grasped both of the Baalist's fists and thrust him forward onto the bar, landing hard on top of him.

Eli knew that the bomb had been armed with the push of the button, a spring-loaded deadman switch, which would detonate the explosives if released. Eli slammed his forehead into the bridge of the bomber's nose and squeezed his fist as hard as he could. Knuckles cracked. Then bones popped. The man writhed on the bar, trying to force Eli back off of him.

The bartender was trying to separate them, advising them to take it outside, threatening to call the police

The doughboy excitedly pointed and announced, "I knew it was him! It's Eli!"

As he smashed the Baalist's own left fist into his face, Eli shouted, "Get out of here! All of you! This guy's a bomb! This place is going to blow!"

The doughboy and his theories were gone in a moment. The bartender lingered. "What do you want me to do?"

"Just get everyone out of here. *Now!*" The bartender obeyed and within a minute the room was empty save for Eli and the terrorist, struggling on the bar.

"Baal is God!" the man bellowed.

"Let's find out, shall we? Why don't we blow up together? You and me." Eli smiled viciously down at the man. Now he knew why he'd been saved alive—to sacrifice himself. To absorb the after-shock of Karmel.

He went on. "You're ridiculous, you know that? You can't even kill yourself successfully. I'm sure today was supposed to be a big day for you devil worshipers. Blow up City Gate. Take a bunch of innocent people with you. But surprise, surprise: you've failed miserably."

The Baalist laughed, low and evil. "That's where you're wrong, superhero."

Eli suddenly remembered the man's obsession with his watch and cranked his wrist around hard. A countdown was in process on the little digital display.

48 seconds . . . 47 . . . 46.

"How many others?" Eli demanded.

"There are twenty of us," the man giggled, high on evil. "You're all going to die for your apostasy!"

"Eli, what is going *on*?"

He looked up to see Zarephath standing at the end of the bar, holding Hiram close, their clothes clean and even dry.

"Zara, get out of here. He's got a bomb!"

The Baalist began to convulse with newfound strength. He yanked his arm as hard as he could, trying to free his hand from Eli's grasp and bring some of the prophet's loved ones with him to Sheol. Zara stood frozen, clutching her son.

Eli pulled the man's upper body a foot off the counter and lurched forward with everything he had. They both flipped over the back of the bar and plunged to the floor. The Baalist's head was the first thing to make contact and his neck absorbed the impact, breaking with a loud *crunch*. His body thudded to the ground.

The stopwatch read 30 . . . 29 . . . Eli firmly held the detonator down with his left hand and, with his right, pulled the tie from around the corpse's broken neck. He quickly but carefully wrapped it as tight as he could around the packed flesh of the bomber's right hand and tied it with a triple knot.

11 . . . 10 . . . He struggled to his feet, grabbed Hiram, and pulled Zara from the bar by her arm. They burst out into the late afternoon sun, Eli screaming, "Everyone get down!"

At once, the windows were blown out of the other buildings in the strip, some launching bodies out into the square. Zara and Eli were thrown to the ground. They were scraped up, but not injured. Eli rolled onto his back, cradling the kid, and looked back at the smoke billowing up from the shells of buildings. The skyscraper stood, but the ground floor was a series of raging fires.

"Oh my God! Oh my God!" Zara was hysterical, examining a cut on Hiram's head where a shard of broken glass had connected. Eli wrenched the boy from her grip and examined the wound. There was a lot of blood, but it was a shallow, superficial cut.

He put a hand on her shoulder and squeezed, trying to calm her. "Zara, listen to me. The hospitals are going to be overrun. They aren't going to have time to deal with this. I have to stay here and help. If you bring Hiram home, can you keep it together long enough to wash and bandage this cut?"

She nodded jerkily, still in shock. Eli slapped her cheek lightly. "Are you sure?"

"Yes." She accepted the boy from Eli and obeyed when he said to put pressure on the abrasion.

"Take the bus," Eli advised. "You'll be home in no time and he'll be fine."

"Pray for me," she said as she hurried away.

Eli said nothing. He couldn't pray.

גוים

goyim

Surveying the damage, Eli's first reaction was horror at the three dozen dead littering the square and the many injured crying out for help. But then he gained perspective at how bad things could have been.

The bartender from the Waters of Merom Pub, the amateur professor of goo-ology, and the rest of the bar's patrons were huddled with a couple hundred others in a tight group. Eli could guess what had happened: they had made such a commotion pouring out into the square, screaming and shouting, that others had come out to investigate—waiters and angry customers especially.

The general sense of panic, coupled with the word "bomb," had spread from the center of the fleeing patrons into the adjacent businesses like ripples in a pond. Many had come running out with a purpose. Others came out to investigate the ruckus. The nineteen terrorists, better at planning than improvising, had all waited until the pre-arranged time to detonate.

It could have been a lot worse.

The sky was darkened with smoke from the explosions and the fires that now burned in their places. Sirens were approaching from all directions. Eli, prickling with adrenaline, wasn't sure what to do first. For just a second, he thought he felt Jah beginning to speak to him, but before he could open his mind to listen, the television monitor on 1 City Gate stole his attention.

On the screen, he saw Obadijah standing in the courtyard at the Ministry of Justice and Conduct. His hands were bound behind his back. The frames of his glasses were bent and one lens was broken out. He had clearly been beaten and his face bore the brunt of the evidence. Still, the servant of Jah stared fearlessly ahead.

Eli stood frozen in fear and despair as he watched. The "Great Moments in Leadership" logo was still there, now animated. A news anchor provided a hushed voiceover.

"Obadijah Uzzi is Ahab's former Chief Officer of Domestic Affairs. He has been convicted of treason for co-operating with an attempted abduction of Queen Isabel last week and for aiding the escape of Eli-Jah Tishbi after the bloody riot at Mount Karmel Stadium last Friday. He was sentenced to death two hours ago. At that time, the regime issued a full statement, indicating that since he was a former member of the cabinet he should—"

Suddenly, two shots rang out, answered by two blossoms of blood on Obadijah's chest. He fell backwards to the ground, landing in an awkward heap.

"No." Eli too fell to the ground, buried his head in his hands, and wept—violently, desperately wept. Over the next few minutes, several EMTs stopped to check on him and, finding him uninjured, moved on. One offered to pray with him, to which Eli responded with a curse and a shove.

When he regained control of himself, the picture on the screen had switched to footage of the death and destruction all around him at City Gate. The caption read, "Live Breaking News: Illegal Religious Rally Ends in Carnage." He wiped the tears from his eyes. *Now* the press had come. There was no justice at all. Eli wished he and the Baalist had gone up in flames. And he wished that he believed in the doughboy's goo story instead of the God of his fathers.

The square was buzzing with emergency personnel. They seemed to have most of the injured stabilized. Some police and firefighters were moving in and out of the burning buildings, quenching the flames and searching for survivors.

Channeling his pain into rage, Eli pulled his phone from his pocket and pushed a speed button. The display read, CALLING OBADIJAH.

A man's voice answered. "Hello?"

"Who's this?"

"This is Eliphaz Terman, King Ahab's Chief Officer. Who's this?"

"This is Eli-Jah Tishbi. Give me Ahab. Now." He walked briskly down the street away from City Gate.

Ahab and Isabel sat in plush chairs in the courtyard, watching the post-execution ceremonies with several government employees and a team of Shomrey-Melek. Eliphaz tentatively approached and offered his phone to Ahab.

"What's this?"

"It's Eli, sir. He's demanding to speak with you."

Isabel sat straight, an evil smile on her face, unable to tear her eyes from Obadijah's twitching body.

"Tell him he's next," she said in a throaty voice.

"I can handle this," Ahab retorted.

"Just make sure you keep him on the line while my people work their magic."

Ahab took the phone from Eliphaz and sent him away with a wave of the hand. "What do you want, you troubler of Ephraim?" he barked into the mobile.

"The treacherous deal treacherously and the treacherous deal very treacherously."

The hate in Eli's voice snatched the king's nerve from him. "I know what you're going to say, Eli. But listen to me first: I can't tolerate traitors in my cabinet. He was leaking secrets. He was deceiving us."

Eli walked faster down the street, eyes narrowed, jaw set. "You had a second chance and you blew it. You couldn't even keep your own wife under control and now you're out of second chances."

"Look, this really doesn't have anything to do with you, Eli. It was an internal matter. Don't—don't go doing anything crazy."

Eli snickered darkly. "You haven't seen crazy yet, Ahab. There is nothing you can do to keep me from taking you down. You will be food for dogs."

"Eli, don't say . . . I really didn't want to—" Isabel glowered at him. He took a deep breath and laid into Jah's prophet. "Bottom line: I can run my kingdom in whatever way I please. You think you can tell me how to do my job? Why don't you just disappear like you always do? And this time don't come back."

"This conversation is over. Just like your time on that throne. And this earth."

"No! Wait! Don't hang up. Listen, I just wanted to tell you that . . . " Isabel signaled him. " . . . that you've now seen what can happen to people when they get in my way.

Watch yourself, Jah lover! You're on very thin ice. It's time you realized: you're not the king of Ephraim—I am!"

Eli stopped abruptly. "You're a dead king."

He flipped the phone shut.

Eli-Sha had arrived at City Gate just before noon. Unsure of exactly what prophets *did* at these sorts of affairs, he just wandered around and started conversations—basically what he would have done anyway. And he met a lot of people. Some had just come by to see if there was any excitement to be had. Others were there to make money. But most had come because they truly wanted to return to Jah. Their hearts were right. Eli-Sha had prayed with these people. He'd cried with some of them. He'd talked with them at length and offered them counsel. And as he did, he could feel Jah's wisdom and power coursing through him.

When the bombs went off, Eli-Sha was off in a corner, praying in solitude. He raced to the site of the destruction and immediately knew by intuition what his job was. There were dozens of critically wounded people lying on the ground. Rushing to the closest one, he laid his hands on the woman's forehead. She was barely breathing. A large gash in her neck was seeping heavily.

He whispered a prayer. "O Jah, my God, heal this woman. She came here to this place to return to you and to worship you. You've promised us that we need not fear the terror of night, nor the bullets that fly by day, nor the pestilence that stalks in the darkness, nor the plague that destroys at midday. My Lord, heal this woman!" Eli-Sha felt healing power coming forth from his bones. The woman's breathing picked up. The blood coming from the split in her neck coagulated almost instantly, closing the wound.

Eli-Sha moved on to the next one.

Eli sat at a bus stop, his chin resting on folded hands, unsure of how to approach the task before him. Should he go after Ahab tonight? No, that would be suicide. Maybe he should take the king's own advice and split town for a while, give himself time to plan. One thing was certain: he couldn't count on Jah for direction. Even if they *were* on speaking terms, his God would never operate in and through Eli's desire for personal vengeance.

The sun was just beginning to dip below the horizon, creating a beautiful pattern on the mirrored skyscrapers across the street and bathing Eli in yellow-orange light. The reminder of the miracle at Karmel did not raise Eli's spirits. He leaned his head back and closed his eyes for just a moment. Fatigue was setting in. He could crash at Zara's house again; that was probably the smartest move. After all, some things were best done on the spur of the moment, riding whatever emotions pulsed through one's veins. Assassinating a king was not one of those things.

He stood, determined to head back to Nadab Circle, and suddenly found the yellow-orange light gone, blocked from overhead. A muted *thwp-thwp-thwp* sounded above him. Eli looked up in time to see four men sliding their way down cables from a sleek black helicopter. They wore body armor, and automatic weapons hung from harnesses on their shoulders.

At first, reason told Eli that they weren't there for him. How could anyone know where he'd be sitting at that particular moment? Then it hit him. They'd triangulated his phone signal. Why else would Ahab have dragged out the conversation the way he did? He was basically carrying a homing beacon for his enemies in his pocket.

Stupid. Outwitted by Ahab. May as well be outwitted by Hiram.

The LOCUST troops were almost out of rope and had spotted Eli. By instinct, he reached for his gun—it wasn't there. He stood stupidly still as the troops hit the ground and formed ranks. Without a weapon, without any advantage, without a single friend, Eli did something he'd never done before—he got scared and ran for his life. The troops slapped off their safeties and took aim.

Eli bent low and tried to move fast and invisible. *Why did I have to wear a bright green shirt today? Way to blend in, dummy!* As he ran, he pulled the cell phone from his pocket and smashed it against the ground. The helicopter quietly hovered forward, tracking Eli. The sun, no longer blocked by the aircraft above, momentarily blinded the four troops, who fired wildly into the glare.

A bullet trilled by Eli's ear, and in its wake came a voice that spoke directly to the prophet's spirit.

Gird up your loins, man of God, the voice said, *and run.* A sudden burst of power entered his body and he took off like a champion sprinter in fast forward. The troops gave chase in a tight formation, but it became immediately clear that they could not match his pace. Tsayid, the squad commander, signaled for the helicopter to come back for them.

Eli darted down Lebanon, eastward. He knew he could outrun the Tsidonians on the ground, but if the previous week had taught him anything, it was to be very paranoid about helicopters.

Sure enough, he looked back to see the quiet little chopper coming up behind him, gaining slowly. He wondered how fast he was running as he passed two moving cars in the right lane. He could feel Jah's spirit within him, giving him strength.

An idea hit him. Maybe he could lose the goyim in the chaos of City Gate. The smoke, the sirens, the inevitable search and rescue teams. At the very least, it would be difficult for a covert special forces team to operate in those circumstances. He turned right and headed back toward the square, the helicopter right on his tail.

Eli flashed into the piazza to a vastly different scene from the one he'd left half an hour earlier. Most of the wounded had been removed. Police were putting up CRIME SCENE tape and paramedics were helping the coroner collect the dead. Unfortunately for Eli, the chaos was no more.

Eli searched desperately for someone who might be of immediate help. Maybe Joab and his men were here. Maybe Joab and his men were in on it. The LOCUST troops were again sliding down the cables to the ground.

None of the police or medics had even noticed Eli tearing through at four times normal human speed. Up on the screen, Isabel was still pontificating—there seemed no shortage of "Great Moments in Leadership."

Automatic gunfire sounded behind Eli. Apparently LOCUST didn't care who saw them. What he wouldn't give for his gun right now. He had always been willing to die for his cause—his God—but there was no honor in dying here.

Not like this, he half-prayed. *Gunned down in the street, shot in the back by goyim. Is this why you saved me alive?*

Approaching 1 City Gate and the strip of burned out restaurants, Eli was drawn to the only one that remained intact. With a last burst of speed, he was through the door of the Waters of Merom Pub just as another burst of gunfire cut through the windows

He dove over the bar, bounced off the back wall, and landed hard. For the third time in a week, Eli found himself lying on top of a dead man. He gingerly pushed the Baalist's mummy-wrapped hand out of the way and began a frantic search of his person. Surely a terrorist would be carrying a gun. He checked his pockets, his waistband, his ankles. No luck. The only thing the guy had on him was a yellowed old handkerchief.

Eli heard the door open. Footsteps—almost silent—moving toward the bar. He squinted in the dark, trying to locate the bartender's weapon under the counter. The light from his phone would—no, his phone was in ten pieces on the sidewalk. He flicked his cigarette lighter to aid in his search.

Nothing. No revolver. No shotgun. Could this be the only bar in the world without a lead bouncer? Eli craned his neck but all he could see were bottles and bottles of liquor. How he hated the stuff.

A burst of gunfire shattered the bottles lining the wall above the bar and rained broken glass and alcohol down on Eli.

The footsteps were drawing closer.

Tsayid was sure he had the fugitive pinned down now.

He'd been the commander of LOCUST's Shin-Squad for fifteen years and he'd never failed to take down a target once he or she was in sight. He was good at what he did. As soon as Eli entered the building, Tsayid had sent a man around back to cover the rear exit. He then secured the front himself and sent his best marksman, Aleph, in for the kill shot.

Pinned down or not, this prophet Tishbi didn't stand a chance. Shin-Squad was air-mobile and they knew the area well. They'd been in and out of Shomron thirty times over the last decade, cleaning up Isabel's messes. They would kill the target. There was no doubt about that. And they would enjoy it.

When Isabel's request had come in for a LOCUST detachment, Tsayid had begged the king of Tsidon to send Shin-Squad. He'd traded in every marker he had for the assignment. Because he and Eli had unfinished business.

A year earlier, when the manhunt began, Shin-Squad was responsible for the Shomron search in three districts. They were unsuccessful. Yet, surveillance footage later placed the prophet in two of those very districts during their search. Months later, his squad was sent to comb the hills of Moab, again coming up empty.

Yes, this was personal for Tsayid. A chance to vindicate himself and tie up loose ends.

"Front room clear, Aleph?" he said into his headset.

"Hold," came Aleph's reply from under his breath.

Tsayid watched through the glass door, straining to see Aleph as he disappeared into the darkened restaurant. Aleph abruptly halted his approach and shot out a row of bottles on the wall. He signaled to Tsayid that the fugitive was behind the bar.

"Perforate it," the commander ordered. "Take him out now."

Aleph obeyed. A dotted line of machine gun fire ripped through the front of the bar, starting at the wall and moving inward. Chewed up wood and sawdust shot up into the air like confetti.

A bottle came spinning out from behind the bar, hard and fast, a burning rag flapping from its mouth. It hit Aleph in the throat, shattered, and engulfed him in flame.

"Gimmel, hold the front and cover," Tsayid ordered. In an instant, he was in the room, gun at the ready. In the same instant the space behind the bar went up in flames and Aleph came charging back the way he'd come, still burning, and smacked head-on into his commander. He was out of control, a throaty roar emanating from deep within him.

"Regain your composure," Tsayid barked. Aleph's hair was on fire and the flesh on his neck was slick and bubbling. He screamed and flailed, trying to shove through his superior to reach the door. A short burst of fire from the commander's gun sent Aleph to the floor, motionless. Tsayid stepped over his burning body and resumed the advance. The place was filling with black smoke, which he waved away as he approached the bar.

Finding the door to the kitchen swinging back and forth slightly, he spoke into his headset. "Gimmel, entering kitchen area now. Fall in behind me. Hold and cover."

He pushed the door open with the muzzle of his gun and stepped cautiously into the back room. A couple of emergency lights poorly illuminated the kitchen. A skillet clacked and popped on a burner, the oil having long since burned away. A cutting board sat filled with chicken and another with vegetables, abandoned mid-task. He performed a precision sweep of the area. No sign of the target.

The kitchen continued off to the left in an L-shape. Tsayid pressed his back to the wall and silently approached the corner. His breathing was even and controlled.

Gotcha. A smile spread across his face. In the window of a double-decker oven on the far wall, he could see the reflection of a man standing in front of the walk-in freezer, his right arm extended over his head. *Got another explosive cocktail for me, my Jah-loving friend? Not this time. This time you get a little treat from me.*

"Backup." He spoke the word into his headset almost inaudibly. Three seconds later, Gimmel entered the kitchen. Tsayid pointed to the reflection and signaled their attack plan. On his count, they flashed out around the corner—one low, one high.

The commander put a burst into the man's head. Gimmel hit him center mass. But the man didn't fall.

"Three-sixty," Tsayid ordered. They assumed a back-to-back configuration, Tsayid facing the freezer, and slowly approached the bullet-riddled man, who was not so much standing as he was dangling by his right hand, slowly twisting back and forth from the impact of the bullets.

They approached in step, Gimmel moving backwards. When they were just three feet away, Tsayid noticed that the freezer door was open a crack. *Ah ha.* Perhaps someone didn't want to be locked inside? He was ready for the door to burst open at any moment, Eli on the other side with another improvised bomb or a mallet or meat cleaver. The selection of makeshift weapons in the kitchen was wide and, in Eli's hands, deadly.

Sweat crowded Tsayid's eyes. He blinked it away. He studied the dead man's hand, which was extended straight above his head, as if in a final salute. It was clubbed, certainly deformed, Tsayid thought, and wrapped in some sort of cloth. It looked like . . . a necktie.

The dead man abruptly dropped six inches as a loop of the tie slipped off. Tsayid flinched and fired a few more rounds into the corpse's chest. He took another step toward the freezer. Another loop slipped off and the man slid another six inches down the door. Tsayid could see something in the man's hand now, beneath the tie. His eyes followed the line of the tie from the hand, up to the crack in the door, back to his hand. Suddenly terrified, he carefully pushed the dead man's black jacket aside with the muzzle of his gun.

"Retreat!"

Inside the freezer, Eli released the necktie and it slipped off the Baalist's hand.

The double concussion of the explosion rocked the kitchen, incinerating the two soldiers and slamming the freezer door shut with such force that it propelled Eli into the dark, where his head collided with a steel shelf.

He rolled to the ground and lay there on the freezing concrete floor, unable to move.

Ten minutes passed. Eli's back grew numb and he began to shake violently. His teeth crashed together like a jackhammer, pounding in his head. It was becoming clear that, if he stayed there, he'd eventually drift off to sleep and never wake up. He wasn't entirely sure how he felt about that.

Making a withdrawal of will power that cleaned out his account, he finally pulled himself to his hands and knees and made his way to the freezer's wall, where he expected to find the door, and felt around. It wasn't there. He felt only a cold textured surface. No shelves, no food, no door.

Coming to his senses, he reached into his pocket and once again pulled out his lighter. The little flame illuminated an intricately engraved wall, overlaid with gold.

He wasn't in the freezer. He turned on his heels and found himself looking straight at an idol of Baal sitting atop a stone altar.

He was in the temple room. But it wasn't a passive dream this time. This was a vision. Looking down, he saw that he was leaving footprints in the ashes, adding a few more to an already extensive collection of various sizes.

Eli took a walk around the room. It was even more impressive in three dimensions. Returning to where he began, he noticed that the statue of Baal was not smiling. Its eyes were not glowing. It looked like what it was—a hunk of stone.

A sliver of white light pierced the room. Eli backed up against the wall as the king and the Prophet of Jah entered. After lighting several oil lamps, the Prophet closed the door and stood respectfully behind his sovereign. He nodded subtly at Eli, but the king took no notice of him.

The king's expression was pensive as they discussed the outcome of the contest. Both men noted that the seal on the door had not been tampered with, but there their agreement ended. The king was shouting the praises of Baal, the winner of the contest. He declared that Baal was great and that there was no deceit in him. He pleaded for forgiveness from the hunk of stone for ever doubting it.

The Prophet of Jah could take it no more and laughed uproariously. He directed the king's attention to the ashes on the floor and asked the king what he saw. Whose footprints were these?

I see the footprints of men and of women and of children, the king answered. His eyes darkened as he considered this development. The Prophet continued to chuckle and invited the king to the center of the temple, to examine the altar.

Eli joined them there. All of the footprints had their source at one floor panel near the altar's base. The Prophet bent over and pushed down firmly on each of its corners. Two of the corners gave a bit, bending down slightly and revealing a void beneath. A secret door, locked from the underside.

Eli laughed.

The Prophet picked up the idol of Baal and hurled it at the wall. It disintegrated in an explosion of stone and dust that swirled around the room. From the point of impact, a shaft of light appeared, illuminating the particles that clouded the temple room. Eli coughed, choking on the dust. There was another impact and more dust filled the air. Then another.

He was back in the freezer.

Light spilled in from the kitchen where several Shomrey-Melek agents had spent forty-five minutes clearing rubble and plaster away from the half-crushed door and were now in the process of prying it open.

One last coordinated heave and it fell off its hinges and clanged to the floor. Eli emerged from the cavern, coughing, squinting, shielding his eyes. The Shomrey-Melek broke into applause.

When the world came back into focus, Eli saw Joab standing front and center, illuminated by floodlights and a gas generator.

"There was one more of those guys," Eli said, indicating the crispy commandos from Shin-Squad, stacked on the floor.

"Yeah, we took care of him." Joab was beaming.

"Why are they clapping?"

"Because it's you. Because everyone who has consistently undermined our authority, effectively neutered us, rendered us superfluous . . . you've taken them out of the picture in the past week. You've made life better for the Shomrey-Melek. Eli, I think I might have been wrong about you."

"Oh." Eli nodded. "So now you can protect Ahab better?"

"Exactly." Joab smiled.

"He killed my best friend today. He killed O."

The smile vanished. "I know."

"Joab, you're going to have to make a choice very soon. You have to decide which one you're going to serve."

Quieter. "I know."

"You couldn't have stopped him?" Eli's voice crackled.

"I couldn't have stopped her."

Eli swayed for a moment like he might topple over, and Joab reached up to steady him. He pushed his hand against Eli's back, then his arm, then his shoulder.

"You're not cold," he said, bewildered.

"Yeah, I wasn't in the cooler. I was in that other place with the weird guy and the ashes."

" . . . "

"Oh, never mind. Get your hands off me."

אדני
jah

Eli walked in and out of streetlights, appearing and disappearing, his face expressionless. He just wanted to get to Zara's apartment. He wanted to see the kid. He wanted to be near someone who felt some kind of a need to take care of him, however manufactured.

Sure, he'd received a vision from Jah. But what did it accomplish? Sure, El-Baal was dead. Luli was dead. The commandos from Tsidon hadn't bested him. But did it matter?

Ahab was still a weakling. Isabel was still in control. Obadijah was still dead. Ephraim was still a shell of her former glory. And worst of all, Eli was completely helpless to bring about any real change.

As he reached Zara's building, he was unsure of what to say, and more unsure of how she'd receive him if he just spoke his mind. He popped a lithium.

On the way up in the elevator, he tried to organize his thoughts, but the antique was in disrepair and Eli thought more about falling to his death than anything else. He ran the distance to her apartment and pounded on the door.

"Hey, it's me."

No answer.

"Zara? Hey, can you open up? I hear you in there." He waited a minute. What was that sound? Maybe she was on the phone.

"Can I come in?" Pause. "I'm coming in."

Eli tried the door and found it unlocked. The only light in the apartment was overflow from the neon and streetlights that streamed weakly between the blinds. In the dark, he could barely make out the form of Zarephath sitting on the couch, crying, Hiram curled up in her lap.

He hadn't been ready for tears. This was not his area of expertise, emotional women. She wouldn't even look at him. A few hundred armed servants of Baal? No problem. But a crying woman . . .

He stood tall in front of the couch and just went for it. "Look, I've been thinking about all this stuff. But everything's jumbled in my mind. I mean, I think I know what I want, but then I don't know if I'm trying to want what he wants me to want . . . or what he *doesn't* want me to want lately, ya know? Do you know what I mean?" She shook her head and cried harder.

"I haven't been drinking. Really. I know I smell like a liquor store, but it was just . . . Look, here's what I know: part of me wants to stay with you. Really, I mean it. It's just that I hadn't heard from Jah in days . . . Then today I had this experience, but then Ahab completely broke trust with everyone. With me, with Jah. I'm not sure if I should just leave or . . . I mean, I know what's funny about the ashes now, but it doesn't help."

She had yet to look up at him. He sighed. "I'm not making sense. Let me start over."

He noticed that she was crying so hard that her nose was bleeding and running down her forearms. "Zara, what's wrong?"

She stared at her lap.

Eli placed his index finger under her chin and tilted her face up to meet his gaze. "Are you okay?"

Her eyes were bloodshot and mascara streaked her face. Eli looked down at Hiram. He was staring off into the distance. Not breathing.

"Oh no," was all Eli could say. He stepped back from the couch.

Zara erupted. "What do you have against me, Man of God?" she sobbed. "Are you here to make me remember where I came from? To punish me for worshiping Baal? Are you punishing my son because I still have *this?*" She wound up and hurled a pop-bottle-sized statue of Baal at Eli. It hit him in stomach.

"Zara, no, I—"

"I don't want your stupid money! I want my son back!" Her crying became uncontrollable. She fought through gasps and hiccups to breathe.

Eli just stood there for a beat, trying to process what had happened.

"Give the child to me," he commanded.

Zara stopped crying all at once and gaped up at him. She opened her mouth to object, but made no attempt to stop him from collecting Hiram's little lifeless form from her lap and carrying him out into the hall.

He walked down to the stairwell and up several flights. Where the stairs ended, Eli kicked open the padlocked rooftop access and brought the boy with him to the middle of the roof. There he laid Hiram's body gently on the ground and knelt over it

Last straw. He and Jah needed to talk. No visions. No dreams. Eli was due an explanation in plain language.

He stared down at the boy and asked his God, "What have I done to deserve this? Why . . .Why are you doing this to me?"

He looked up into the heavens and repeated, "Why are you *doing this to me?!* My friends are all dead. My enemies are still in power. And now you've even brought tragedy on this woman who hides me from Isabel. Did I curse her house by walking through the door?"

He tipped his head back, exposing his throat. "Just take my life! Take me instead of this little boy! I'm tired. Tired of this. I've had enough. I don't even want to live."

There was no response from above.

"Are you even listening? Hello!"

A brief gust of wind blew across the rooftop, flicking Eli's clothes. He cricked his neck. "What's that? You're going to 'pass by?' My whole life is falling apart! I'm crying out to you for deliverance, and you're going to *pass by?* That's so very good of you."

He stood. The wind picked up strength, slowly working up to a huge gale. Eli could barely keep his eyes open. His clothes billowed and flapped.

The wind blew stronger still. Peals of thunder skipped in from a distance. Eli stopped fighting it and stretched his arms out straight, eyes closed, and leaned into the wind, letting it hold him up.

As quickly as it had appeared, the wind died out. His eyes snapped open. "That's it? That was 'passing by?' Where are you? Where *are you?!* "

A slow rumble began to vibrate the building. His eyes sweeping the landscape, Eli saw that all of the surrounding buildings were trembling as well. A sudden violent shaking knocked Eli back down onto his hands and knees. Hiram's little body quivered with the rumbling of the rooftop. It felt like the building might come down at any moment. Even Eli's thoughts seemed to be shaken loose by the quake.

After a minute the tremor subsided.

He stood again and looked around defiantly. "Still waiting."

The sky took on a familiar orange tint. Thunder cracked and rumbled in a sharp crescendo. Massive flames once again filled the sky, churning around in a circle, producing a huge jet engine noise, lending the whole city a red-orange tint.

"I've already seen this trick!" he shouted against the thundering in the sky. "You're not here! This isn't you! I know you! I need you to talk to me! I need you to tell me what to do!"

Like a light switched off, the flames disappeared and the sky was once again dark. Eli glanced side to side, impatient.

A gentle breeze came blowing over his face, softly, comfortingly. He fell to his knees and buried his face in Hiram's chest.

"Jah . . . "

Jah's voice came still and soft and deep—a whisper. "What are you doing up here, Eli?"

He didn't look up. "I have been very zealous for you, my Lord. But your people have rejected your covenant, torn down your altar, and executed your prophets. I'm the only one left, and now they seek my life too."

"You are not the only faithful man in Ephraim," Jah assured. "Do not be afraid any longer and do not be silent, for I am with you, and no man can destroy you. Know that I have many people in this city. I have reserved unto myself seven thousand whose knees have never bowed to

Baal and whose lips have never kissed him. They will be your strength. So be strong and very courageous.

"And now this is what you are to do: go and anoint Jehu son of Nimshi as king over Ephraim, for Ahab has rejected me and I have rejected him. And go anoint Eli-Sha son of Shaphat, my beloved prophet, to replace you. For your time is short. Soon I will gather you up to myself. Now go and serve me faithfully, as I have been faithful to you." Eli was crying hard into the boy's chest. Jah's voice faded away with the breeze.

When it had gone completely, Hiram abruptly sucked in a huge gasping breath. Eli recoiled. The little boy took a few more breaths, then sat up and stared at Eli, mouth hanging open.

Eli smiled at him. He smiled back.

Zara hadn't moved since Eli left with her son. She couldn't let herself believe that he might be doing what she hoped he was doing. He was probably performing some prophetic ritual, preparing the body for burial.

Burial. He was three years old. There was a plot next to her husband's that was meant to be hers. There she would bury Hiram, she decided. The reality of his death hit her anew and a fresh wave of tears came to the surface.

Then everything went completely still as the door from the hall swung open. She fought against the light to see what was out there, now coming in. Eli. Smiling and completely at peace. And holding his hand, Hiram, very much alive and happy to see his mother.

"Mommy!" he yelled, and broke away from Eli. She caught him in an embrace and squeezed until she was afraid she'd smother him. Then she kissed him and fawned over him for some time, until he'd finally had enough and squirmed out of her grasp. That over with, he turned his attention to a couple of toy trucks on the carpeted floor and began to play.

She watched him play for twenty minutes, unable to stop saying, "Praise Jah. Praise Jah."

Eli emerged from Hiram's room, showered, having shed the torn khakis and green golf shirt. He wore a black suit and tie with a deep purple shirt. Zara whistled playfully at the change in wardrobe.

"Bringing some grievances against the king?"

"Something like that."

"If you're going out, bring a jacket," she nagged. "It's supposed to get down into the forties tonight."

"I'm leaving now, Zara. I don't think we'll be seeing each other again. Not in this life."

She forced a smile. "You don't know that."

"Yes, I do."

"Oh, yeah." She quietly added, "Prophet."

Eli picked up the idol from the floor. "You don't need this thing, you know."

"And I don't want it."

"Remember what you asked me the other day? About whether he's real? Well, the answer is that Baal is nothing. Footprints in the ashes. He's what happens when we worship ourselves."

She nodded.

He lingered by the door, not wanting to go.

"Are you hungry?" she asked. "I still have a bunch of leftovers. I could pack you a lunch."

"You are such a mom." They laughed together. "Actually, I wonder if you have any cooking oil. I just need a little bit."

"That I do have. It's strange; that's the one thing I never ran out of, even when things were at their worst." She was into the kitchen in a flash, filling a little bottle with olive oil. Her urgent need to be near him was fading, but she still wanted nothing more than to repay him in some small way.

"Is this enough?" she asked, pressing the bottle into his hand.

"More than enough. Thank you." She stood close to him, her breath tickling his neck. With some difficulty, he forced himself toward the door. "Well, I'm out. Be good. I'll be checking up on you both."

Her smile contradicted her eyes. "I'll keep a chair open for you, if you ever want to drop by." She gave him a hug and a kiss on the cheek. "You've saved our lives. You saved us."

"Nah. It wasn't me. It was Jah. He just *used* me." A grin broke out between Eli's ears. "He just used me."

"Take care of yourself, Eli -Jah Tishbi."

"He'll take care of me."

יהוא
jehu

Eli was wide-awake now, despite the lack of sleep. He stood straight and smart, clutching a hand strap in the sparsely populated metro bus. His fatigue had rolled away as the bus rolled up Jehorash Avenue toward the projects.

You can sleep when you're dead, he told himself, and Eli knew it wouldn't be long. He had it from the mouth of God: his time was short. Everybody dies. But not everyone gets a heads up and one last *to do* list before joining his fathers in glory. Jah was surely good to him.

The bus bounced, rattled, and hissed, but all Eli heard was Obadijah's voice loud and clear as the conversation of a week earlier replayed itself in his mind.

Then it hits me— the perfect solution.
Which was . . . ?
Massive reorganization of the housing projects . . . We've got a bunch more homeless on our hands. So, we build a few more low-income units, juggle everybody around, and before you can say "shibboleth" we have a building in the projects solely dedicated to housing the prophets of Jah.
How many?
A hundred. Up in Kishon Heights.

Eli moved quickly through the midst of the projects, trying to blend in. Yeah, right—in a tie. He was still

233

unarmed and the last thing he wanted was for more trouble to materialize and sidetrack him from his objectives. The certain knowledge that just about everyone in this neighborhood was packing, many looking for trouble, kept him pushing forward at a good clip.

Despite his attempt at alertness, he was almost entirely consumed in his thoughts, which were on his two outstanding missions. He had to find Jehu. He had to find Eli-Sha, the son of Shaphat. He had no idea where to find either of them. He needed help.

As he neared his destination, Eli surveyed each building he passed, rejecting each in turn. Each unit bore a large numbered sign, liberally tagged with graffiti. Even at 1 AM, throngs of residents were milling about, drinking and talking. Some played basketball. Others busied themselves with less wholesome activities.

"Eli!" came a pixy voice from in front of Unit 33. A petite woman in her thirties came rushing up to him. She had short hair and a mocha complexion with a dusting of freckles. "Is it really you?"

She half-hugged, half-tackled him.

"Miriam? What are you doing in the projects in the middle of the night?" He held up a finger. "Wait, don't tell me. You joined a gang."

She giggled, her voice almost reaching a pitch above Eli's range of hearing. "We all live down here. Didn't O tell you? Unit 33. We call it the Cave."

He noticed a faint tongue of fire flickering above her head. "*We?* You're a prophet now?"

"I still prefer prophetess, actually. And yes, I am. Commissioned two years ago."

"Prophetess?"

She nodded, her eyes bright. Eli noticed that everyone who passed nodded respectfully at Miriam and stepped around her. No catcalls, no advances, no trouble of any kind.

"Maybe you can help me," he said. I'm looking for a guy named Jehu. You know him?"

"Everybody knows Jehu. He kind of . . . took your place when you disappeared."

"A prophet?"

"No, but a gifted leader. And a zealous servant of Jah He may be the only guy I know who's more intense than you. Come on, I'll introduce you."

Miriam led Eli by the hand down the main hall of the Cave and up to the door of room 307. She knocked once.

"Come in," came Jehu's measured voice from inside.

They entered the dimly lit apartment and found themselves in the living room, which bore a striking resemblance to a firearms dealership. Guns of all sizes hung on pegs along the long south wall. Jehu sat at a small desk, cleaning a Maqil .60, a glaring desk lamp illuminating his work.

"We've been expecting you," he said evenly. He abruptly stood, slid a clip into the gun, and held it out by the barrel to Eli. "I believe this belongs to you."

The image of Jehu in the rail station flashed into his mind and everything clicked for Eli.

He accepted the pistol gratefully. "I owe you my life. Thank you."

"Believe me, it was my pleasure." Something in his eyes turned Eli's blood cold.

Jehu continued, "So I suppose you're here to assume command."

"Not at all. I've actually come with a message for you."

"For *me*."

"Yes, but I can't tell you here. It's something the prophets need to hear as well." He glanced over to Miriam. "Shall we start knocking on doors?"

"Knocking on doors?" Jehu shook his head. "I heard you were old school. Check this out. Obadijah set it up."

He reached over to a beige telephone on his desk and held down a red button for a few seconds. A pager on Miriam's belt began beeping and flashing. Jehu punched a four-digit number into the phone.

"That code basically means Ahab's men are on their way here to kill us all, but it'll do the trick. O was a little obsessed with being ready for the worst, Jah rest his soul."

"Huh. Never noticed."

Miriam laughed. Jehu almost laughed.

One hundred prophets of Jah, braced for the worst, had assembled in the small parking lot behind Unit 33. They were armed to the teeth, on edge, each looking for information, but none possessing any. Eli stood back in the shadows amused by the irony of a hundred prophets without a clue waiting on information from a civilian. Well, not a civilian for much longer.

Jehu walked out onto the top of an old, black school bus parked against the brick wall of the building. A streetlamp shone down on him like a spotlight on a performer. The prophets' voices went to mute and they offered him their full attention.

"Friends, I've got good news and bad news. The good news is: they're not coming for us at the moment." The tension in the crowd began to melt away. "The bad news is: look who showed up at my door tonight."

Eli stepped from bumper to hood to windshield and up next to Jehu. There was a moment of shock from the men and women below, and then frenetic applause. Eli looked down into the faces of his admirers. Most of them he'd known for years. Some were new, practically kids. He remembered the fresh passion of those first months and years after his commissioning. He was nineteen then. Everything seemed so new and exciting. It felt like there was no limit to what Jah might accomplish through him—like he could actually change the world.

It felt exactly like this.

He raised his hands for silence. For some reason, this set the prophets off even more. It took him a full minute to regain control.

Why hadn't he come here from the beginning? How much easier could this whole ordeal have been with a hundred loyal friends at his side?

"It's good to see you all," he said. "Really, really good." And with that out of the way, he turned to Jehu and commanded, "Kneel."

Jehu obeyed, kneeling before Eli, head down, his hair falling over his face. Eli retrieved the bottle of oil from the pocket of his coat—the one Zara had insisted he wear— and spun the plastic cap off. He poured a few drops over Jehu's head.

"Our God Jah, the Creator of Heaven and Earth, has anointed you king over this kingdom. You will rule this land in a manner that glorifies him. You will tear down the altars to Baal and the Ishtar poles and smash the idols wherever you find them. You will lead the hearts of this people further and further into the hands of our Lord. You will promote justice for the oppressed and equity for everyone, native-born and sojourner alike. If you do this, Jah will bless you and he will bless his people."

Jehu stood, ran his fingers through his thick hair and tied it back with a rubber band. "I am honored and humbled," he said.

Eli turned and addressed the group. "And now we have a big problem on our hands. An imposter and his devil-worshiping wife are in our king Jehu's home, ruling our king Jehu's country. We have to go and take it back."

These were the words that many of the prophets had been waiting years to hear.

"Jah has assured me that there remain many in Ephraim who have not worshiped Baal. Surely, you must know some of these. I need you to call them. All of them. Anyone you know who is loyal to Jah—call them and tell them this . . . "

Dawn outside the Ministry of Justice and Conduct headquarters. Drizzling and gray, the first depressingly rainy day in three and a half years. A crowd about a hundred and fifty strong stood in the courtyard, crowding around the statue of the now-defeated god of Tsidon.

The protesters had cut a large alternate entrance out of the barbed wire fence, giving them access to the lawn.

"Jehu is king! Jehu is king!" they chanted. Some among them held signs, streaked and weakened by the rain. Others brandished bats and axes, thrusting them into the air to punctuate the slogan. They'd been at it for fifteen minutes, without response or even acknowledgment from those inside the building.

Someone threw a bottle at the statue. Everyone liked that idea and, before long, it was under full-scale attack. A short, fat man gave Kohath—his mugger days now behind him—a boost, and the wiry man scaled the idol like a spider. He threw his leg over Baal's shoulder and, balanced there like a parrot, began pounding the idol's face with a sledgehammer. Pieces of the god's head began cracking off and plopping down into the fountain.

Ahab and Isabel sat at the breakfast table in the executive mansion, four empty seats between them. Their plates were filled with a variety of pastries, breads, and nuts. She ate hers daintily, while Ahab just pushed the food around, his fork producing a scraping noise against the plate with each move.

Isabel clapped her palm to the table and shot him a look.

Ahab met her gaze defensively, his eyes rimmed with dark circles. "What?"

She furrowed her brow and sucked her teeth.

"Sorry," he offered feebly, and set his fork down on his napkin.

Ahab was beyond tired. He'd finally fallen into a fitful sleep at about 4 AM, only to be awakened by his wife noisily stalking around their bedroom at 5:45, blow-drying, clinking bottles, opening the curtains. She had re-discovered religion with a vengeance and had begun insisting that they arise before dawn to pray to Baal.

Joab entered the room, all business. "Sir, there's a situation downtown at the J and C headquarters. I've prepared a conference with your advisers. We'll meet in…"

"Joab, it's 6:15 in the morning. I'm trying to enjoy a nice, restful breakfast with my lovely wife. Can you just do your job and take care of this?"

"You don't understand, sir, it's—"

"No, *you* don't understand. I've slept four hours in the last two days. I don't want to deal with this right now. Justice and Conduct can take care of itself."

"With all due respect, Your Highness, this looks like the beginnings of a riot."

Ahab let out a long, self-pitying sigh. "A riot? What for? It's raining out, for Baal's sake. What could these people possibly have to riot about?"

Joab planted a hand on the table and looked the king in the eye. "They're shouting *Jehu is king*, sir."

"Who's Jehu?"

"I have no idea."

Out of habit, Isabel assumed command. "That's not a riot. That's a coup. That's a call to revolution!" She addressed Joab. "You will take as many men as you can summon down to this uprising and put it down *hard*. And don't leave any of them in a condition to riot again. Do you understand?"

Joab ignored her orders. "Sir, it's only a few hundred people. It's not a revolution. It's a temper tantrum. We could probably put it down with a domestic detachment. I'd advise against giving Justice and Conduct a free hand with this. Remember our discussion the other night."

"Listen to me, my husband," Isabel seethed. "These people are defying us! They're calling someone else their king. It's perfectly clear what you need to do: Make an example out of each and every one of these insurgents. Bring the traitors to their knees. And find out who this *Jehu* is and have him publicly executed."

"Is that your answer to everything?" Ahab said.

Joab remained frozen a foot from the king's face. "What would you like me to do, sir?"

Isabel slipped into the chair next to Ahab's and slid her hand over his. "Trust me, I know what's best for you. When you were crying in your room, pining over Naboth's little vineyard, who went out and got it for you?"

"You did," he answered quietly.

"And when the king of Jehudah wouldn't form an alliance, who found the leverage you needed?"

"You."

"Your captain is waiting for your orders."

Ahab chewed the corner of his lower lip for a moment. "Send in three riot squads from Justice and Conduct. Your people are backup. Give them a warning first. If they don't clear out, take care of them."

Joab nodded and stood at attention. "Yes, sir."

As he headed out the door, Ahab added, "And bring me this Jehu's head in a box."

A caravan of armored vehicles emerged from beneath the Justice and Conduct compound, circled around behind the building and skidded to a stop, boxing the protesters in. Standard operating procedure. A moment later, four trucks of Shomrey-Melek came roaring in from the west and screeched to a halt behind them.

Riot troops came charging out of the armored cars, batons in hand, tear gas grenades jingling from their waists. Their sleeves bore the insignia of Justice and Conduct: the lord Baal commanding the world in power.

They were ready to bash heads, to quickly and efficiently crush this gathering as they had at the Executive Offices a week earlier and at a dozen riots before that. This time, though, they were particularly bloodthirsty. The priests of Baal had comprised three quarters of their number before they'd been killed at Karmel.

It was payback time.

The front line stood shoulder-to-shoulder, wielding transparent polycarbonate riot shields and facemasks, streaked with rain. Their orders had described a violent rebellion underway and advised them to approach with extreme caution. Taking in the sight of this little band of activists, whom they easily outnumbered, the riot troops were confused and disappointed. Still, they would make the best of it.

Several others had joined Kohath on the statue and were working together to systematically destroy it. Baal was now missing an arm and most of his face had been chipped away, a new and rather goofy cartoonish face spray painted in its place. They paused and stared down at the troops surrounding them, like so many kids caught shoplifting.

A burly Shomrey-Melek agent assumed command and issued orders through a megaphone. "Cease this demonstration immediately and return to your homes in an orderly fashion. If you comply, you will not be harmed or detained. This is your only warning from King Ahab, your kind and wise sovereign."

The black school bus rumbled down the road, trailing a ribbon of black smoke from under the hood, a mohawked, lip-ringed prophet behind the wheel. Sixty others were filed into the seats of the bus, riding and waiting silently, intently. Most of them held various weapons in their laps. Shotguns, revolvers, machetes. Those in the back two seats were empty-handed. Their commissioning did not permit them to fire a weapon; their support would take a different form.

The chanting had resumed outside the ministry of Justice and Conduct. This time, "Ahab lies; Jah gives rain."

Joab's Lieutenant tried once more. "I repeat, disperse now, or you will be treated as traitors!"

The chanting grew more insistent. Asa, the new acting Minister of Justice and Conduct, approached the agent.

"You've warned them," he barked. "Now it's our turn. They persist and we take them down." He waved a fax in his gloved hand. "These orders come through Joab, your own captain."

The Shomrey-Melek agent firmly clarified, "You know the new regs. You're authorized for non-lethal weapons only."

The minister looked hurt. "Of course. What do you take us for?"

"I know how you've dealt with unarmed citizens in the past."

"No guns." Asa grinned, and held his hand up as if taking an oath. "I promise."

The lieutenant nodded his submission and set the megaphone down.

Asa signaled two of his men. "Give them what they want."

They opened a side compartment of an armored car and pulled out a large coiled fire hose. Two other agents went to work with a wrench and spun the end off a hydrant. They quickly connected the hose and opened the valve.

"You like rain, huh?" The riot troops directed the blast of water into the heart of the group, blowing people onto their backs like paper dolls. From there, they moved up to the men scaling the statue, blasting them from their precarious perches to the ground below.

The minister smiled and ordered, "A few minutes of this to wear them thin. Then the fun begins." His subordinates thumped their batons against their shields in anticipation.

חֵצִי בְּמִקְרֶה
an arrow at random

Jehu's little Neshur two-seater zipped down the road in the faint pre-dawn light, swallowing yellow lines as fast as they came. Eli rode shotgun and prepared his handgun, chambering a round and clicking on the safety. It felt good to have its familiar heft back in his hand for this last ride. He spat a little on the barrel, using his tie to rub away a smudge before slipping it into his coat pocket.

The CB on the dash came to life. "Jehu! Er—Your Kingship. Or . . . what should I call you?"

"Today only, you may call me Jehu. Go on."

"We'll be at the rendezvous point in about twenty minutes. Should we just hang tight?"

"Do the Capitol Loop again. We'll meet up with you shortly."

"Yes, sir. Sire. Whatever."

"Everyone in there locked and loaded?"

"Yeah, I think so."

"Good. Remember, we're not there to talk. And don't ever call me *Sire.* Out." He hung the mic on its cradle and gripped the wheel with both hands.

Eli glanced at him uneasily. "Jehu," he said softly.

"Mmm?"

"When we get there, make sure no one kills Ahab. Not unless we absolutely have to."

Jehu smoldered. "You're joking, right?"

"No. That's the way it's going to be."

"You're out of your mind."

"Maybe, but that doesn't change anything."

"He killed O, man! He *publicly executed* Obadijah!"

"I know."

"Then what are you— *What?!* "

Eli couldn't believe what he was saying. "Make room for God's wrath."

"You've got to be kidding me. After the body count you've racked up this week . . . "

"Jehu . . . "

"No, hold on—and after you got yourself in over your head with those pale freaks, and Jah had to wake up Jah-El in the middle of the night and tell him where I'd find you so I could save your sorry butt. You didn't seem upset when I killed them."

"Look, you're the king now and—"

"And Ahab's not. He's going down, Eli. Deal with it." He sped up, as if to try and arrive before the prophet could say another word.

"Pull over," Eli demanded. "Stop the car."

"We don't have time."

"Stop the car."

Jehu begrudgingly obeyed, pulling up to the curb, cranking on the parking brake.

"Look at me," Eli articulated. "This is how it works: you're the king. You rule with the wisdom that Jah has given you. When your *ego* gets in the way, that's when Jah's prophet will come to you and tell you the way it is, what Jah would have you do. His prophet will interpret the Law for you, enforce the covenant for you. If you don't accept that, then you'll end up exactly like Ahab. Do you accept it?"

Jehu looked away and had a brief, angry pout. Then violently grabbed the radio mic off its cradle and called to the others: "All prophets, change of plans. No one is to harm codename Henpecked if it can be helped. From what I can gather, Lilith is still fair game. Do you copy?"

A series of answers came in the affirmative.

"Good choice," said Eli. "Don't let your personal vendettas get in the way of the mission. Trust me, there's nothing there but a world of pain and regret. Let him call the shots. Sometimes it'll be what you would do anyway—like blowing the dust off El-Baal's dental records in Kishon Valley. And sometimes it'll be the polar opposite—like letting your sworn enemy choose life or death, and then living with that choice. Remember your Torah: *Jah has said, 'To me belongs vengeance and retribution. The foot of the wicked will slip away in due time, for at hand is the day of his calamity.'*"

He gave Jehu a friendly shove. "It will get easier. Believe me. Now let's get this thing done with; I still have one more loose end to . . . no way."

Eli noticed that they had parked next to a storefront boasting a big, old-fashioned tin sign that read *Shaphat and Son Mercantile.*

"What is it?" Jehu had his hand on the shifter. "Should I go?"

"The son of Shaphat," Eli laughed.

"You know Jeshua?"

"Hmm? No, Eli-Sha, son of Shaphat."

"He's calling himself 'Eli-Sha' now?" Jehu scoffed. "Sounds like a girl's name."

Eli sat back and ran his hand along the surface of his budding hair, a habit he'd picked up since it started growing back in. "Tell me about him."

"Well, for starters, he's your biggest fan. I mean, a great guy—he'd do anything for Jah. Anything. But real stalker potential as far as you're concerned. You wanna make somebody's day sometime, pop your head in there and say hello."

Eli opened the car door. "Come on. We're bringing him with us."

"Wait. We're what?"

Eli bounded up to the storefront and tugged at the door. "It's not open."

"Of course not. It's barely six in the morning."

"Where's he live?"

"Just upstairs. I'll show you."

Jehu led him around back and up the stairway to the second-story apartment.

Eli checked his watch. "We need to wake him up and get him going quickly."

"I guarantee he's already up. Regimented guy." Jehu pounded on the door.

There was clomping.

And then the door was yanked open and Eli-Sha and Eli-Jah stood face to face. The first thought that went through Eli-Sha's head was that he'd have to stop shaving it every morning, try and catch up. Then it hit him that his hero was standing right there in his home and he grabbed Eli in a bear hug.

The awkwardness amused Jehu. He savored it a moment before again rescuing Eli, this time by whacking

Eli-Sha on the shoulder and telling him, "Let's go for a ride."

The bus full of prophets hurtled along down Canaan Road. From three different directions, six cars merged in behind it.

One was Jehu's sports car, now transporting Eli-Sha, awkwardly squeezed into the hatchback. He occasionally shot an indignant look at Eli, whose star power was fading fast. *Sure, put the big guy in the back.* His right leg was prickling from lack of blood flow.

Eli's mind was on even bigger things. It had just dawned on him that he'd completed both of his tasks. Jehu: check. Eli-Sha: check. Jah could take him any time now. As they neared their destination, Eli felt his insides tie up in knots.

It wasn't his impending death that bothered him. It was Isabel's words from a week earlier. She'd called him Zimri, the insurgent who turned on his own king and tried to replace him. Was Eli any different? He was about to walk into a king's home with the express purpose of overthrowing him. Then again, this wasn't one of the nations of the West. Ephraim had a covenant with Jah, and if Jah said Ahab had to go . . .

He picked up the CB microphone and announced, "Okay Levi, it's 6:35. Call our friend and make sure Ahab took the bait."

Surrounding the executive mansion was a massive stone wall with a single entrance and five arcane looking watchtowers—one adjacent to the ten-foot-tall iron gate and one at each corner. In each tower, two men stood guard with high-powered rifles. The tower at the gate was also armed with a mounted Matzor machine gun.

At 6:45 AM, the guards in three of the five towers reported hearing the unmistakable sound of dozens of vehicles approaching from the west.

The Southwest tower radioed the others, "Sounds like an army headed this way. Do we have any intel?"

The gate tower responded, "We hear it too, but no idea what it might be. Sounds like a caravan. Fifty Amasa Fighting Vehicles, a helicopter or two, maybe a tank. I can't believe how loud it is. Do we have any manpower left here to go check it out?"

"Not nearly enough to deal with *that*. Most of the Shomrey-Melek are dealing with the uprising at Justice and Conduct. I think we've just got bare bones security personnel on site. Let me call Joab a minute."

The thundering got louder and the men at the gate swiveled the Matzor toward the west and locked it down in firing position.

"Joab sees nothing coming eastward on radar. But if anyone approaches without clearance, we're to fully engage, ask questions later. He's sending a recon team out presently."

The sun was just rising above a chain of tall trees, just beneath the ceiling of rainclouds, opening up visibility to the west as far as the mist and drizzle would permit. The guards clicked off safeties and peered through scopes. Whatever it was out there sounded like it was almost on top of them. They could see the ground and the trees shaking from the heavy vibrations.

Two Shomrey-Melek agents came revving their way up from the garage in a TrailMaker SUV. The driver paused at the gate and told the guard, "If it's trouble down there, we'll try and really slow them down just as they come into range. Use the Matzor to take out the tires on the lead vehicles, then everyone goes for kill shots. Just make sure we're behind you before you start shooting. Joab is calling back the troops from Justice and Conduct. But for now, it's just us."

The guard nodded and hit the release. The iron gate slowly swung inward, discharging the TrailMaker, then clumsily began to creak closed again.

The Southeast Tower dispatched, "There's something coming from the east as well. I can't make anything out through the rain—sun's in my eyes— but I think—" He squinted off into the distance. "I think we're getting it both ways."

Suddenly, an old black bus blew past the Southwest Tower and turned a slight right to catch the iron gate head-on just short of the latch. The bus won the argument and charged up the half-mile drive toward the mansion, six cars following close behind at seventy miles per hour.

The two guards at the gate frantically grappled at the Matzor, unable to turn it in time. Large caliber bullets came roaring down from the other watchtowers, but in a matter of seconds, the prophets were off in the distance, out of range, almost to the king's house.

A handful of Shomrey-Melek came charging out of the mansion, sending a spattering of small arms fire at the bus.

Their courage proved finite, however, when the bus was undeterred. They dove and rolled from its path.

Joab burst into the dining room again, this time not seeking orders, but issuing them. Two other agents followed close on his heels.

"Sir, we're under attack!" he barked. "We need to get you to a secure location *now!*" He physically pulled Ahab from his seat by the collar of his bathrobe and rushed him out the door. Isabel was up from the table in an instant, hurrying the agents out in front of her. She was panicked, a network of worry lines crisscrossing her perfect white face. Everyone she had relied on for a sense of security now dead, she was feeling small and alone.

Into a small two-way radio, Joab ordered, "Escape chopper on the roof in three minutes!"

They rushed down a narrow corridor, through a huge, lavish ballroom, and began ascending a giant curved staircase up to a wide landing.

The helicopter would be at least another five minutes. Probably closer to ten. This was going to be close.

A wave of riot troops had moved into the crowd, pounding the protestors with fist and baton. Some put up a fight, while others simply covered their heads and took the beating. The troops had yet to work their way to the heart of the crowd, where a burly tow truck driver was lassoing Baal around what was left of his head with the cable from his winch. The third try proved the charm.

A flash of black in his face and the trucker found his nose crushed by a metal baton. He absorbed the next blow in his ribs and snapped the stick from his attacker's hand. A shove sent the armored thug off balance, and the end of the baton found its way up under the face shield to connect hard with the man's chin. The trucker kept him down with a kick to the ribs.

The senior Shomrey-Melek agent on site stood back from the fray and watched the drubbing with disgust. His job was to protect the king's life. He lacked the imagination to convince himself that he was doing that now.

From inside the truck, the radio squawked, "The executive mansion is under attack! I repeat: we are under attack. Withdraw immediately from Justice and Conduct Headquarters and divert all units to the king's residence."

The agent snatched the megaphone from the front seat. "Shomrey-Melek, return to your assigned vehicles immediately," he bellowed. "Justice and Conduct, you have been reassigned to my command. The king and queen are under attack! I repeat: there is an attack underway at the royal residence. Follow us. You'll be armed on site."

The riot troops were out of the courtyard in a matter of seconds, and filing back into the armored vehicles. The remaining band of bruised and battered protesters managed a feeble cheer for their victory, helping each other to their feet.

The cable around Baal's neck went taut. As the long line of trucks and armored cars snaked its way up away from the mob, the god of Tsidon fell like a giant redwood to the ground.

The men of Justice and Conduct, now purged of goyim but not of their love for Baal, watched the rioting crowd grow smaller behind them. Asa stretched impatiently. Very little could have torn him away from that particular task, but Isabel was in danger. If the Shomrey-Melek were the keepers of the king, Justice and Conduct were the unofficial protectors of the queen. The riot at headquarters had been a good warm-up. There would be no nonsense about non-lethal weapons at the royal mansion. Whoever had come for Isabel would pay with their lives.

Joab and his men had just cleared the top of the stairs when the south wall of the ballroom exploded and an old black bus came charging in, shooting debris everywhere. Joab shoved the king and queen toward two agents and ordered, "Saferoom 12 is just down the hall. No one goes in. You guard them with your life!"

The agents spirited the royal couple away as dozens of prophets poured from the black antique and the remaining cars entered the house through the bus-sized hole in the wall. The prophets left their vehicles and stood out in the open, guns at the ready.

Ten Shomrey-Melek raced into the ballroom from the main house. Two of them rushed to Joab's side. The rest spilled out into the gallery, drew large handguns, and took aim at the prophets below.

Eli emerged from the pack and hoarsely shouted, "Have you made up your mind yet, Joab?"

"Have you *lost* yours?" Joab was hysterical. "Eli, this is beyond crazy. You're committing treason here!"

The prophet slowly scratched his head. "I was hoping you'd see things my way this morning."

Another ten agents came charging onto the landing behind Joab, fresh from the towers outside. Wearing helmets and bulletproof Shiryon vests and armed with rifles, they positioned themselves strategically around the landing.

The captain shook his head. "You've got me in a very tough spot, old friend. I really ought to have you all executed where you stand as traitors. But, lucky for you, Eli, I've got a soft spot for bipolar, gun-wielding religious fanatics. So I'm going to give you this one chance: if you surrender to me right now, I can guarantee you a fair trial."

"That's not going to work this time, Joab. Put down the pea-shooter. You've got nowhere to go. If Ahab and what's-her-name weren't close by, I don't think we'd be having this conversation, would we?"

At that moment, Ahab and Isabel were hidden away in Saferoom 12, one of thirty such chambers, about four feet tall and five feet deep, concealed behind secret panels in the wall. There was just room enough for the two of them to sit side by side. Their knees pushed up to their chests like children, they could hear nothing of what was happening outside the four walls. Isabel clutched a statue of Baal—she kept one in each saferoom, just in case—and issued a stream of prayers and promises to the idol.

Sweat streamed down Ahab's face. "What's happening out there?" he asked, his voice quivering. "We should be on a helicopter headed for Tsidon. We need more muscle around here. Your old man needs to take over." Tears joined the rolling sweat on his cheeks. "I don't even care if we *do* become a colony of Tsidon like that teacher said. Our son will still rule this land after we're gone. It's okay."

"No." Isabel tipped her head back, resting it against the concrete wall. "If we showed up in Tsidon this afternoon, we'd be dead by tonight. My father is all out of patience and so is Baal. It's up to you, Ahab. You've got to be a man for once." She rolled her head toward her husband and added, "I'm not going out there."

Ahab hugged his knees all the harder. "Well, if you think *I* am, you're crazy. This is exactly what we pay Joab for. He'll take care of it."

"Joab is the last person we want writing our kingdom's future. We both know that Eli is behind this. Who else would it be? Joab will make a deal with him." She set Baal down between them.

"No, I don't think he'd do that," Ahab countered. "Joab's my best friend." *Joab's my only friend.*

Isabel wheezed. "Did you see how he acted at Karmel? He's a closet Jah-lover just like Obadijah." Her fingertips brought Ahab's face in to meet hers. "I'm certain he killed El-Baal's snipers that day. He can't be trusted."

Ahab threw his shoulders up. "What do you want me to do about it? I'm no soldier."

"Just go stand at his side," she encouraged. "He won't turn on you if you're right there with him."

"Certainly not. No." He was silent for a beat and then added another "no" for good measure.

She narrowed her eyes. "Everyone says you're a coward—everyone—but I've never really believed it until now."

Ahab cringed. "I can't take a chance with my life. I'm too valuable to Ephraim."

Isabel leaned in, her breasts pushing against his side, and whispered into his ear, "Go and fight for me. Go be that husband and that king. Go be your father. I know you can."

The idol tipped over with a clink and rolled up against Ahab's leg. He looked down at Baal's empty face. What did they all see in him? Of course Baal would be no help. Gods were for people who couldn't do anything on their own.

Ahab felt a hand rest firmly on his knee. He shrieked. His wife was gone. Sitting next to him in the saferoom was his father Omri. He was not presently decaying—in fact, he looked very much alive. Omri was silent, but his eyes spoke loud and clear: *You are a coward. You are a weakling. You are a monumental disappointment.*

Ahab shoved his palms against the back wall and sent the hidden door open with a frenzied kick to the release bolt.

The guards in the hallway were staggered so as not to reveal the location of the chamber. Two Shomrey-Melek stood ten feet up the hall, another agent five feet down. The one closest to Ahab, clad in helmet, Shiryon vest, and combat boots, came rushing over, shouting in a whisper, "Sir, what are you doing? Get back in there!"

The king awkwardly emerged from his chamber into the hall and clicked the door shut behind him. "No. I'm going out to face them."

"Sir, no. My orders are to keep you—"

"Your orders come from me! And I'm telling you that I'm going out there."

"With all due respect, Sir, your servant is only concerned for your safety." He bowed his head.

Ahab stood as tall as he could. "My father didn't need a god to help him defeat his enemies and neither do I."

"A . . . god?"

"That's right. I'm done with the lot of them. Now take off your helmet, vest, and boots. And your pants."

The agent hesitated.

"I can't go out there like *this*, can I?" He indicated his bathrobe and slippers.

Fifteen yards away, in the ballroom, the posturing was continuing. And growing tiresome.

"What exactly is your purpose here, Eli?" Joab was joined on the landing by another agent with rifle and body armor, his blue pajama pants almost totally concealed by protective padding.

Eli sensed that Joab was stalling, waiting for the odds to stack themselves further in his favor, so he escalated. "You people keep telling me that I'm fighting progress, so today we've brought some progress with us. The new king is here to take over." He took another step forward, knowing that he was immortal until Jah's purpose for him was complete. "Ahab is relieved of duty. And so are you."

Joab tried a laugh, but convinced no one. "You think you can just show up here and take over? This isn't the Wild West! We're not Shophatim here, okay? We can't all just do what's right in our own eyes. There are laws in this kingdom. Now throw down your weapons and place your hands on your head. You're all under arrest. I'm not going to tell you again."

Eli walked up two steps. Several prophets filled in behind him. "You don't have the authority to arrest us; you do not work for the current king." His gun remained at his side, barrel to the ground. "There are, what, twenty of you? Your men are outnumbered five to one. Do the smart thing and surrender. We won't hurt you. We won't even hurt Ahab. I promise."

"We may be outnumbered, but we have the high ground, Eli. How long are you people prepared to stand down there? Reinforcements are on their way as we speak and if you hang around long enough, the military is putting together a breach team by my order." He decided not to tell Eli about the escape chopper, which should be landing on the roof any moment.

The standoff was broken abruptly when a truck full of Shomrey-Melek careened through the hole in the wall, slamming the bus and sending it lurching forward ten feet, through a line of banquet tables. Outside, three more trucks arrived from their brief assignment at Justice and Conduct, followed by a dozen armored cars, bursting with Baal's riot troops.

The Shomrey-Melek flooded the ballroom, surrounding the prophets, guns drawn. As the riot troops hit the ground, each was handed a shotgun from an armory vehicle parked just outside the missing section of wall. They pushed in behind the Shomrey-Melek—seventy of them—and spread out along the back wall.

The ballroom was getting crowded.

Joab took the rifle from the agent next to him and put Eli in the crosshairs. "Okay, then. I'm quite sure that you no longer outnumber us. Your cause is dead, Eli. The king and queen are safe. They'll be boarding a helicopter any minute now. If you have a grievance of any real substance, we can provide you a forum. But put those guns down.

"The way I see it, if you all drop your weapons, you're only guilty of destruction of public property and disorderly conduct." He lowered the rifle an inch and added earnestly, "Don't make us kill you."

Eli dropped his pistol to the floor and ascended a few more stairs. This might be it, he thought. Death at Joab's hand was something he could live with.

"Shomrey-Melek," he called out, "listen to me. Ahab has rejected Jah. And now Jah has rejected Ahab. He is no longer king! You're serving an imposter. Remember your oaths. The true king is among these prophets today!"

Half the agents lowered their guns, glad for the excuse. After all, this was Eli-Jah Tishbi, the great prophet of Jah. There was no one they'd rather *not* shoot.

Joab clicked off his safety and held his ground. He wouldn't be swayed.

Isabel sat in the saferoom, clutching the figure of Baal. She was droning a prayer.

"Lord Baal, I come to you in this secret place, seeking your favor." She pushed her forehead against the stone figure. "I have failed you Baal, and you demand an act of ruthlessness as proof of my dedication. Today, I have sent to you a Treachery Offering—my husband, the king. He will serve to seal myself and this land to you."

She was glad to be rid of the weakling and hoped this would be enough. If Ahab was killed—and she was certain he would be—she might be forgotten in the chaos. And Baal loved nothing more than a treachery offering. If he could not have your children, your spouse was almost as good. And getting back in Baal's good graces meant re-entering her father's as well.

Eli was halfway up the stairs now and still climbing slowly. "You've seen what Jah can accomplish," he continued, "yet you persist in giving your loyalty to that idol-worshiper and his satanic wife! If you will truly serve Jah, then join me in deposing these pretenders."

Eli was three steps from the landing and Joab knew he couldn't pull the trigger. He dropped the rifle to his side and looked at Eli with pleading eyes. "Give him one more chance."

Eli shook his head. "No more chances. Where is he?"

"He's safe. You said you wouldn't hurt him."

"And where is *she*?"

"Yes, where?" Asa called from below. His men moved from the back wall at his command and into a formation near the base of the steps. Asa moved quickly up the stairs behind Eli, riot gear clacking, shotgun ready.

"As Minister of Justice and Conduct, I demand that you turn the queen's protection over to us immediately. I don't care if you return that useless whelp Ahab for a refund—I know I would. But no one dethrones our queen.

Long live Isabel and all praise be to Baal!" Asa's troops roared their approval.

"You say this 'new king' is in amongst these Jah-lovers?" Asa asked sharply. Seventy shotguns took aim at the cluster of prophets. "Give us the queen or we'll slaughter them all where they stand."

Joab hefted the rifle again, this time centering Asa's nose in the crosshairs. "Shomrey-Melek," he ordered, "pick a target. No one threatens the king's life!"

Half of Asa's troops turned their aim back to the Shomrey-Melek. There was a thick dread in the room—apprehension of the chain reaction that would result if anyone fired.

"We've got ourselves a genuine Moabite Standoff," Asa observed. "What's it gonna be?" He moved up another five steps. "We're ready to die for our god. Are you?"

"Rubber bullets," Joab said.

"What?"

Joab snickered. "Your shotguns. They came from our armory. They're loaded with rubber bullets. Riot rounds. Non-lethal weapons only. Didn't you get that memo? You think I'd trust you goyim wannabes with live ammunition?"

"You're bluffing."

"Try me."

Asa fired. So did Joab. Thirty more shots rang out around the ballroom.

Face shields were shattered and Baal's troops cut down by a shower of lead.

Agents and prophets were slammed to the ground by rubber rounds.

Eight were dead, including Asa. His surviving men abandoned their worthless weapons and retreated through the hole in the wall, scrambling back into their armored cars and fleeing for their lives.

"Cease fire!" Joab ordered.

The fallen prophets helped each other to their feet. None of them had lost his life, or even an eye.

The Shomrey-Melek celebrated their victory with a military grunt. They too were all alive and unharmed—except for one agent at the top of the stairs. He had been hit by a random bullet, which skipped in through the seam of his Shiryon vest and entered his side. The injured man stumbled down a few steps, every eye on him, then tripped and tumbled to the bottom, his helmet bouncing off in the process.

Joab recognized Ahab's face, now pale and blood-stained, and scrambled down the stairs to his side.

"Sir, are you badly hurt?"

Ahab groaned, tried to talk, and gave up. Each breath was accompanied by a spasm of pain and a high whistle from somewhere beneath the vest. Finally, he found his voice. "Get me out of the fighting, Joab. I'm wounded."

Joab cradled Ahab's head. "The fighting is over, sir. I'll get a doctor."

"She was right about you. Betrayed me. What were you . . . " He launched into a coughing fit.

Joab fought tears and lost. "I'm sorry, Ahab. You know that my oath is to Jah's anointed. You're not the one anymore. You always had a great king somewhere inside. You were just too afraid to embrace him."

Ahab gripped Joab's hand hard and grunted, as a fresh wave of pain hit him deep inside his chest. "I'm on my

way out I think. Tell Eli he won. The troubler of Ephraim."
His voice scooped up to a falsetto sob.

Joab looked off, embarrassed.

Eli stood back away from the scene, not at all happy to
see the former king reduced to this. He had always
dreamed that when Ahab went down, it would be . . . fun,
really. But now that it was happening, it was unmistakably
tragic on every level.

The captain regarded Ahab with pity. "Go and join
your fathers in peace, Ahab. You've been a good friend."

At the word "fathers," Ahab's eyes flew wide in terror.
He pointed above him. *"No!* Get him away!"

"There's nobody there," Joab comforted.

"He's a dragon! A snake! He's coming for me!"

"Who?"

"My father! It's Baal! It's my father!" He gulped his
way through several aborted breaths.

Eli took another step back from Ahab, repulsed. *You
reap what you sow.*

The one-time king of Ephraim let out a guttural
scream, slapped his skull twice against the floor, and
expired.

Most of the prophets hung their heads in sorrow. Jehu
just shook his and quickly ascended the staircase.

"I am Jehu, king of Ephraim," he declared, reaching the
top. "Who's with me?"

סערה
epilogue

"Eli-Jah."

The voice came from out in the courtyard, drifting in through the new makeshift entrance. It was a whisper, but somehow the sound filled the whole ballroom, drowning out everything that was happening around him.

No one else seemed to have heard it.

Eli-Jah. It came again—his name, stretched out, wandering in through the opening in the wall and swirling around him. There was no doubt; the voice was Jah's. Eli slipped out of the mansion. No one noticed. Every eye was on Jehu.

He walked around a few trucks, through the wet grass, and began the journey down the long, winding drive.

It was a beautiful morning. The rain had stopped and the clouds dissipated. A rainbow was barely visible against the still-rising sun. Various pinks and oranges were competing for space in the sky to the east.

A hundred yards out from the house, he heard footsteps clomping up fast from behind him. Labored breathing. It occurred to him at the same time that he didn't have his gun and that he really didn't care.

He stopped and let Eli-Sha catch up to him.

"What is it?" Eli-Jah asked.

His successor leaned over a moment, hands on his knees, and caught his breath. "I was supposed to tell you: *At the appointed time, it is written, you were destined to calm the wrath of God before it breaks out in fury, to turn the hearts of parents to their children, and to restore the tribes of Ja'acov. You've done well."*

"Thanks." He was about to send him back into the house, but saw a hesitation in Eli-Sha's eyes. "There's something else, isn't there?"

"Yes." He cleared his throat—unsure how to ask—and decided to just go for it. "Give me a double portion of your spirit."

"Do what?"

"I want to inherit a double portion of your spirit."

"That's a difficult thing, Eli-Sha. It's not exactly mine to give. But I tell you what—if you see me go, you'll have it." He took off his trench coat and hung it on the shoulders of his slouching successor. "Now I'm off."

He walked thoughtfully down the asphalt drive at a medium clip, the brisk morning air invigorating him. At the entrance, he skirted around the bent iron gate, crumpled on the ground, and out of the compound to the empty road.

Out of nowhere, he felt himself slammed to his knees. The stone wall, the trees, the street beneath him all disappeared. Instead, he saw Isabel. She was up in the gallery of the ballroom, surrounded by Shomrey-Melek agents—no one he recognized. She was dressed in purple and scarlet, covered in pearls and gold, and smiling, smug, victorious.

Baal was at her back, shifting and slithering behind the agents, barely visible to the prophet. Something was different about him. He seemed to be everywhere at once. What was it? Eli winced. It was Baal's head, or rather, his *heads*. He had seven of them. One hung limp and dead, but the other six glowered and snarled, emerging from between the agents long enough to growl and snort at Jah's prophet, then disappearing back into the darkness.

Isabel looked Eli in the eye and produced an evil grin. Suddenly, one of the agents grabbed her by the back of the neck and hurled her forward. She slammed into the railing, flipped it, and began the thirty-foot descent, gracefully spinning head-over-foot in slow motion.

As she began her third turn, the floor got in the way, producing a muffled *crump*. Her body stood on end for a moment, violently convulsing, before slumping to the floor in a twisted heap.

Eli's surroundings came back into focus, replacing the macabre scene. The sound of birds singing drifted down from the branches above. Off to the west, he saw a cloud of dust in the distance, rising up off the road. Something big was on its way to the mansion. Whatever was approaching sounded to Eli like ten trucks. Maybe a helicopter too. Another attack on the mansion?

Pulling himself to his feet, Eli wondered what was out there. And what would do him in. He hadn't expected to make it this long. His lungs felt scarred, his heart heavy and sluggish. He was sure he could feel a pinching kind of pain where the bullet had gone through.

Out of the cloud of dust came a long, shiny stretch limo, zipping down the road at ninety miles per hour. As it approached, the deafening noise faded away. The vehicle moved, light and smooth, almost hovering along the ground, and came to a soft stop in front of Eli, a deep purr emanating from under the hood.

Eli studied the car. Something was off about the color. The dark reds and oranges were fluid, shifting slowly like burning embers. In the tinted window, he caught a glimpse of his reflection. A tall, blue tongue of fire burned and flickered above his head.

He reached out and tentatively touched the door handle. It was as real as he was, and cool to the touch. Where his hand made contact, the door smoldered a bright red.

He gave the handle a pull.

Sitting in the back of the limo, hands folded in his lap, was Obadijah.

"You ready to come home?" he asked.

Eli grinned, nodded. He was glad to see his friend and even gladder to be headed where he was.

Everybody dies, right? Wrong.

He climbed into the limo and pulled the door shut behind him. The oiled leather seats were softer than anything he'd ever felt, and he sunk deep into them.

"That's it?" he asked. "I'm done?"

Obadijah smiled. "For now."

סוף דבר

Zachary Bartels is the pastor of a church in Lansing, Michigan, where he lives with his wife Erin and their son. He holds degrees from Cornerstone University and Grand Rapids Theological Seminary.

Zachary enjoys film, fine cigars, gourmet coffee, reading, writing, and chopping down idols of Baal. Look for his new book *Playing Saint*, hitting stores in October of 2014.

www.zacharybartels.com